KAPPY KING AND THE PICKLE KAPER

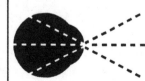

This Large Print Book carries the
Seal of Approval of N.A.V.H.

KAPPY KING AND THE PICKLE KAPER

AMY LILLARD

THORNDIKE PRESS
A part of Gale, a Cengage Company

Farmington Hills, Mich • San Francisco • New York • Waterville, Maine
Meriden, Conn • Mason, Ohio • Chicago

LIBRARY OF CONGRESS CIP DATA ON FILE.
CATALOGUING IN PUBLICATION FOR THIS BOOK
IS AVAILABLE FROM THE LIBRARY OF CONGRESS

ISBN-13: 978-1-4328-5561-1 (hardcover)

Published in 2018 by arrangement with Zebra Books, an imprint of Kensington Publishing Corp.

Printed in Mexico
1 2 3 4 5 6 7 22 21 20 19 18

To Stacey:
Thanks for being the Edie
to my Kappy or the
Kappy to my Edie. Or the . . .
well, you get the gist!
These books wouldn't be
the same without you!

ACKNOWLEDGMENTS

The list that goes here is of the usual suspects, er, wonderful people. My editor, my agent, my family, and my friends. But the biggest thanks go to the readers. You make it all worthwhile! And I'd also like to thank the people of Kishacoquillas Valley for "lending" me their beautiful corner of Pennsylvania. I am both honored and blessed to be able to set a series in this lovely area.

CHAPTER 1

A car horn honked outside. Well, *honked* was a kind word. It was more like the driver pressed the wheel and didn't stop.

"I'm coming!" Kappy called, though there was no way Edie could hear her.

She let Elmer, her beagle pup, out the back door. "And stay in the yard this time," she called, but the puppy didn't even break stride.

Yesterday, Kappy had filled all the holes that Elmer had dug, even the ones around the small fence she and Edie had put up to keep the pup from roaming across the valley. The dog liked to dig. And get out of the yard. Hopefully, today he would behave, but she wasn't counting on it.

Kathryn King, otherwise known as Kappy since as long as anyone could remember, grabbed her purse, checked her prayer *kapp* in the mirror in the living room, then locked the door behind her.

Finally, Edie took her hand off the horn and silence filled the air. For about a second and a half.

"Kappy, would you hurry? You know how Jimmy gets when I'm late to pick him up."

Kappy grumbled to herself and hustled to the car. "Is it my fault that you're late picking me up?"

Edie barely made sure the door was closed before putting the car in reverse to back out of the drive. "You were supposed to be ready."

"I was ready. Fifteen minutes ago."

Edie waved away her protests. "It's okay." She turned the car onto the main road and headed toward the Peachey Bait Shop.

"Tell me again why you thought Jimmy should go to work at Mose's shop."

"He needs to get out more. I worry about him. I mean, the only time he goes anywhere is church." She shrugged, her off-the-shoulder top slipping a little farther down her arm. "And sometimes to the grocery store. He needs to socialize."

"I'm not sure working at the bait shop can be considered socializing."

Edie cast her an exasperated look. "It's a start."

"*Jah.*" Kappy turned to face front, the glare of the sun off Edie's bright-pink outfit almost more than her eyes could take.

If anyone saw her, they would never know that Edie Peachey had once been Amish. Or that she had only recently returned to take care of her special-needs brother. Jimmy Peachey had Down syndrome, but all Kappy really knew was that he was one of the sweetest people she had ever met. Despite her new responsibilities, Edie looked carefree, bohemian even. At least Kappy thought that was the word. Or maybe it was *eclectic*. That one was on her word-a-day calendar, and she knew it applied.

Edie seemed to wear whatever was at hand. Kappy wasn't sure if the clothes actually went together or not, but one thing was certain: Edie didn't dress like the other *Englisch* women Kappy knew. Not that she knew many.

"It gets him out of the house a couple of days a week. And I think it gives him a sense of importance."

"He can't get that from taking care of the puppies?"

After her mother died, Edie had inherited more than the care of her brother. She had also gained her mother's beagle-breeding business. For a while, it seemed as if Edie would return to her life among the *Englisch,* but after working side by side with Kappy to uncover the truth behind her mother's death, Edie had decided to stay. For a time, at least. She hadn't wanted to take Jimmy away from his friends and support system. Not after just losing their mother. But Kappy wondered if Edie was as unhappy with the *Englisch* as she had been with the Amish. Not that Edie would ever admit such a thing.

"No," Edie finally said. "Taking care of the puppies is not a challenge for him. This way he's learning all about bait and fishing poles and a whole bunch of other sportsman things like that."

Kappy nodded. "I see. This is about a father figure."

Edie sent her a shocked look. "Of course not."

Then why would Mose, who had a fifteen-year-old son who helped him, need the help of a twenty-something, special-needs man?

Unless he was doing this as a favor to Edie

"So how did you get Mose to talk to you?"

Edie sniffed. "He didn't actually talk to me." She gave another of those shirt-slipping shrugs. "Jimmy went in and talked to him."

"Alone?"

"I was with him, of course."

"Of course," Kappy murmured, hiding her smile. All that meant was Edie had been behind Jimmy, feeding him lines while Mose pretended she wasn't there. Oh, the joys of being shunned.

And Edie was shunned. She had joined the church, then left the Amish. Now she was back and unwilling to rejoin the church. But at least she was providing a steady home for her brother. In light of Jimmy's trouble after their mother's murder, Kappy was glad that Edie had decided to stay.

"What in the world?" Edie slowed the car, drawing Kappy's attention to the road. Normally, she didn't like to watch where they were going. Edie's driving was a little . . . well, scary. She drove too fast as far as Kappy was concerned and seemed to take too many chances. Anytime Kappy said anything, Edie scoffed and laughed, leaving Kappy to pretend that they weren't hurtling down the road in a dangerous car with an inattentive driver. No, that wasn't the case at all.

A line of cars stretched in front of them as far as Kappy could see. They all had their back lights on, *brake lights* she thought they were called, indicating that they had all stopped for something. Hardly any traffic came from the other direction, and Kappy

13

wondered if the two were connected. Were there cars backed up on the other side of the road, just farther down and out of sight?

"What's happened?" Kappy asked.

Edie stuck her head out the window and craned around to better see. "I don't know. An accident, I guess." She reached for the radio knob, then pulled back with a sigh. "I guess we can't listen to the traffic report and see if there's any news."

"Not until you have that bulb replaced," Kappy returned.

"Fuse," Edie corrected.

"Right."

The radio in Edie's car had gone out not long ago. And though Kappy didn't know two cents' worth about the details, she knew that it wouldn't work.

Edie hung her head out the car window once more. "I can't see anything but cars," she complained. "A whole bunch of cars." She gave the steering wheel a quick pound. "We are going to be so late."

But being late wasn't the real problem. It was how Jimmy would react to the fact they were late that was potentially troublesome.

"Maybe he'll be okay," Kappy murmured. She was trying to be encouraging, but Edie just shook her head.

"You weren't with me the last time." She

shook her head some more. "He was not happy."

"Maybe you should leave a little earlier," Kappy suggested.

"Like I have any control over this." She waved a hand toward the long line of cars.

True, with this sort of delay there was no way anyone was getting anywhere on time for a while.

"Why don't you call Mose and tell him? Maybe if he prepares Jimmy, it won't be such a surprise to his system."

Edie tossed her an appreciative look. "Hey. That's not a half-bad idea." She fished her phone out of her purse and pulled up the number, setting the phone to call before she tossed it to Kappy. "You tell him."

Kappy frowned, but couldn't say anything as Mose picked up the phone at his bait shop.

They inched forward as Kappy explained the situation to Mose. The man was more than happy to help. Kappy promised to be there as soon as possible, then handed the phone back to Edie.

"Thanks," Edie said, and pushed on the screen, effectively hanging up.

"With any luck that will help."

Edie nodded. "With any luck," she repeated. Though Kappy knew what she was

15

thinking. They were backed up so badly, it was going to be a while before they got past and on the other side of whatever had happened.

"I really hope no one's hurt," Kappy murmured. She hadn't planned on being gone this long. At the speed they were going and the fact that they would have to most likely take an alternate route back home, they could be gone over an hour. She said a quick prayer that God would help direct Elmer's mischievous puppy steps and he would stay in the yard today and not dig his way out.

Then she immediately felt a little guilty. With all the problems in the world, she shouldn't take up God's time with her dog's bad habits.

"I think we're moving a little faster now," Edie said, but Kappy couldn't tell. "I wish I knew what was going on up there."

"I don't know," Kappy murmured. With the way traffic was lined up and the number of cars barely inching forward, Kappy had a feeling whatever was ahead of them was pretty bad indeed.

But Edie was getting impatient. Kappy had grown used to most of Edie's *Englisch* habits, but her urge to just . . . go was not one of them.

"We'll get there soon enough."

Edie shot her a look. "You sound like my mother when you say things like that."

Kappy sniffed and smoothed a hand over her apron. "I'll take that as a compliment."

Edie laughed, shook her head, and turned her attention back front. "I think we're moving better now."

Not knowing how else to respond, Kappy nodded.

"Look." Edie pointed to a spot up ahead.

Kappy saw the flashing lights of multiple emergency vehicles, but not what they were tending. Kappy counted three police cars, a fire truck, and two ambulances. A stretcher had been pulled out and whatever was on it had been covered with a sheet. "That looks serious."

Oddly enough, the cars were moving a bit quicker, slowed only by the other drivers twisting their heads around to see everything of the accident.

And Kappy was certain of that now. This was definitely an accident.

"Maybe one of those big trucks turned over," she said.

"Maybe," Edie murmured, still trying to see what was in front of them.

Finally, they were close enough.

The yellow buggy was almost unrecognizable. Just the sight of it made Kappy gasp. That and the acrid smell of vinegar that rent the air. The buggy was turned over onto one side and off in the ditch. The back wheel that was up in the air was cracked in half, tilted like one of those crazy rides at the county fair. The buggy itself . . . well, Kappy only knew what it was because of its distinctive color.

"Holy cow," Edie breathed.

"You can say that again."

Only the gravity of the situation kept Edie from actually repeating it. Having traveled in carriages most of their lives, they both knew: Whoever had been in that carriage was hurt. Badly. If not —

"What is that smell?" Edie asked, pulling the wide neck of her shirt up to cover her mouth.

"Vinegar, I suppose." At least that was what it smelled like. But why would this particular spot in the road smell any differently?

"From what?"

"Maybe the other vehicle was a vinegar truck?" Kappy speculated.

Edie rolled her eyes. "There is no such thing as a vinegar truck."

"How am I supposed to know?"

But Edie had moved on to other issues.

"Is that glass on the road?" She pointed in front of them where something sparkled like diamonds in the sun.

"I guess." What else could it be?

"And . . ." Edie leaned over her steering wheel, squinting ahead of them as if that could help her see better. "Are those pickles?"

Stacked on the side of the road were several wooden cases, their contents a mystery except for the jars and jars of pickles littered around. Some had been turned upright, but still others lay willynilly as if they had been tossed aside. Or flung out when the car or whatever had rammed into the buggy. And not just any pickles, but the white church pickles Big Valley was known for. Kappy had never thought twice about the white pickles and the white cucumbers used to make them, but here with them lying all over the road and off in the grass, some in jars and others not . . . well, they were downright eerie.

"That looks really bad," Kappy said. There was no horse to be seen. And no car. Or even a vinegar truck. Kappy looked even though Edie had already knocked out her theory. The other vehicle could have already been towed. And the horse . . . ? If the horse had managed to make it through the crash, someone could have already taken it to the large-animal vet clinic. But from the looks of the carriage . . .

"You don't think . . ." Edie turned wide eyes to Kappy.

"I don't know."

"Do you know who it belongs to?"

They were almost past now. Kappy turned in her seat to look behind them. Cars still lined the highway as far as she could see. Vinegar, pickles, wooden crates. "It has to be Jonah Esh."

Edie whirled around as if to get a better look.

"Turn around!" Kappy yelled. Edie's driving was bad enough without her being distracted by pickles and broken buggies.

"Jonah Esh is just a kid."

"He was a kid when you left. He's seventeen or eighteen now." If she was remembering right.

"And his family still makes pickles?"

"His mother has turned it into an empire," Kappy said with a quick nod.

"A pickle empire?" Edie asked.

"Something like that." At last, they were through the wreckage. Kappy was glad. Just the sight of all those pickles and that broken carriage was enough to give her chills.

Lord, please take care of those involved.

Heal them and watch over them. Amen.

As far as prayers went it was quick and to the point, but she figured the victims in the accident could use every prayer they could get.

"That was a lot of pickles." Edie glanced in her rearview mirror as if checking for pickles once again. They were a ghostly white against the darkness of the road.

"Jah," Kappy whispered and faced front. She was beginning to get a little sick to her stomach turned around like that and driving faster than a buggy pace. Or maybe it was the stench of vinegar.

"I'm sure what happened will be all over the valley by dark."

"Maybe," Kappy said. She closed her eyes, almost haunted by the sight of the stretcher being loaded into the ambulance, pickles lying all over the place, and the strong smell of vinegar. And the broken buggy. Don't forget that.

"We are never going to make it now." Edie flipped one hand at the dash clock. They should have been at the shop ten minutes ago, and they had at least five minutes left before they arrived. Well, Kappy *thought,* anyway. She wasn't practiced at determining arrival times in cars.

"Maybe he'll be okay," Kappy reassured

her. And she hoped it was true.

That was the thing about Jimmy. He was as sweet as they came, but things could set him off. Kappy wasn't sure why some things bothered him more than others. Like why he wouldn't eat red foods. Ever since his mother died, things had been a little harder for him, but he was trying for Edie's sake. Kappy was just glad that Edie had decided to stay in Blue Sky, allowing Jimmy to do the same.

But despite Jimmy's usually positive and amicable attitude, Kappy could tell that Edie was concerned. *Amicable.* That was another one from her word-a-day calendar. It meant friendly, and that was one word that fit Jimmy Peachey for sure.

A thoughtful silence fell between them as they continued toward Mose Peachey's bait shop.

"Oh, no." The car started to slow as Edie whispered the words.

"What?" Kappy glanced at the dashboard as if somehow she could determine the problem, but Edie wasn't staring at the car's gauges, she was looking ahead, at the bait shop's graveled parking lot.

Jimmy was out front, pacing back and forth, shaking his head. He held the fob on the alert necklace he wore in case of emergencies. Even from this distance, Kappy could tell that his face was creased with a frown of worry.

Edie pulled the car into the lot, a little too quickly as far as Kappy was concerned, but she knew that Edie wanted to get to her brother as soon as possible. Her friend might be a little flighty, but Kappy knew she loved Jimmy above all else.

Edie shoved the gearshift into park and hopped out of the car with it still running. "Jimmy. Hey, Jimmy."

He stopped pacing and lifted his head, pinning his sister with a hard gray stare. "Where have you been?"

"There was an accident on the highway. Are you ready to go home?"

"Accident?" His gaze swung wildly around as if making sure everything in their corner of the world was still intact.

"Yeah, of course." Edie's tone was offhanded. She was trying to downplay the emotions and get Jimmy into the car without a meltdown. Whether she would be successful or not still remained to be seen.

Jimmy held up the fob. "Do you know how many times I almost pushed this button? This one right here. Do you know?"

"You didn't push it, though, right?"

"Five times." He held up his fingers to

emphasize his point.

"But you didn't?" Edie asked again.

"When *Mamm* . . . when *Mamm* . . . you told me that I should have pushed it. Today I thought I would have to push it." Tears welled in his eyes, but whatever anger he had drained from him. "You worried me."

Edie reached for him, then remembering he didn't like to be touched, she lowered her hands to her sides. "I know. And I'm sorry."

"I thought you were . . . I almost pushed the button five times."

"I know. But I'm here now. Are you ready to go home?"

He looked from his sister to where Kappy waited in the car. "Now?"

Edie smiled with apparent relief. "Yes. Now."

Jimmy nodded. "*Jah.* Okay." He started toward the car, then stopped and captured the alert fob in his grasp once again. "But next time you're late, I'm pushing it. How else is anyone going to know if something happens to you?"

CHAPTER 2

They were halfway home the long way before Edie finally convinced Jimmy that he should only push the button in case of emergencies, and her being late picking him up from work did not an emergency make.

They drove around the back side of the valley on the road closest to Jacks Mountain and came around the opposite side of the area. Driving the long way may have taken them around the scene of the accident that happened earlier in the day, but it still took twice as long to get home. Everyone else was trying to avoid the main road as well, it seemed. When they passed Jay Glick's house, Kappy couldn't help but stare. Not all that long ago, chickens once pecked around the yard and cows mooed from the barn. Now the house was devoid of life.

"Is that . . . ?" Edie peered over the steering wheel as she pulled into Kappy's drive.

"What?" Kappy half expected to see

Elmer on the front porch — even though she had put him out back — with some poor animal in his jaws. That was the one thing she hadn't anticipated when she got a beagle. They were hunting dogs, a fact that came home with every "present" he brought her. But it wasn't Elmer on the front porch. It was Martha Peachey.

No one in the valley knew exactly how old Martha was. Kappy wouldn't even hazard a guess, but Martha had been old as long as Kappy had known her.

"What's she doing here?" Edie asked.

"She's sitting on the porch," Jimmy said helpfully.

Kappy shot Edie a look. "How am I supposed to know?"

Edie stopped the car and shifted the gear into park. "Go ask."

Kappy would have liked to refuse, but the woman was on her porch.

Martha pushed herself to her feet, leaning heavily on her cane as she waited for Kappy to get out of the car.

"Kathryn King," she called. "I thought you were done running around all over the place in a car." Only Martha Peachey called Kappy by her given name.

"Hi, Martha. It's good to see you, too," Kappy murmured as she shut the car door

26

and made her way to the porch. She was only half aware that Edie had gotten out of the car and was following behind her.

"What brings you out today, Martha? Need a new *kapp*?"

Martha pointed the tip of her cane toward Kappy as she climbed the steps. "I will. Going to be a funeral soon." She shook her head sadly as Kappy tried to find the words to ask whose funeral that might be. But she thought she knew. Bad news traveled fast.

"That accident on the highway," she said. "Jonah Esh?" The thought was heartbreaking. Jonah hadn't even started his baptism classes or joined the church and just like that his life was gone. Kappy knew it was all part of the Good Lord's plan, but she couldn't say knowing that made her understand it any better.

But Martha shook her head. "Sally June."

Kappy blinked and cast a quick glance at Edie. The only Sally June she knew was Sally June Esh, Jonah's sister. And if she was having a funeral . . . then that could only mean . . . "Jonah wasn't driving the pickle delivery today?" she asked, her voice barely above a whisper.

Martha shook her head. "That's what I'm trying to tell you, but you aren't listening. Sally June was in that buggy crash."

"And she's . . . dead?" Kappy asked.

"That's a shame," Edie said. Though Kappy figured the two had never met. Sally June was nineteen or so and couldn't have been more than nine or ten when Edie had left.

"A tragedy," Kappy agreed.

"It's the Lord's will." Martha gave a stern nod as if her statement settled it all.

And though both Kappy and Edie had been raised to accept God's will for what it was, Kappy couldn't help but wonder why God would will something so heartbreaking to happen.

"Now about that new *kapp*," Martha started.

Kappy sighed. "Come around back, and I'll get you set up."

A rustling noise sounded outside shortly after noon the next day. Kappy checked to make sure Elmer was still close. He lifted his head, his ears falling back as he pointed his nose into the air. He sniffed, then laid his head back down as if declaring that nothing was amiss.

He was starting to get used to the fact that people came and went as they pleased, letting themselves in Kappy's basement to pick up special orders, pre-made *kapps*, and bonnets for travel. The first couple of weeks he'd barked his head off, but lately he'd come to expect the noises of her customers.

And there had been a lot of them. Just this morning she had lost count of the people stopping in to buy a new *kapp*. At the rate this was going, she would have to replenish before the end of the week. Sally June Esh's funeral was Friday and Kappy could be completely out of stock by then.

A knock sounded at the front door and Kappy jumped, startled by the change.

"People never learn," she muttered to no one, maybe Elmer. Then louder, "Around back. Down the basement."

The knock sounded again.

Elmer hopped up and trotted to the front door. He dropped his rear to the floor and stuck his nose in the air as he let out the perfect beagle howl.

On the other side of the door, a voice sounded, but Kappy couldn't make out the words over Elmer's baying.

"Who is it? Elmer, hush!" But the dog kept on. Kappy scooped his wriggling form into her arms and flung open the door, preparing to tell whoever it was that she sold *kapps* around back and in the basement only. It was good to have boundaries. But Edie stood on the other side of the threshold.

"Why didn't you answer the door?" she asked, barging inside.

"Hi, Edie. It's good to see you, too."

Edie whirled around and shot her an apologetic grin. "I wish the Amish were allowed to have phones," she mused, one hand propped on her hip. "It would make this so much easier."

"This?" Kappy shut the door and turned to face her friend.

Elmer, having decided that Edie was no immediate threat, circled her and tugged on the legs of her skin-tight black pants. To Kappy they looked more like winter tights than a garment to be worn by itself. The only difference she could see was the bright green whip-stitching that snaked up each leg at the outside seam.

"Quit it." Edie shook her pant leg out of his mouth and made her way toward the kitchen. "This." She held out her phone even as she plopped down into one of the kitchen chairs.

"Hold it still," Kappy fussed, grasping her hand to steady it. Unsuccessful, she sat down across from Edie with a shake of her head. "What is it?"

"A text."

"From?"

"That's the thing." Edie threw up her hands. "I don't know."

Kappy shook her head. "Start at the beginning."

"Okay." Edie took a deep breath. "I got a text this morning, and I don't know who it's from."

"Jah."

"It says —" Edie thumbed her phone and sucked in another gulp of air. *"Some accidents aren't accidents."*

Kappy waited for her to continue, but Edie just stared at her with eyes wide. "That's it?"

"Don't you see? They're talking about the buggy wreck yesterday."

Kappy shook her head. "What makes you say that?"

"Well, it was an accident, wasn't it? And somebody died. What if it wasn't an accident?"

Kappy closed one eye as if that could bring Edie's argument into focus. "I don't understand. Was it an accident or not?"

"Exactly." Edie sat back triumphantly in her seat, a self-satisfied grin spreading across her face.

Kappy frowned.

"Don't you see?" Edie leaned forward again and propped her elbows on the table.

"We call those things accidents, but what if it was an 'on purpose'?"

"And someone tried to kill Sally June?"

"Yes!"

A pang of unease thumped in Kappy's midsection. "But why? Why would someone want to do that?"

"Why does any human do the things they do?" Edie shrugged.

"Have you shown that to the police?"

"Of course not. It's not like I have any proof. Just a theory."

"A crazy theory," Kappy grumbled. She had almost let herself get caught up in Edie's dramatic ways once again.

"It might be a little crazy, but it's also very possible."

"Again, who would want to kill Sally June Esh?"

"I don't know. Maybe a rival pickle maker?"

"Now *that* is crazy. Why would anyone kill another over pickles?"

"Stranger things have happened."

Kappy shook her head, starting to feel a little dizzy from all this. "You're talking about Amish folks here."

"Maybe," Edie conceded. "Or maybe not. I read in the paper today that the police are looking for the driver of a dark-colored car.

I don't know many Amish who drive cars of any color."

Kappy frowned, trying to understand it all. "You're saying that a rival, *Englisch* pickle maker ran Sally June Esh off the road?"

"It's possible." She sniffed. "But when you say it like that it doesn't seem as likely. I suppose there's only one way to find out."

"How?" Kappy was certain she would regret asking.

"Friday's the funeral. I say we go and see who shows up."

There were so many problems with that idea that Kappy didn't know where to begin. "Last time I checked, you were shunned, and I wasn't invited." Nor would she be. She might make the *kapps* for the entire valley, but she somehow always remained just on the fringes of the community.

"I'll dress in my old Amish clothes, and we crash it."

Amish funerals were as big as Amish weddings, and like weddings, they required an invitation to attend.

"I know what you're thinking," Edie said. "But there will be so many people there, no one will notice if we sneak in."

"And what will this prove?"

Edie flicked an expressive hand in Kappy's general direction. "They're always talking on the TV shows about how murderers return to the scene of the crime."

"You're talking about the funeral, though."

"Same thing. Chances are the murderer —"

"If there even is one."

"— will attend the funeral out of guilt."

"You think the Eshes will invite them?"

"I'm thinking they're *Englisch* and won't know the rules of funerals. They'll show up and be easy to spot. All we have to do is find them once they get there."

Kappy wasn't sure, but this could be the dumbest thing she had ever done. In her entire life.

She flicked the reins over the horse's rump and tried not to feel like every eye was on them. Beside her, Edie pulled on her apron and frowned.

"I never thought I would be dressed like this again." She messed with her prayer *kapp,* obviously uncomfortable.

"This was your idea."

Edie shifted again. "Don't remind me."

Kappy hid her smile and pulled into the lane that led to the Esh farm. A line of buggies was already parked down one side in

34

front of the pasture, and the horses milled around, accustomed to being turned out in strange fields.

Kappy and Edie had purposefully waited until it was a little late before heading out. Kappy thought it best that they arrive after everyone else. The more people who were already at the service, the less chance they had of being noticed.

They were just late enough that most of the buggy parkers had already gone in. Kappy unhooked her mare, June Bug, and turned her out into the pasture before any of the helpers left could come over to assist her. The less interaction they had, the better.

"Did you see that?" Kappy nodded toward a line of cars and trucks parked off to one side.

"Mennonites?"

"Probably. But are we going to be able to tell them from the *Englischers*?"

Edie shot her a look. "Yeah, I believe so." She nodded toward a woman with a handkerchief covering.

But not all of the non-Amish there were Mennonites. Kappy spotted several *Englischers* in the crowd. "How are we supposed to know if any of them are guilty?"

Edie shrugged. "They'll be acting nervous

and stuff."

Kappy scanned the crowd. No one looked particularly nervous or frightened. Most just looked sad. A group of Sally June's friends stood clustered together, the girls wiping their eyes as the boys shifted uncomfortably. Kappy hadn't been particularly active in her youth group, but she knew most Amish teens were. These bonds grew strong during the runaround years. Even as adults the members got together on a regular basis, eating, laughing, and playing games. Sally June would be missed.

"I don't see anyone who looks like they might have kil— hurt her."

Edie shook her head. "It could be anyone here," she said out of the corner of her mouth.

Kappy looked around again. Mr. Roberts from the supermarket was among the *Englischers* there. But she couldn't believe that he could be guilty of harming another human being. Mild-mannered. That was the only way to describe him. Jimmy was more capable of violence than Mr. Roberts.

"Was Jimmy upset that he had to work today?" Kappy gave a quick nod to Mose Peachey. Jimmy had gone into work even though it was one of his days off so that Mose could attend the funeral.

Edie shook her head. "He likes the money. He says he's saving for a skateboard."

Kappy drew back, her attention swinging from Mose to Edie. "A what? Isn't that dangerous?"

"I didn't say I was going to let him have one. Only that he was saving for it."

"You should stop that dream before he gets his hopes up."

"I don't know." Edie gave an offhand shrug. "Maybe it'll be good for him."

"They're dangerous," Kappy repeated while Edie just smiled. "At least make him save for a helmet, too."

"And I'll be sure to tell him it was your idea."

"Not funny." Kappy looked around the crowd again. Nothing seemed out of place, just a bunch of solemn-faced funeral goers who looked as though they would rather be anywhere but there.

Englisch, Mennonite, Amish . . . all seemed equally upset. No one seemed jumpy or like they didn't belong.

"Maybe that text wasn't supposed to go to you," Kappy mused.

"I've thought about that. And I think it was. After all, who else here has a cell phone and could look into this?"

That was true. "Does it show the number?" Kappy asked, trying her best to remember all she knew about the phones. "If it shows the number, then you could call it right back."

"I tried that." Edie frowned. "But no one answered. It's not like I can make the other person pick up."

And that was true as well. Even with the number, they were no closer to discovering who had sent the text.

"And there was no voice mail, just one of those automated recordings, telling me that the person at that number couldn't answer. No name or anything."

"You don't think the kil— person responsible for the accident sent the text, do you?"

"It's possible, I guess." Edie tilted her head to one side as if mulling over the question. "But why?"

"You know, out of guilt?"

"You mean they want to be caught?"

Kappy shrugged. "It was just a thought."

"Hmmm . . ." Edie looked around the crowd. Kappy wondered if they looked the same to her. Edie had been gone from the Amish for almost ten years. She saw things both ways: as a woman raised Plain and a woman who lived in the *Englisch* world.

Had the killer texted Edie? Or was that person waiting in the crowd? "It could have been a witness," she muttered.

"What?" Edie turned her attention back to Kappy.

"The text. It could have been from a witness."

"I suppose." Edie shifted her gaze to the crowd once again.

Kappy tried to see it from her perspective. Or at least differently from how she had before. There were *Englisch* people in attendance, most of them merchants in Blue Sky, owners and managers of the places where the Eshes sold their famous pickles. The Mennonites milling around were friends and neighbors and the owner of the Country Store, which sat across the road from Hiram's store, Sundries and Sweets.

And speaking of Hiram . . . his store carried the Eshes' pickles. And she supposed that he was around somewhere. She hadn't seen him in a few days. And things hadn't been the same between them since Ruth Peachey died. Her death hadn't caused the change but rather the events surrounding it. Hiram hadn't exactly been supportive when she and Edie had tried to solve the murder. But the more things had happened, the further Edie and Kappy had been drawn into the mystery.

Which meant . . .

She shook her head. "What am I saying? This isn't a murder. That text means nothing. We're just wound up from all the trouble with your *mamm.* There is not a mystery here."

"Maybe." But Kappy could tell that Edie said that only to appease her. "Let's get a plate. Maybe we can find out more in the food line."

Amish funeral fare was always the same: cold roast beef, mashed potatoes, rolls, and prunes. Always prunes to strengthen the body.

Edie took a bite and made a face. "I always hated these. They make you go to the bathroom, you know."

"Then why did you get it?"

"Do you think I had a choice? Bertha Troyer came up right behind me."

Kappy tried not to laugh. "Serves you right for crashing a funeral."

"Quit fussing at me and keep your ears open for anything interesting." She popped the rest of the prune into her mouth and grabbed her stomach. "Uh-oh."

"Edie, be serious. There's no way the prune worked that fast."

"I don't know what it is, but . . . I gotta go." She rushed off, head ducked so she could wind her way between the people without being recognized.

"Kappy King."

Kappy tried to smile as Mary Raber sauntered up. "Hi, Mary."

"Who was that you were with?"

"Just a cousin . . . from the west." *Lord, forgive me the lie.*

"Really? I didn't know you had family out there. I didn't know you had family at all."

Kappy did her best not to just walk away. Mary Raber was the biggest gossip in all of Blue Sky. If Kappy was anything other than as sweet as pie, then it would be all over the valley by sundown.

"Oh, there's a few of us left."

"Strange. For a minute there she looked a bit like Edith Peachey."

"*Pbth. . . .*" Kappy blew a raspberry, something that Edie did on a regular basis. "No. I haven't seen Edie in . . ." She trailed off, willing her mouth to quit talking and for Mary to quit asking questions.

"You know what I heard?"

"No."

"I heard that on top of this tragedy with Sally June, the Eshes found out that Jonah has been dating a girl they don't approve of."

Kappy didn't keep up with the youth of their district, but news was shared both

41

good and bad. There weren't many teens in the area who were disobedient. At least not many that she had heard about. "Someone from the valley?"

"I don't know." Mary's eyes twinkled with excitement over having a captive audience. "That's the thing. No one has seen him out with a girl. And he's not committed to dating anyone. Pretty interesting, *jah*?"

"I . . . I guess." She supposed it could be considered interesting, but more than that she felt for the Esh family. They had lost their daughter and now rumors were being spread about their son.

Kappy had never known Jonah Esh to be anything other than a polite young man. She had heard he was preparing for his baptism classes, but it was still too early to know if that was actually true. They had just had this year's baptism classes, and there wouldn't be another until the year after next. Until that time, he wouldn't be free to date. But that didn't mean he couldn't stake a claim on a girl who had already been baptized.

"I've heard it was a Mennonite girl," Mary continued. "But someone else said that she thought it was a girl from Lancaster. An *Englisch* girl."

"Did she say who she thought it was?"

Mary drew back as if she had been scalded. "Oh, no. That would be gossiping. Excuse me. I think I see Alma over there."

Mary moved away before Kappy could say anything else. She did look to see where Mary was headed, but Alma Miller was nowhere around.

"Whew. I didn't think she would ever leave."

Kappy whirled around as Edie came up. "You were hiding from her?"

"Of course. She's got the biggest mouth in three counties. I couldn't chance it. I've been getting enough looks since we got here."

"It might have been better if you'd worn the correct apron."

Edie smoothed a hand over her front. "Whatever do you mean? This apron is not the right one?"

"You know good and well it's not." The district's clothing rules had been drilled into them since they were old enough to sit up without help. A person didn't forget that in just a few years living with the *Englisch.*

"Hmmm . . . I guess I forgot."

Kappy debated on whether or not to call her on the lie, but as she prepared what to say next, a voice sounded behind her.

"Fancy seeing you here."

Kappy whirled around to find Jack Jones, detective, standing behind her.

"And dressed like that, no less." He let out a chuckle, and Edie started toward him with murder in her eyes.

CHAPTER 3

Kappy could almost hear Edie's teeth grinding together. As she watched, Edie stilled her steps and propped her hands on her hips as she coolly stared down Jack Jones. "And what's wrong with the way I'm dressed?"

"Nothing." Jack laughed, but his mirth was cut short as Edie took two steps forward and punched him in the arm.

"Ow!" He rubbed the spot where her fist struck. "Aren't the Amish pacifists?"

"Yes," Edie said and punched him again.

"If this is what you call peace, I would hate to see violence." He rubbed his arm once more.

Kappy had a feeling his pride was hurt a little more than his arm.

"What are the two of you doing here?"

"I think I could ask you the same thing," Edie countered.

Jack nodded. "Of course you're here. It is

a funeral and all." He shifted his weight, then frowned. "But why are you dressed like that?" He flicked a hand in Edie's general direction.

"What's wrong with the way I'm dressed?"

"Nothing, if you're Amish. Are you joining back up?"

Edie looked ready to answer. She opened her mouth, then shut it. She opened it again, and closed it once more.

Anything she said could be incriminating. It wasn't like they could tell the police that they were there investigating a crime. But maybe if Kappy told Jack Jones about the text he could help them.

"Edie got a strange —" She got no further. Edie stepped down hard on her foot.

"Ow!" Kappy cried.

"I don't think it's strange," Edie said, her teeth clenched as if daring Kappy to contradict her.

"Now *that* wasn't suspicious at all," Jack drawled.

"There's nothing to be suspicious about," Edie shot back.

Jack looked from Edie to Kappy, then back to Edie again. "Uh-huh." He did not seem convinced. But that didn't mean Edie was going to give up her secrets.

"And are you here in an official capacity?"

Edie asked.

That's the way. Change the subject.

But Jack was nothing if not smart. He stopped just long enough for Kappy to know he was allowing the shift, then he turned his full attention to Edie. "Something like that."

But Edie couldn't press him. If she insisted on knowing what he meant, he could just as easily turn the tables on them once again. "Well, good luck with that." She grabbed Kappy's arm and pointed her in the direction of the buggies.

"Are we leaving?" Kappy asked, stumbling along beside her.

"Might as well," Edie grumbled. "We're not going to find out anymore today."

"Kappy." She turned as someone called her name.

"Hiram," she greeted him in return.

"I didn't know you would be here."

Kappy shifted from one foot to the other, unwilling to admit that she and Edie had crashed the funeral.

"I don't believe we've met." He turned toward Edie, hand out to shake, but his expression froze as he saw who she was. "Edie Peachey, is that you?"

Edie just smiled.

Hiram shook his head. "Should I ask?"

47

"No," Kappy replied. "Are you okay?" He looked tired with dark circles under his eyes and a pinched look around his mouth. Surely that wasn't because she had told him they could only be friends for now.

"It's Willie. He's gone again."

Kappy wasn't sure if she should feel relieved that she wasn't responsible or saddened because the look was caused by his brother's disappearance.

During the last couple of years, Hiram's younger brother, Willie, had been having a tough time, leaving the Amish for greener pastures only to return a month or so later. But he had left and come back so many times, Kappy couldn't understand why this time would be so upsetting to Hiram.

"Did something happen?" she asked.

Hiram shrugged. "It just feels different this time. *Mamm*'s worried. Everyone's worried."

Kappy wanted to ask why this time was different, but she kept quiet. She and Hiram had agreed to be friends and only friends, but that didn't mean she should pry into every aspect of his life. "I'm sorry," she murmured instead.

He nodded. "Just keep him in your prayers, please. I have a feeling he's going to need them."

■ ■ ■ ■

"What was that all about?" Edie asked once they had hitched up the buggy and started back for their houses.

"Hiram or Jack?"

"Hiram. I know what Jack wanted."

Kappy shot her a quick look. "You do?"

Edie nodded. "But Hiram . . ."

Kappy explained as best she could about Willie's choices and how they were affecting the family. "His *mamm* has been beside herself for years, doing everything she can to keep him happy so he won't leave."

"Willie always was her favorite," Edie muttered.

"That's not very nice," Kappy countered.

"But true."

Okay, so maybe she couldn't agree with that point. It was true that Willie was Janet Lapp's favorite child. Or maybe it just seemed like it since he required so much more attention than his siblings. Ever since Kappy had known him, his mother had done everything in her power to make him happy, keep him comfortable, keep him with her. But the older he got, the more restless he seemed to be, until he started leaving the Amish for months at a time. Kappy fully

49

expected that one time he just wouldn't come back and that would be that. Maybe that was what was different about this time. Maybe the rest of the Lapps could tell that this time Willie meant it.

"I guess we should stop by and pick up Jimmy, *jah*?" Kappy asked.

"I can go get him in the car," Edie said.

"Or we can pick him up in the buggy."

"The car would be easier," Edie countered.

Kappy shook her head. "It's not about easy. But I guess you never learned that while you were here." Or she had forgotten it.

"You know what I think? I think you are trying to make me Amish again."

"It was your idea to dress Amish and go to the funeral."

"But it was your idea to take the buggy."

Kappy shot her a look. "Really?"

Edie shrugged. "Just sayin'."

At the main road, Kappy turned the buggy in the direction of Mose Peachey's shop.

"Why do you suppose Hiram said this time was different?" Edie asked. "You know, Willie leaving."

"I didn't think you were paying that much attention."

Edie tugged the prayer covering off her

head, then shook her hair free. "I was trying not to." She was still a little put out that she was shunned, even though she had to expect it. After all, she had left the Amish after joining the church. Rules were rules.

"I don't know. I wanted to ask, but . . ."

"Why didn't you?"

"It's not my business."

Edie nodded. "Don't you feel a little . . . vulnerable on the road like this?"

Kappy glanced over to see Edie's white-knuckle grip on the dash. "Not particularly."

"Even after Sally June's accident?"

"You believe it's an accident now?"

"Just sayin'."

"Well, don't. You can't worry over God's will."

"God's will . . ." Edie mused.

"Things that are out of our control."

Edie let go of the dash and sat back in her seat. But she didn't respond.

Kappy gave her one small glance, then turned her attention to the road ahead. They rode along for a time, the only sound the rattling whir of the wheels on the pavement and the clop of the horse hooves.

"We're early," Edie said, as Kappy pulled the buggy into the parking lot at Mose's bait shop.

"Amazing what happens when you leave

51

on time."

"Yeah, yeah." Edie swung down and started for the shop, leaving Kappy to hitch up the horse and trail behind.

"Good afternoon." An Amish woman nodded toward them as she walked past them to her own parked buggy. Kappy had never seen her before. She was tall and thin with dark hair streaked with gray. At least what she could see of it was.

"What do you suppose she's doing here? I mean, it's a bait shop, and she doesn't look like a fisherman," Edie said.

"Buying honey."

Edie turned around, Kappy supposed to stare at the stranger. "She doesn't have a bag."

"Quit being so suspicious."

The inside of the small shed was dim and cool. And mostly geared toward the male. Crossbows hung from hooks in the ceiling. A large cooler hummed and gurgled in one corner. It was filled with hellgrammites, the odd-looking larvae of the dobsonfly that apparently fish couldn't get enough of. At least that was what the handwritten sign above the cooler said. Several other types of hunting and fishing equipment were displayed around, though Kappy couldn't identify most of it. Fishing poles and rifles, and that was where her knowledge ended.

Jimmy's face lit up like a firefly when he caught sight of them. "Edie, Edie, come look." He grabbed her hand and dragged her toward the cooler.

She shook her head, resisting his efforts. "I've seen those things, and they give me the creeps."

Kappy had to agree; they were a little like fat millipedes with several legs to propel them along.

"Not them. We got something new in today. Look, minnows."

Kappy frowned. "Mose didn't have them before."

Jimmy shook his head. "No, but he got them in for me. I like the fishing stuff, and he said he would expand his business, but I have to take care of them."

Edie's mouth twisted into a frown. "Are you sure you're up for it?"

"Of course I am. I can take care of puppies and gerbils, ducks and rabbits. I can take care of fish, too." He beamed her a proud smile.

But unlike puppies and gerbils, someone was going to feed these fish to other, bigger fish. But Kappy wasn't about to tell him that. A job like that belonged to his sister.

"That's great," Edie said, though her tone

53

was anything but excited.

"*Dat*'s trying to build up the store a bit more." Fifteen-year-old Mel Peachey took a proud step forward. "I'm going to run things soon."

"Good for you," Edie murmured.

"That lady who just left? She wants to sell canned goods," Jimmy added.

"What did you tell her?" Kappy asked. Not that she wanted to sell any of her own canned stock, but it was still good to know. *Kapp* making kept her busy, but it was never a bad idea to keep one's options open.

Jimmy made a face. "That she would have to come back when Mose was here."

"I could have made the decision," Mel grumbled.

"Maybe, but if you made the wrong one your *dat* would be mad," Jimmy countered.

Mel had no comment for that and instead went to straighten the jars of honey stacked to one side of the cash register.

"He's also talking about bringing in some birdhouses and baskets made by the Mennonite woman who lives at the bottom of the hill."

"I've seen her work." Kappy nodded. "She's good."

"That was my suggestion." Jimmy jerked a thumb proudly toward his chest.

Edie smiled. "Aren't you the businessman all of a sudden."

"One more reason to keep the puppies," Jimmy countered.

"You're still thinking about selling off the puppies?" Kappy had thought Edie was happy taking up her mother's breeding business. As far as she knew this matter had been settled long ago.

"Jimmy, go get your coat."

"I don't have a coat, Edie. It's summertime."

"Edie," Kappy said.

"Well, get your lunch box."

"I didn't —"

"Oh, for heaven's sake." Edie tossed her hands into the air. "I only said I was thinking about it."

"But why?" Jimmy and Kappy asked at the same time. Yet Kappy was afraid she knew. Edie was still thinking about returning to her life outside of Blue Sky. And where would that leave Jimmy?

"They're a lot of work," Edie admitted.

"But I do most of the feedings."

"I mean the books and the registrations. And the shots. Let me tell you, the vet isn't very happy with me after this deal with *Mamm*."

"Maybe we shouldn't have questioned

him so blatantly about the murder," Kappy mused.

"Blatant?" Edie asked.

"It's on today's word-a-day calendar."

"I see," she replied.

Jimmy bounced up and down on his toes, a sure sign he was getting anxious. "But I love the puppies."

"Even though you have to give them up?" his sister asked.

"That's the best part," Jimmy said. "I always get to have a puppy. As long as we have a litter."

"I suppose," Edie muttered.

"I'll come help you," Kappy said. She gave a fierce nod, not realizing until that moment that she couldn't let Edie leave Blue Sky. If not for Jimmy's sake, then definitely for her own. Edie was the one person who fit in less than she did. They were made to be friends, and she couldn't allow her best friend to leave without a fight.

"You have your own business to run."

"What if I bring Jimmy to the bait shop on the days he works? That will give you more time. Or you could let Jimmy drive himself."

"Yes." Jimmy gave a quick fist pump.

Mel rolled his eyes.

Kappy felt Jimmy was fully capable. After

all, he had driven to her house and painted her front door not so long ago. But it seemed that Edie was picking up the role of overprotective mother right where Ruth Peachey left off.

"I just said I was thinking about it," Edie groused. "No one needs to get their drawers in a wad."

"Just don't make a decision yet," Kappy pleaded.

Jimmy moved behind her, nodding the whole time. "Please." He clasped his hands together as if in prayer.

"Fine," Edie exhaled, then turned and headed out to the carriage.

"You're not really thinking about selling all the puppies, are you?" Jimmy asked on the way home.

He might have actually voiced the question, but it was on Kappy's mind as well.

"I don't know," Edie mumbled, her voice sounding like she had no energy left at all.

"Why do I feel this has less to do with dogs and more to do with something else?" Kappy leaned close when she asked, hoping that Jimmy wouldn't overhear.

Edie shrugged one shoulder. "I dunno."

"You don't know, or you're not ready to talk about it?"

"Both."

Kappy straightened and shook her head. Something was definitely up with Edie, but as to what was anyone's guess.

"I don't belong here," she finally said.

"What?" Jimmy screeched. "Of course you belong here. This is your home. It always has been."

"Something happen?" Kappy asked from the corner of her mouth.

Jimmy continued to extol the benefits of Blue Sky and its many Plain residents.

Extol. That was another from her word-a-day calendar. It meant to praise enthusiastically, and that was exactly what Jimmy was doing. But the more he talked, the more miserable Edie looked.

"Tell me," Kappy demanded.

Edie let out a frustrated growl. "Did you see how Mel treated me? He wouldn't even look at me."

"He's a fifteen-year-old boy," Kappy pointed out. "He's supposed to be that way."

Edie shook her head. "No. I don't believe that. He was shunning me hardcore."

Kappy wasn't sure exactly what *hardcore* was. It hadn't been on her calendar. Would it be two words? She mentally shook the thought away. Whatever it meant, she got the gist. "You are under the *Bann.*" She said the words as apologetically as possible, but she knew they carried a sting.

"That's just it!" she cried.

"What's just it?" Kappy asked. Somewhere along the way she had lost the thread of this conversation.

"Never mind." Edie blew out a breath, lifting her bangs off her forehead in the process.

"If you don't like being under the *Bann* you could always rejoin the church."

"*Jah,* Edie, that would be great." Jimmy gave her a toothy grin.

"I am not rejoining the church."

Jimmy fell back in his seat, his expression crestfallen.

That was when Kappy understood: Leaving the Amish had been difficult, but for Edie Peachey, returning was twice as hard.

"You could, though, right?" Jimmy asked.

Edie sighed. "I guess so." But her heart wasn't in it. Kappy could tell. How terrible to not belong in either world.

Kappy didn't exactly fit in with the normal crowd, so to speak. But she knew where she belonged. God had made her Amish for a reason.

So why had God laid it on Edie's heart to leave? Or was it as the bishop said and thoughts of a better life outside the district were the devil's handiwork?

She cast a quick sideways look at Edie.

No. That wasn't it at all. But she surely didn't understand it herself.

"It's not a decision that you have to make right away," Kappy murmured.

Edie swallowed hard and gave a quick nod.

"You have Jimmy to think about, too, you know."

"What about me?" He pushed himself forward in his seat and stuck his head between theirs.

"Nothing," they said at the same time.

Then they burst out laughing, the tense moment gone so quick Kappy had to wonder if it had even happened.

"Did you bring me a piece of funeral pie?" Jimmy asked as they continued along.

"No," Edie said without explanation. "But I can make you one. I found *Mamm*'s recipe book last week."

Jimmy made a face. "Isn't that bad luck? To eat funeral pie that didn't come from a funeral?"

"It's just raisin pie," Edie said.

Jimmy shook his head. "No," he adamantly stated. "It has to be bad luck."

Kappy couldn't help but slow down. They were in the spot where Sally June's buggy went off the road. There were a few tire

60

marks and a streak of yellow on the asphalt, but other than that, nothing out of the ordinary to signify that someone had died there on that very spot.

The thought sent chills down her spine. Or maybe it was all this talk about funeral pie.

"Is this . . . ?" Edie asked, not finishing the question.

Kappy nodded and kept the horse at a steady pace.

A car went around them, and Kappy instinctively closed her eyes, fearing the worst.

Edie's talk of vulnerability had her jumpier than a jackrabbit.

But the car continued forward just as the buggy did, only faster.

Kappy breathed a sigh of relief when she turned onto School Yard Road. A few more minutes and they would be home. Safe.

"Who is that?" Edie asked as they pulled into Kappy's drive.

The man on her front porch stood, and she immediately recognized him, her neighbor, Ephraim Jess, one of the oldest men in the district. Ephraim was tall and lanky, a bit stooped in the shoulders, with craggy features like the rock that made up Jacks Mountain.

"Kathryn King," he called as she hopped down from the buggy.

Kappy stole a look at Edie. Her eyes were wide. No one called Kappy *Kathryn* except for Martha Peachey, the older woman who lived on the other side of Jimmy and Edie. No relation that anyone could remember.

"Uh-oh," Edie whispered.

"What brings you over today, Ephraim?"

He hobbled down the porch steps, meeting her halfway between the house and buggy. "There's a murderer running loose, and I want to know what you're doing about it."

CHAPTER 4

Kappy looked at Edie. Edie looked at Kappy. They both looked to Ephraim.

"What?" Edie was the one who broke the intense silence.

"There's a murderer running around," he patiently repeated. "And I want to know what you are going to do about it."

"I — uh . . ." Kappy wasn't sure how that sentence should end. Or begin. "Ephraim, that's a strong accusation."

"Are you saying you're not going to take responsibility for your ill-mannered pup?"

Pup? "Are you talking about Elmer?"

Ephraim flicked a hand in her direction as if the details were not important. "I don't know what you call him. But he's a killer. I lost three chickens this morning."

"There are plenty of birds and squirrels here in Kappy's yard," Edie said. "Why would he run all the way to your house to chase other animals?"

Ephraim raised his gaze, but to Kappy it looked as though he were staring through Edie instead of at her. "Kappy, you must do something."

Edie let out a sound that was half-sigh, half-growl. She still hadn't gotten used to being shunned. Kappy supposed it had to be a little like arriving at a party where everyone ignored you.

Kappy shot her a quick, sympathetic look, then turned her attention back to Ephraim. "I'll bring by some chickens in the morning," she promised.

"Chickens?" Ephraim shook his head. "You think this is about chickens?"

"I . . . well, it seems . . . That is . . ."

Jimmy picked that moment to get out of the buggy.

"Hang on, Jimmy," Edie called to him.

But he kept coming. "We could build a fence," he said, that adoring grin on his face. He was so proud of himself for finding a solution.

"Kappy already has a fence," Edie said gently.

Jimmy shook his head. "Not a fence-fence, but one like we have for the puppies. They never get out."

Except for that one time, but they'd had a little help.

"Thanks, Jimmy." Kappy reached out a hand toward him, then dropped it back to her side before actually touching him. Still, the thought was there.

Ephraim looked off into the distance, then spat.

Edie shuddered.

Kappy hid her smile. It wasn't really funny, and yet it was.

"I don't think you'll do it," Ephraim said.

"Build a better fence?" Kappy asked.

"Jah."

"I'll build the fence," Kappy promised. "And I'll bring three chickens by in the morning as well."

Ephraim stared at her a moment, then spat again. "Better make it five."

"That's blackmail," Edie screeched once Ephraim was heading back to his own house and well out of hearing distance. Not that he would have acknowledged her words.

"Maybe," Kappy said absently. "But I'm still taking him five chickens."

"Does that mean we're not building the fence?" Jimmy asked, his expression falling.

"Of course not," Kappy and Edie said at the same time.

"But chickens first," Kappy added.

"Are you saying we're loony tunes?" Edie asked.

Kappy shook her head. "I don't know what that is, but if it means that we've started seeing problems where there are none, then yes. We're lonely tunes."

"Loony," Edie corrected. "Loony tunes. Not — never mind." Edie braced one elbow on the table and propped her chin in her hand. "There's something weird happening in Blue Sky."

"Only in our imaginations."

"We didn't dream it up last time."

Kappy nodded and set two glasses of water on the table. The third glass, the one for Jimmy, she left on the counter. He had gone out back to play with Elmer, but Kappy suspected that he was secretly measuring the existing fence for improvements.

After Ephraim had left, Kappy and Edie had headed inside for a drink. It wasn't hot outside, but it was warm enough. And considering the morning they'd had . . .

"Fine." Edie grabbed her glass and gulped half of it down in one swift swallow. Kappy wondered if she wished it were something stronger. But she hadn't had anything stronger than liqueur in the house since her aunt, Hettie, died, and then it was only for special occasions. Kappy had inherited the

66

house from Hettie, who had raised her after the terrible buggy accident that killed her mother, her father, and her two brothers. Hettie might have been a little bit odd, but she had values. Drinking alcohol was not among them. Plus, alcohol had never been known to solve even one single problem.

I thought you said there wasn't a problem.

Kappy pushed that voice away and sat down across from her best friend.

Strange, but up until Edie Peachey had returned to Blue Sky, Pennsylvania, Kappy had never had many friends.

But that didn't mean they agreed on everything. "Why didn't you tell Jack about the text you received?"

Edie gave a quick little shrug. "There really wasn't anything to show, now was there?"

"You seemed to think there was."

"If I had told him about the text, he would have taken my phone. I don't have the money to buy a new one."

Kappy studied her expression. But she couldn't see any deceit. "And that's all?"

"Yes. Maybe."

"Edie!"

"I know. I know. I get it. But it's so unbelievably boring here."

Kappy tilted her head to one side. "I

67

thought you had adjusted to being back."

Edie made a motion with her head and shoulders that could have been considered a shrug.

"No?"

"Everything's changed."

Kappy frowned at her. "Of course it has. You didn't expect to come back and have everything the same. Did you?"

"Did you know that Jacob Detweiler got married?"

"How did you find that out? Did someone tell you at the funeral today?"

"Did you know?" Edie asked again.

"Of course, I knew. I live here, *jah*?"

Edie nodded a bit sadly. *"Jah."*

Kappy wanted to remind her that life had gone on after she left, but there was no sense rubbing salt in old wounds. Jacob and Edie had been quite a couple way back when, before Edie decided that *Englisch* life held more appeal.

"Just because you're bored doesn't mean you can go around looking for things to be trouble."

Edie frowned. "How weird is it that I actually understand that?"

Kappy propped one hand on her hip. "Stop trying to change the subject."

"What about you? You thought the same

68

thing I did."

"I admit that I may have let my imagination run away with me, but now I've thought about it more, and I realize that nothing strange is going on here."

"Except for us."

Kappy grinned. "You said it, not me."

The front door opened, and Jimmy poked his head inside. "Kappy! Hiram is here."

Edie was on her feet in an instant. "I'm gone." She was out the door in a flash. "C'mon, Jimmy. It's time to feed the dogs." Before she could protest, Edie motioned Jimmy to walk through the house and together they disappeared out the back door.

Kappy started toward the front door, which Edie had left open. Hiram came in with Elmer at his heels. "Hi, Kappy."

She stopped in her tracks. "Hiram."

"I just wanted to . . . uh, come by and talk to you."

She gave him a small smile. She didn't want to be too encouraging. After all, she hadn't made up her mind yet. Well, she almost had. He had yet to convince her that he could love her as much as he had loved his first wife, Laverna.

Just the thought made her feel selfish. Hiram was a good man, and he deserved a good wife. But she hadn't convinced herself that was where she needed to be.

"We just talked a couple of hours ago."

He nodded. "*Jah.* I know. But I wanted to talk about . . . other things."

"And not . . . Willie?" Willie was a safe topic.

"*Mamm* wanted me to invite you out to supper tonight."

She was shaking her head before he even finished. "I don't think that's a good idea."

"My family will be there."

And your mamm *doesn't think I'm right for you.* The last thing she wanted was to hear the virtues of Hiram all laid out to make her feel useless. Or unworthy.

But the problems with their relationship had deeper roots.

Kappy had been best friends with Hiram's wife, right up until her death. If Kappy was being honest with herself, she'd had feelings for Hiram as long as she could remember. But she knew he was still in love with Laverna. As selfish as it seemed, she wanted more than a second-place love. They both deserved more.

"No. *Danki.*"

"Will you come sit on the porch with me?"

She nodded despite herself. She was supposed to be thinking about the two of them and if their relationship deserved another chance, but instead all she had been thinking about was an imagined crime. But it was easier not to give Hiram a second thought when she hadn't seen him in a couple of weeks.

She followed him onto the porch, Elmer bouncing around her ankles. The beagle puppy crouched on the planks, waiting for what was next.

Hiram settled down on the porch bench and patted the seat next to him.

Kappy eased in, careful not to let her skirt brush against him as she did so. She wouldn't want him to get any ideas.

They sat for a moment, staring off toward the road. Neither spoke. The wind rustled the leaves in the trees. Elmer flopped onto his belly and let out a sad, doggie sigh. From the road she could hear the cars zooming back and forth. There was an occasional horn sound and the squeal of tires. But in front of them, the road was empty.

"So," Kappy said, needing to fill the quiet between them. Despite the sounds all around, she couldn't stand the silence that separated them. "Willie left again."

He opened his mouth to protest, she was certain, but he simply nodded. "*Jah*. It's been a couple of days now." He shook his head as if trying to sort it all out. "He usually comes home by now."

It was hard out there for Amish young people to fit in. They needed help if they really wanted to leave. Edie was one of the rare ones who left once and never came back. Well, she was back now, but not the same as some who returned. She might be planning on staying for a while, but Kappy seriously doubted she would ever make amends with the church.

"Has he called the phone shanty or anything?"

"No." He studied his hands as if the answers were written there in some sort of unbreakable code.

Kappy frowned at him, trying to get ahold on what was happening. "You're more worried than I've ever seen you."

He nodded again. "I am worried. This time it's different."

"You said that already."

He sat back in his seat, surprise registering in his eyes. "I did?"

"At the funeral earlier."

"Oh." He went back to examining his fingers. "Well, it's the truth."

Kappy looked out over the yard to the straight ribbon of asphalt that joined her neighborhood to the main highway. "Why is this time so different?"

Hiram sucked in a breath, then let it out slowly. It seemed to take forever for him to answer. "Last time he started talking about *Englisch* stuff about two weeks before he actually left. The time before, it was even longer. But this time . . . One day he was home and the next he was gone."

"I see." Though she found it perplexing. That was tomorrow's word of the day. She had peeked this morning. "And this is why you think he's not coming back?"

"It's even worse than that," Hiram admitted. "I'm afraid something's happened to him."

"Like?" Kappy managed to squeeze the word around the lump that suddenly formed in her throat.

Hiram gave a small shrug. "You know. Sally June died because she was run off the road. And Ruth Peachey was found dead in her barn. What if something like that has happened to Willie?"

It seemed the crazy events of the last couple of months were getting to Hiram, too.

"You don't think . . ." she started.

"I don't know what I think. But I'm worried."

Kappy wanted to reach out and touch his

hand, offer him comfort, but she was afraid that he might misconstrue her intentions. "Give it some time," she finally said. "He's only been gone a few days."

"I know."

"What does your *mamm* say?"

Hiram gave a bitter smile. "She's either crying or threatening to never speak his name again."

Kappy nodded. "That's understandable."

Hiram pushed to his feet. "I was hoping that maybe . . . well, you've been going around with Edie Peachey. And I thought maybe if you would, you know, keep a listen out for any news or talk."

"Wait . . . first you didn't want me hanging around with Edie and now you want me to use it to your advantage?"

"It's not like that."

Kappy stood and nudged him toward the steps. She didn't touch him, just started in that direction, leaving him no choice but to move or get stepped on. "That's exactly what it's like. Good-bye, Hiram."

He hesitated for a fraction of a second, then loped down the steps and hurried over to his buggy.

But she knew that she would be listening for any information to help him. After all, they had agreed to remain friends. And she liked Willie. She would hate to see anything happen to him.

"Are you going to leave your door that color?" He nodded toward the blue-painted front door.

"As a matter of fact, I think I will." Kappy crossed her arms and dared him to contradict her. Everyone in the valley knew the myth, that a blue door meant a girl of marriageable age and availability lived there. And Jimmy hadn't meant any harm when he'd painted it earlier in the year. He had heard that she and Hiram had called off their wedding and wanted to help her find another suitor. Maybe she was being a bit strangely sentimental, but she wasn't changing the door.

Hiram shook his head and climbed into his carriage.

She stood there as he turned his buggy and pulled out onto the road.

"I didn't think he was ever going to leave."

Kappy slapped one hand over her mouth to stifle a scream as she turned to find Edie standing on the porch behind her. She had changed out of her Amish clothes. Now she wore a pair of plaid jeans in red and black with a bright yellow shirt that hung off one shoulder. At least this one had a sort of strap to keep it from falling completely off.

"How did you get there?"

Edie shrugged. "Back door."

Kappy brushed past her and into the house. "I thought you had puppies to feed."

"I do. But I have something I need to show you first." She held her cell phone toward Kappy.

Kappy took it, but didn't check the screen. "Were you just waiting for him to leave?"

"Of course. Now read that." She motioned toward the phone.

"There's nothing here." Kappy held it up so Edie could see the dark, blank screen.

Edie sighed, took the phone, touched the screen, then handed it back.

If you still think it's an accident, where are the skid marks?

"When did you get this?" She handed the phone back to Edie.

"Right when I got home. I came over immediately, but you were outside talking to Mr. Thinks He's Better Than Us."

Kappy started to address the nickname, then changed her mind. "What did you do? Hide behind the shed until he left?"

Edie rolled one shoulder. "Maybe."

"What do you suppose it means?"

"It means that there are no marks on the road, so whoever hit Sally June meant to."

Kappy shook her head. "I still don't get

76

it." She whistled for Elmer to follow behind her. He trotted into the house, his ears bouncing and nearly brushing the ground with each step. She shut the door behind them and made her way into the living room.

"When someone is about to hit something, they usually brake. Hard. And that leaves marks on the road." Edie flopped onto the couch and waited for Kappy's reply.

Kappy eased into the rocking chair and eyed her questioningly. "Were there skid marks at the scene of the accident?"

Edie made a face. "I don't remember."

Kappy couldn't, either. She hadn't been looking at the road when they passed the first time. The smell of vinegar and the crates of pickles had distracted her from everything else. And she hadn't looked the second time she passed through, either. She had been praying for peace and closure for Sally June's family. "We could go look."

Edie shook her head. "We have to feed the puppies first. Then we eat. You know how Jimmy gets when his schedule is off."

"And by the time you eat supper . . ."

"It'll be dark."

Kappy gave a quick nod. "I guess I could go by myself."

Edie was on her feet in an instant, the motion so quick that Elmer jumped to his feet and started barking.

"Hush, Elmer."

The puppy didn't stop. Kappy grabbed the newspaper sitting on the table. She rolled it up and pointed it at the dog. Elmer immediately fell silent.

"Impressive," Edie said.

Kappy set the paper back onto the table, then gave Edie a rueful smile. "I've never actually bonked him with it, but it seems to work just fine."

Edie laughed, then started toward the back door. Kappy followed behind her.

"Promise me you won't go look at the crash site without me." Her voice held a deep, pleading note.

"I won't." Though she wanted to. Oh, how she wanted to. "Hey," she said. The words had Edie stopping and turning around. "At the funeral I heard that Jonah Esh is dating a girl his parents don't approve of."

"Like it's the first time that's ever happened."

Kappy nodded. "I know, but this bothers me for some reason."

Edie shifted her weight from one foot to the other and waited for Kappy to continue.

"Jonah's a good kid. I mean, I don't keep up with the youth, but I've never heard of

Jonah doing anything rebellious."

"They think he's dating an *Englisch* girl?"

"No one knows. That's all part of the speculation."

Edie gave a quick nod. "And who gave you all this info?"

"Mary Raber."

Edie laughed. Literally doubled over with her arms wrapped around her stomach. "You're kidding, right? You're going to believe anything Mary Raber says? She's the mouth of Pennsylvania."

"I know."

"I mean, there are three types of communication: telephone, television, and Tell Mary Raber."

"Fine. Fine. I get it. She likes to spread rumors."

"That she does."

"But how is it that you can remember that about Mary Raber, but you can't remember which apron to wear?"

"The wonders will never cease." Edie gave a quick wave and started across the yard.

Kappy shut the door behind Edie and leaned against it. She felt as if she were missing something, though she had no idea what. It was a strange feeling to think that something was amiss, even though everything seemed in the correct place. Even with

Mary Raber going around spreading rumors. Actually, that made the uncomfortable feeling all the more real.

She made herself a cup of tea, then sat down at the table. She needed to stitch up a bundle of *kapp* strings, but something about the text message had her glued to her seat.

She unfolded the newspaper and stared at the headline: Amish Teen Killed in Hit-and-Run Accident.

Farther down the page was a picture of the buggy turned over on its side, just waiting to be flipped back to rights.

She was missing something. She just knew it.

She examined the picture, wishing she still had that magnifying glass she'd had as a child. Maybe then she could make out a few more details.

Then she saw it. A smudge of blue streaked along the back side of the yellow buggy. If the car had gone after a black-topper or a brown-topper, she didn't think the mark would have shown up at all, but there it was, plain as day.

Which meant the car that hit Sally June was blue. Which helped . . . not at all.

She really needed to get down and see that road. Without skid marks on the pavement, only one thing would hold true. Sally June Esh had been murdered.

CHAPTER 5

Saturday morning, Kappy was dressed and out the door as soon as the sun came up. She had spent half the night thinking about blue paint, wrecked cars, and cryptic text messages.

And really, she was no further decided about Sally June's death than she had been the day before. But something in her gut told her that the killer was the one texting them.

"Why?" Edie asked.

Kappy had headed over as soon as she could. She wanted to tell Edie about the blue paint. It was a good clue, even if it didn't help them at all. Not until they could find that blue car. But in an area as large as Kishacoquillas Valley, finding that one car would be like finding a needle in the proverbial haystack. Now they would have to know what kind it was, and even then Kappy wasn't sure they had any use for the information. It wasn't like they would know who it belonged to or anything.

Jimmy was in his happy element, feeding the puppies and cleaning their cages. Watching the dogs racing around and playing in the new, warm sunshine made her wish that she had brought Elmer over for a visit. He might have liked playing with the other dogs. And it could help him be a little happier in his own yard. Yesterday she had found the hole where he had been sneaking out and plugged it with a piece of firewood until she could devise a more permanent fix. Until then, the split log should keep him on the proper side.

"Why do I think the killer is texting you? Or why did he kill Sally June?" Kappy asked.

Edie cocked her head to one side. "Both, I guess."

"I don't know." Those simple words seemed to tear her theory all apart. If there was no why, there was no motive. "Maybe he's feeling guilty," Kappy pondered out loud.

Edie seemed to think about it a moment. "Could be," she said. "That's entirely possible. I once saw this police movie and the bad guy kept leaving notes at the scene of all his crimes. Of course the police caught him and said that he really wanted to get caught and that's why he left the messages."

Kappy shook her head. "You lost me somewhere after police movie and before messages."

"It's simple, really." Edie turned as Jimmy called out that he was heading into the barn for new hay. He was as determined to do a good job with the puppies as Edie was up in the air about selling the whole business. It was heartbreaking. Jimmy could lose all that he had on a whim from his sister. Kappy would just have to convince her to stay. "The killer is texting us because he wants to get caught."

Kappy thought about that a moment, but couldn't decide if she believed it or not. "Are we going?"

"To look for skid marks?"

Kappy nodded.

"You bet your sweet cheeks we are."

"What are you looking for again?" Jimmy asked.

As soon as the chores were complete they had all piled into Edie's car and driven to the site of the accident. They parked in the packed gravel lot at the cemetery and walked across the main road for a closer look. Everything had been cleaned up, and Kappy was sure that to Jimmy it appeared they were looking at nothing.

In a way, she supposed they were.

"Skid marks on the roadway. You know, those black tire marks?"

Jimmy nodded. "Can we go back across now? I don't like standing here."

Kappy had to admit that it was a little unnerving, standing on the side of the road where so recently a young woman had died. She felt vulnerable and found herself looking over her shoulder for a blue car.

"We just need to find that car." Edie smacked her fist into the palm of her other hand.

"And then what?" Kappy asked.

"Well, we could tell the police, for one."

Kappy shot her a look. "Like you told them about the texts?"

"We," Edie corrected. "We're in this together."

"Nuh-uh." Kappy shook her head. "Your phone. Not mine."

"Sister." Jimmy bounced on the balls of his feet, his anxiety apparent.

"Just a sec, Jim." Edie examined the blacktop as her brother fretted, then she turned on her heel and together the three of them marched back across the road.

"Can I go see *Mamm*'s grave?" Jimmy asked when they were back by the car.

Edie nodded.

"Come with me?"

She hesitated. Kappy didn't think Jimmy noticed, but she did. Just a fraction of a second. Things between Edie and her mother had been strained at best. Kappy wasn't sure the last time the two of them spoke. And now Edie was faced with the very hard task of learning to live with past mistakes. Her mother was gone now, and there was no way to make up for lost time.

Finally, Edie gave a small nod, swallowed hard, and allowed her brother to lead the way.

Kappy wandered in the opposite direction, allowing them privacy to visit with their mother.

The cemetery was a unique one. The Amish and the Mennonites in the area shared the space, much as they did their farms. Some of the graves dated back decades, while others were just last year. Earlier that year. And earlier this week.

Kappy stopped and stared down at the small wooden cross that marked the spot where they had laid Sally June Esh to rest. It would be months before the actual headstone was in, but someone in her family must have erected the cross until then.

Gone too soon was what the *Englisch*

would have carved into her headstone, but as it was, *Beloved sister and daughter* was all it said. A variety of flowers lay scattered around. Someone had even left a stuffed bear, a panda that somehow looked sad with those black circles around his eyes.

Kappy couldn't say she'd known Sally June all that well. But she knew of her and knew what folks who came to buy a *kapp* said about her. Everything that Kappy could ever remember anyone uttering about Sally June Esh was good. She was a kind person, a good neighbor. Beloved sister and daughter, just as her temporary grave marker proclaimed.

A sound from the direction of the road drew her attention. Kappy turned, expecting to see other mourners coming to pay their respects. Instead she saw Jack Jones get out of his unmarked police car and push a pair of mirrored sunglasses onto his slightly bent nose.

She looked back to see if Edie had noticed. She had. Jimmy followed behind her toward the detective.

Kappy made her way over to the three of them.

"Pretty day," Jack commented as she came up beside them.

"Very." Edie nodded enthusiastically.

"Going somewhere?" He gave a pointed look at Edie's eclectic outfit.

She wore another pair of those tight stretchy pants but these only reached her knees. Over them she had a flouncy skirt made of insubstantial material like wisps of smoke. She wore another one of those off-the-shoulder shirts that looked as if it had been cut around the neck instead of designed to be worn that way. Her hair was in a ponytail but crooked, sort of off to one side, and her bangle bracelets jangled with every move she made. At least today she wasn't wearing a pair of those noisy flip-flop shoes, though Kappy wasn't sure her shocking-pink canvas sneakers were much better.

Edie shook her head. "Laundry day."

Now *that* Kappy could believe. Well, sort of. Edie wasn't about to use her mother's old-fashioned wringer washer to clean her clothes. It stood to reason that the clothes she had on were the only clean ones she had at the moment and her trunk was full of all the dirty ones.

"As much as I love the Madonna Tour 1987, what are you doing here?"

Edie took hold of the fabric of Jimmy's shirt, careful not to touch him as she urged him forward. "We came to see *Mamm*'s grave. Right, Jimmy?"

Jimmy studied the toes of his plain black lace-up boots before giving a quick nod. "That's right. Visiting *Mamm.*"

Jack Jones turned to Kappy.

"I'm just along for the ride."

"Uh-huh." Jack looked from one of them to the other, the set of his jaw clearly stating that he didn't believe any of them. He was too much of a gentleman to press Jimmy for the truth. Or perhaps he thought that it was best not to. After all, what sort of trouble could the three of them get into at a cemetery?

"And you being here has nothing to do with the fact that the Esh girl's buggy was run off the road just over there." He jerked a thumb back over one shoulder, indicating the general direction of the accident. It wasn't quite a question.

Edie studied the spot for a moment. "You don't say."

Jones crossed his arms and stared at Edie. At least Kappy *thought* he was staring at Edie. She couldn't see his eyes behind those dark glasses. "You know that any clues you find should be turned in to the police."

"Clues?" Edie asked innocently. "Why would there be any clues?"

"Evidence, then," Jack corrected.

"Evidence of what?" This time Kappy thought Edie's wide-eyed innocent look was a little over the top.

"If you find anything, you just be sure to let me know."

"Of course," Kappy and Edie said at the same time.

"How's the investigation going?" Edie asked. At least this time she had toned down her innocent act.

"As well as can be expected."

"And you're not at liberty to discuss the details with me," Edie continued.

Jack shot her a confused look.

Edie shrugged. "I watch *CSI.*"

"Yeah, well, hit-and-runs are hard to solve. Witnesses are hard to find, if there even were any. Can't track them down, you know. There's no real way to know who would be driving on this road about the time Sally June Esh was."

Kappy nodded.

Edie gave Jack a small grin. "Be careful there, Detective. You keep talking like that, and you'll let something slip."

"There's nothing to let slip." Jack nodded at each of them and moseyed back over to his car.

They stood that way for a moment, all three of them huddled together, until Jack

Jones was well and truly gone.

"What evidence do you suppose he was talking about?" Edie asked.

Kappy shrugged. "I don't see any evidence. Do you?" She made a sweeping gesture toward the road. There were no skid marks, no tire tracks. Whoever hit Sally June had not bothered to slow down, not even right before impact.

Somehow Kappy kept all her questions to herself as they drove back to Edie's house. She could tell Edie was having as much trouble as she was, but neither mentioned it. Jimmy sat in the back and chattered on about coming again. He liked visiting his mother's grave, and he wanted to make sure that he had flowers to bring the next time.

Edie muttered something in return. Kappy didn't know what she said, but it seemed to be enough to satisfy Jimmy. He sat back, but continued to plan his next visit with his mother.

"You should bring him more," Kappy said in an aside to Edie.

"I know." Edie's fingers tightened on the wheel until her knuckles were white. "It's just that . . ."

"It's hard to visit her, knowing that you will never have the chance to make amends."

Edie swallowed hard and gave a quick nod. "I would give anything to go back in time and stop that last argument we had. But I can't. And I didn't listen. Oh, Kappy, if I could take back the things I said . . ."

"We all feel that way," Kappy answered as Edie pulled her car to a stop to one side of the house. They didn't have a proper driveway, just a packed gravel lane with a strip of grass running down the middle.

"What about Jack Jones?" Kappy asked as they got out of the car.

"What about him?" Edie slung her purse strap over her shoulder, then shut the car door. A little too smoothly.

"I think he likes you."

"Pbbfftt . . ." Edie blew her bangs out of her face and rolled her eyes.

"Don't be coy," Kappy said. "Are you going to make me walk home from here?"

Edie looked around as if she was confused as to where *here* was. Then she gave a quick shrug. "I thought you might help us feed the dogs."

"Jah," Kappy muttered. She didn't mind helping Edie. Not at all. But Edie had driven home without thinking, forgetting that she needed to drop Kappy off at her house. Had the encounter with Jack Jones bothered her so much, or was it the trip to

the cemetery? Kappy figured the latter.

With the three of them working side by side, they made short work of feeding and cleaning up after the dogs.

"The gerbils, too?" Kappy asked. She wiped her sweaty brow on the hem of her apron and motioned toward the small hutches where Jimmy kept his gerbils. He had started the business on his own last year, and to date had been quite successful selling the cute rodents to Amish and *Englisch* alike.

"No." He puffed his chest out proudly. "They are my responsibility. You two go on in the house and rest. And don't forget to save me a glass of lemonade."

"You got it." Edie motioned for Kappy to follow and together they left Jimmy in the barn to complete his chores.

"Thanks for helping," Edie said as they made their way to the house. "Another set of hands makes it go so much faster."

Then the idea struck. "I could come every day," Kappy offered. "And help, *jah*? It would be good for Elmer, too. I could bring him to play. Maybe that would keep him in his own yard more. And maybe then . . ."

"Maybe then what?" Edie asked.

"Maybe then you won't think so often

93

about selling everything and taking Jimmy away."

By now they had reached the porch, Edie turned as her brother bustled out of the barn, a metal bucket in each hand. He didn't even notice them as he made his way to the water spigot and started filling the buckets, whistling as he waited.

"He loves it here," Kappy said quietly. *And it would kill him to leave,* she thought. But she didn't say it.

They let themselves in the back door and headed for the kitchen.

Edie poured them each a glass of lemonade as Kappy settled at the table.

"It's just confusing, you know," Edie said. She slid into the chair opposite Kappy and took a long drink. She didn't meet Kappy's gaze.

"What's confusing?"

Edie shook her head. "Maybe that's not the right word. I worry. Am I doing right by him?" She didn't have to tell Kappy she was talking about Jimmy.

"Of course you are."

Edie frowned and sat back in her seat. "How would you know? You've never been out there."

"I don't have to be out there, as you say, to know that Jimmy is right where he belongs. Right where God put him."

Somehow her words brought Willie Lapp to mind. He had been where God put him, but that hadn't been enough. Was he wrong in leaving?

"What if he's missing opportunities?" Edie said.

Kappy pulled her attention from Willie and settled it back on the woman in front of her. Edie Peachey might dress a little strangely, and she seemed to have no desire to bend her knees and repent for her time spent with the *Englisch,* but she loved her brother and wanted what was best for him.

"What if he could have more education," she continued, "and I'm keeping him from that by allowing him to stay in the church and raise gerbils and beagles?"

"Did you see him out there? He's happy raising beagles and gerbils."

Edie shrugged. She fished her cell phone out of her pocket and pressed the screen. "You really think the killer is the one texting us?"

Kappy knew a change of topic when she heard it. "Well, you said yourself that the killer always returns to the scene of the crime. He wasn't there today. And he didn't come to the funeral."

"We don't know if he did or not," Edie

pointed out.

"Maybe this is the next best thing." She pointed toward the phone Edie still held.

Edie pressed her thumb to the screen.

"If you still think it's an accident, where are the skid marks?" she read. "It's almost like he's bragging."

"Like he's proud of himself," Kappy agreed in a hushed whisper. What kind of person found satisfaction in such actions?

"We can't let him get away with this," Edie said. "This is where we live and he can't come here and start killing people." She furiously pressed her thumbs to the screen, her mouth a thin line, brows furrowed, eyes determined. "There."

"What did you do?" Kappy was almost afraid to ask.

"I'm texting him back. *We know who you are and we know what you did. No crime goes unpunished.*"

"That's what you wrote?" Kappy frowned.

"Yep. And send." She pressed her thumb to the screen one last time, then sat back with a smile. "Let's see how Mr. Killer likes that."

CHAPTER 6

Sunday. Kappy loved Sundays, especially church Sundays. She spent most of her days sewing *kapps* and taking care of her small garden and hardly got off her property for anything other than a quick trip to the market. At least that had been the case until Edie had come back to town. Still, church Sundays were the best.

She got up with the sun and did her necessary chores. She let Elmer out the back, picked a few cucumbers and tomatoes, then went inside to wash up and get dressed.

There was something special about donning that crisp white apron after thirteen days of wearing a black one. Kappy appreciated the ritual. She had heard others grumble behind the bishop's back about changing the old ways, but she enjoyed the specialness of dressing differently, presenting herself differently on the church Sabbath. It made it important somehow, as if her manner of dress was there to remind her, *Today is special.*

After she fixed a small breakfast, ate, and cleaned up the mess, she hitched up her buggy and headed over to Edie's.

Since Ruth Peachey had died, Jimmy had taken to riding to church with Kappy. She didn't mind; in fact she kind of enjoyed his company.

She pulled up in front of the Peachey house and secured the reins before climbing down.

Jimmy rushed out onto the porch, his sweet lopsided smile lighting up his entire face. "Hey, Kappy. Happy Sunday to you."

She smiled in return. "Happy Sunday to you, Jimmy. Is Edie still asleep?"

He shook his head, then climbed into the buggy. "No," he yelled out the window. "She's inside. Where's Elmer? Is he not going with us?"

"Elmer's a dog. He has to stay home."

"Not always. I read in the paper that some dogs go everywhere with their owners. Wouldn't it be great if Elmer could come with us like one of those *Englisch* dogs?"

The image of Elmer in the Rabers' barn pulling on the pant legs of the bishop as he preached the Sunday sermon almost made her laugh out loud. Somehow she managed to keep her composure. "That would be great, Jimmy. Too bad it can't happen."

He held up his alert necklace. "They let me have this for emergencies. Why wouldn't they let me have a dog to help me?"

Help you what? was on the tip of her tongue, but she didn't have time to answer as Edie came out onto the porch.

"Any text back?" Kappy asked.

"Good morning to you, too," Edie quipped.

Kappy shook her head. She had hardly slept the night before. Between the excitement of knowing that the following day was a church Sunday and the accusing text that Edie had sent to the killer, sleep had been the furthest thing from her mind. "Sorry. Good morning, Edith."

"Never call me that." Edie pointed a finger at Kappy, her tone and expression stern, but Kappy knew she was putting it on.

"Uh-huh. Any word?"

She shook her head. "Maybe we'll hear something later."

"Jah," Kappy said, flipping over a rock with the toe of one black lace-up boot. "Maybe."

"Thanks for taking Jimmy to church."

"No problem." She understood how awkward it had to be for Edie. Jimmy still wanted to attend services as he had since he was born. What was his sister supposed to do? Drive up in her *Englisch* car and drop him off at the door?

Plus, Jimmy was something of an outsider. And that made him and Kappy two of a kind.

"When you get back, I'll whip us up something for supper. We can sit and stare at the phone together."

Kappy laughed. But it wasn't really funny. Perhaps this entire investigation thing had gotten out of hand.

"Sounds good," she said, then hopped in her buggy and drove them back down the lane.

Even as much as she loved church, Kappy wasn't able to concentrate on the sermon. Every little sound, every shift of the congregation, every sigh, every baby hiccup, every *everything* seemed to draw her attention away from the message. From there it was a short jump to Sally June Esh.

She should be there, at church, sitting with her mother a few rows in front of Kappy. She chanced a quick look toward the men's side. Sally June's brother, Jonah, and her father sat side by side, their attention centered on the deacon as he delivered today's message. Their expressions were solemn, a bit pinched and overly focused. Kappy knew that look well. She had worn it the first year after she had lost her family. It had been nearly sixteen years since her parents and her two brothers were killed in a car-buggy crash, and still she missed them every day. The Amish might understand better than most that everything was part of God's will, but that didn't mean it automatically popped into their thoughts. Understanding took time. And with time, their lost look would be replaced with one of resignation and then acceptance. She prayed for the Eshes that it would happen quickly.

After the final prayer, the men carted the benches outside and flipped them over to form their tables for eating. The women got the food ready. It was a beautiful day to be outside. The sun was shining, but not too hot. The wind created a stir that was just enough to keep everything cool. In the blue, blue sky, clouds moved across, creating floating shadows on the valley below.

"I don't know what she thought, bringing those here." Frannie Lehman frowned at the jars of pickled green cucumbers resting on one bench top. The frown didn't concern Kappy. Frannie was always frowning about one thing or another.

"That's what she's used to," Alma explained. As the bishop's wife, Alma felt it her duty to keep the peace, even over something as small as pickles.

But Kappy had to admit that the fat green cucumbers did seem strange.

Kish Valley was known for its church pickles, solely on the basis of color. All the ladies in the area made church pickles with white cucumbers. They tended to have a ghostly look about them, but Kappy only noticed after someone — an *Englischer* — pointed it out in front of her. Kappy had been at the farmers' market stand at the end of the valley. She had needed to pick up a few extra green beans since hers had fallen prey to the beetles. The women hadn't known that she was listening as they went on and on about the strange color of the pickles. Kappy had never thought much about it. That was simply what the church pickles looked like, and she hadn't given it much attention up until then. But she supposed to someone who hadn't grown up in the valley, white pickles would look a little odd. But they tasted the same. Or rather close enough so no one thought much about it.

"She lives in the valley now."

"What are you saying?"

Kappy didn't recognize the third voice. It sounded familiar, but she simply couldn't place who it belonged to.

"I'm saying Bettie Hershberger may have grown up in Lancaster, but she's in the valley now and the pickles here are white."

"I think there's enough room for all the pickles." Alma smiled at the other two women in turn, then began fishing the green pickles out of the jar for the hungry churchgoers.

For whatever reason, Kappy couldn't stop thinking about those pickles. She ate her meal as quickly as possible, then walked around looking at plates to see if anyone had opted for the green pickles. Not seeing anything on anyone's plates, she headed back over to where the pickle jars had been set up.

All the white pickles were gone, but just a few of the green pickles had been taken.

It was strange. Were the white pickles that much better? Or was it simply a habit? Was everyone eating the white pickles because they liked them more or because it was just what they were used to?

"I would tell you that the green pickles are just as good as the white ones, but since they are the only ones left . . ."

Kappy turned, dragged out of her thoughts by the man approaching.

Silas Hershberger smiled, showing her his even white teeth. She had never really noticed before, but they were as straight as if he had been to one of those fancy *Englisch* doctors who prescribed braces.

"Hi, Silas."

"Come to get some pickles?"

She shook her head.

"You don't want any pickles?" He frowned. "I mean, you've been standing here for a while, just looking at them."

She shrugged. "Sorry. I guess I just got lost in thought."

"Oh." He almost looked disappointed.

"Why are you so interested in pickles today?" she asked.

He leaned in as if telling her a great secret. "My aunt made the pickles."

"All of them?"

He gestured toward the full jars of green pickles. "She made these," he explained. "And it would make her really happy if you would eat some of them."

She hesitated. She had a feeling they couldn't be very good if no one was willing to try them. Or was it just because they were green? Had she ever decided?

She really wasn't hungry, and she had

never been much of a pickle person, but she took one anyway, cupping her hand under her chin as she took a large bite. The vinegary juice dripped down her chin as the spices tickled her tongue. She swallowed the bite even as the heat intensified.

Silas handed her a paper napkin, and she cleared her throat so as not to cough.

"They're a little . . . spicy." She stifled another cough.

Silas smiled. "They are different. But my aunt is determined to convert everyone in the valley to green pickles."

Kappy glanced at the empty jars where the white pickles had been. She was careful not to let her gaze linger too long. "Your aunt?"

"Bettie Hershberger." He discreetly pointed to a group of ladies huddled together talking about after-church, Sunday afternoon things on the opposite side of the yard from where the men did the same. A tall, middle-aged woman stood out among the others. Maybe because her dress was green, not blue, and her stockings didn't appear to be the same as the ones Kappy — and every other woman present — were wearing. The Amish of Kish Valley might dress similar to the Lancaster Amish, but Kappy could spot the differences right off.

"She's my father's sister," Silas explained. "Never married." The last two words were uttered in a hushed tone, as if Silas didn't want everyone around to know such a family secret. Like Bettie Hershberger would be the only old maid in Blue Sky. Kappy herself was right on track to never marry. And it didn't bother her. Not one bit.

It's a sin to lie.

She pushed that little voice away and concentrated on what Silas was saying.

"She just moved up here . . ."

He really was handsome. And nice. Edie would say that he was a good catch, but Kappy wasn't entirely sure what that meant. It sounded like a fishing reference. Perhaps she should ask Mose. She allowed her gaze to quickly scan the crowd for him, then once again directed her attention to Silas. The man was a distraction, for sure.

"She was living in the *dawdihaus* at my uncle's in Lancaster, but his wife's *dat* fell and broke his hip. He had to move in so they could care for him." Silas shrugged.

"And she moved here."

He nodded. "She's a nice lady. Let me introduce you."

Before she could utter so much as a word of protest, Kappy found herself face-to-face with Bettie Hershberger. Strange, really.

106

Kappy felt almost pulled across the yard in Silas's wake, even though he hadn't laid so much as a finger on her.

"Silas." Bettie tugged on her shirtsleeves and looked down her long nose at Kappy. Actually, the woman had no choice. She was a good six inches taller than Kappy with an imposing presence like that of Jack Jones.

"Bettie, this is my friend, Kappy King."

Friend? They were friends? She liked the sound of that. To date, she thought that Edie was the only soul in Blue Sky she could really call friend. Well, Edie and Jimmy.

"Kappy?" One dark brow shot up almost under the edge of Bettie's prayer *kapp*. And it might have, had her stern hairline not stopped it. "That's an interesting name."

Kappy gave her a quick nod. "It's a nickname. Short for Kathy. I mean, Kathryn."

"Really?"

"Kappy makes all the prayer coverings for the ladies," Silas said.

"And that's how you received your nickname?"

Close enough. Kappy nodded, not willing to explain that her youngest brother, Danny, couldn't say Kathy correctly and the rest was simply part of God's plan. "When it's time for a new *kapp,* come by and see me. I can sew one just for you or I have stock

107

always available. Special orders take a bit longer, of course."

"Of course."

"And be sure to go around back," Silas said. "Kappy won't do business on her front porch." He grinned, and she wondered if he was poking fun at her. His dark-blue eyes sparkled like the sapphire ring Heather at the Sheriff's Office wore. They didn't appear to be making a joke of her, but she just couldn't tell.

"I'll bear that in mind." Bettie half turned as if dismissing Kappy, her nickname, and her business practices. Kappy tried hard not to be even a little miffed that the woman ignored her like yesterday's newspaper, but there was something about the hard set of her mouth that made Kappy realize that she probably treated everyone the same way.

Bettie Hershberger appeared settled with her lot in life in all aspects but pickles. At least as far as Kappy could see.

"It was nice to meet you," Kappy said, turning on one heel and making her way back across the yard.

"Kappy, wait." Once again Silas was at her side. "Don't pay her much mind. She's just a little put out from having to move."

"I can understand that."

"Good." Silas grinned, tipped his hat, and

started backing away from her. "I'll see you in a couple of Sundays, Kappy King."

Something in his tone was a little intense, a little familiar, and she found that she liked it. "See you then."

She watched him walk away, thoughts of pickles taunting at the veil of her distraction. She didn't want to think about pickles or maiden aunts, car wrecks or new *kapps*. She only wanted to watch Silas Hershberger walk away. Why had she never noticed how nice he was before?

"He likes you."

She whirled around as Jimmy came up behind her.

"I would hope so." Kappy gave a small cough to hide her joy at the thought of Silas Hershberger actually liking her.

"No," Jimmy continued. "He *likes* you likes you."

"What would you know about that?" Kappy asked, searching for a way to change the subject. "Did you eat some of the green pickles?"

Jimmy shook his head and made a face. "They're not church pickles. Church pickles are the white ones."

"What makes you say that?"

"It's just the way it's always been."

Those words rang through Kappy's head all the way back to Edie's house. They ate the white pickles because they always had. Who decided that?

Then along came Bettie Hershberger, who wanted to change the system. Was it only that she was proud of her own pickle recipe? Or maybe the white pickles held less appeal for her. Kappy didn't know.

But of this she was certain: The one way to get acceptance for one thing would be to cut the supply of the other.

Bettie's stern face rose into her thoughts as she pulled to a stop in front of the Peachey house. The woman was . . . determined, if nothing else. Though why she couldn't accept the white pickles as the favorite in the valley was a mystery to Kappy.

Live and let live.

Wasn't that what Aunt Hettie was always saying?

Of course, Aunt Hettie was on the fringes more than Kappy.

But still . . .

"Are you coming?"

Kappy jerked herself out of her thoughts

and centered them on Jimmy.

He had already climbed out of the buggy and was waiting for her to do something . . . go in the house . . . leave.

"Oh. *Jah.*" She climbed down as Jimmy secured her horse. Together they walked to the porch.

They no sooner got to the door when it was flung open. Edie reached out, wrapping a firm hand around her arm and pulling her inside the house.

"I know who killed Sally June!"

Kappy stumbled to a stop, dully aware that behind her Jimmy did the same thing.

"Someone killed Sally June? I thought she was in an accident," Jimmy asked.

Edie shook her head. "Of course she was." She pasted on the biggest and brightest smile Kappy had ever seen. It was also the fakest.

Jimmy looked unconvinced for a moment, then he slowly nodded. "No one would hurt Sally June on purpose. Not like *Mamm.*"

They had done their best to shield Jimmy from the details of his mother's murder, but since Jimmy had been the first suspect in the crime, that had been a near-impossible feat.

But that didn't mean they couldn't keep him from knowing so much about the accident that killed Sally June.

"That's right," Edie said.

Jimmy let out a long breath, his shoulders relaxing in obvious relief. "That would be terrible, *jah*?"

"That it would." Kappy felt a little like one of those bobble-head dogs she had seen at Hiram's store. She quit nodding and thankfully Edie did the same.

"I'm going to check on the ducks," Jimmy said, bypassing the kitchen and heading toward the back door.

"That's a great idea." There went that strange smile again.

Kappy and Edie watched and waited as Jimmy let himself out.

"I know who killed Sally June," Edie said when he was out of earshot.

"So do I."

CHAPTER 7

"What happened?" Edie dragged her into the kitchen and fairly forced her into one of the wooden chairs surrounding the table. "Tell me."

Kappy shook her head. "You first."

"Age before beauty."

Kappy opened her mouth to reply, then changed her mind and closed it again. She decided to ignore Edie's comment and tried again. "At church today, I learned that Silas Hershberger's aunt Bettie has moved here from Lancaster."

Edie stared at her with rapt attention. "Go on."

"Well, she had a bunch of green pickles for the church meal."

Edie frowned. "Green pickles?"

"You remember. Valley church pickles are white."

"And bland." Edie made a face.

"Well, the congregation doesn't agree with

you. She brought all those green pickles, and I don't think anyone ate even one. But the valley pickles were gone."

"And why would this make her want to hurt Sally June Esh?"

"Well, if I have to explain it to you . . ."

Edie smiled like a cat lapping cream and pulled her cell phone out of her jeans pocket. The garment fit so snugly that Kappy was a little curious as to how she actually fit the phone into the pocket, but that was a question for another day. "I heard from the killer again."

Kappy gasped. "No way!"

"Oh, yes." She waggled the phone in the air between them.

"What did he say about your text?"

Edie stopped, a frown wrinkling the space between her over-thinned eyebrows. "He didn't." She shook off whatever funk had overtaken her and laid her phone on the table. "He just said he saw the car that hit Sally June that day."

"Of course he did. He was driving it."

"Maybe."

"It's obvious." Kappy gave a quick nod to reinforce her theory. "He's feeling guilty. That's why he didn't mention your text. But he wants us to discover the truth so he doesn't have to carry this burden forever."

Edie drummed her fingers against the wooden tabletop as she stared at the opposite wall. The expression on her face was so faraway that Kappy wondered if she was really even looking at it at all. "Then we're doing him a favor," she mused.

"I suppose, *jah*." Kappy hadn't really thought about it that way. She had been more concerned that they had imagined the crime. But after today's church meal, it was clear there was definitely something going on here. "And he just texted you this morning . . . out of the blue?"

Edie turned the perfect shade of pink to complement her shiny lipstick. "Well, I may have texted him first."

"Edie." Kappy flopped back into her seat and crossed her arms. "Why would you do that?"

"We texted him yesterday."

"*You* texted him, and at least the two of us were together."

"It doesn't matter now."

"It could have. You could have ruined everything."

"But I didn't. And he told me that a blue car hit Sally June's buggy."

"We already know that."

"And that a woman was driving."

"How did he know it was a woman?"

"She had long dark hair."

Kappy thought about it a moment. "But what about Bettie Hershberger? If she wants to corner the pickle market . . ."

"Maybe she was driving the blue car." Edie stood, her excitement palpable.

"What would an Amish woman be doing with her hair down and driving an *Englisch* car?"

"I don't know." Edie threw up her hands in frustration. "It sounded better inside my head." She paused, then whirled on Kappy. "Corner the pickle market?"

Kappy shrugged. "What else would you call it?"

"Good point." Edie slipped back into her seat and propped her elbow on the table, bracing her chin in her palm. "Maybe she hired someone to hurt Sally June."

"But why?" The stern, pinched-faced woman's image swam before her mind's eye. Bettie Hershberger looked mean enough, she supposed, but Kappy wasn't sure how much hatred it took for one person to hurt another. She had no idea.

But she was overlooking one important detail. "Are pickles worth killing another?"

Edie shrugged. "Who knows what pressure this woman has been under?"

"True. I mean, Silas told me that she had

to move here from Lancaster. I don't think she was happy about the move." Unhappy enough to commit murder?

"Maybe it was an accident," Edie offered.

"And you still think she was driving the car?"

"He said the woman had long dark hair."

That sort of fit Bettie Hershberger. She had mostly dark hair, and it stood to reason that it was long as well. After all, Amish women didn't cut their hair, not even a trim.

"Pickles?" Kappy asked, not having to elaborate.

Were pickles so important? Or had Bettie been pushed past her limits? Neither seemed plausible. And yet Sally June was gone, called home and buried. And someone was texting them, pointing fingers away from himself. Or maybe herself.

"I once read a story about a woman who killed her husband because he wore a shirt from the dirty clothes."

"Please tell me that's not true."

Edie shot her an apologetic look. "People are crazy."

"And we'd have to be crazy to think that Bettie could be behind this."

"There are a lot of holes in our theories," she mused.

"Maybe that's a sign we're sticking our

noses where they don't belong." The longer the thought stayed in Kappy's head, the less plausible it seemed until she knew it was impossible. One person couldn't kill another young, innocent person over pickles. That sort of thing didn't happen. Not even in the worst *Englisch* movies.

Edie held up her cell phone. "He texted me first."

That was something Kappy couldn't argue with.

"I'm hungry." Edie pocketed her phone as if the discussion was over. "Let's go get something to eat."

Kappy started shaking her head before Edie even finished. "I'm not sure how the bishop would feel about me riding in a car on a Sunday, but I know he wouldn't want me out eating in a restaurant."

"He can only get upset if he knows."

Kappy braced her hands on her hips and shot her friend a scathing look. At least she meant for it to be scathing. Edie didn't blink an eye. "Really?"

"You're not hungry?" Edie smiled in that cajoling way she had. *Cajoling,* that was today's word of the day, but it wasn't working on Kappy. Not today.

"Yes, I'm hungry, but the last thing we need is both of us shunned."

Edie crossed her arms and pouted. "That's the dumbest thing anyone could be shunned for. Eating in a restaurant."

"On Sunday," Kappy reminded her.

"It matters?"

"It does to the bishop." Sundays needed to be spent at church, home, or in quiet reflection with family and friends.

"Edie." Jimmy opened the back door and stuck his head inside. "I'm hungry. What's for supper?"

Kappy flashed Edie a quick smile. "Never fear, Jimmy. Your sister was just about to go get takeout."

The valley was a very conservative area for Amish and *Englischers* alike. So Kappy shouldn't have been surprised when Edie returned with a handful of sacks from the local convenience store.

"That smells good." Jimmy rubbed his hands together in anticipation.

"What did you get?" Kappy eyed the bags with more skepticism than she wanted to show.

"Fried cheese curds, fried mozzarella sticks — and marinara sauce." She listed each item as she unpacked the bag. Jimmy made a face at the mention of the red sauce.

119

"Popcorn chicken, french fries, and a pretzel."

"At least there's one thing that isn't fried." Kappy reached for the pretzel, but Edie held it out of her reach and shook her head.

"This one is mine."

Kappy looked in the sacks, scattered across the table. "Where's mine?"

"See, that's the thing. They only had one ready."

Jimmy started wolfing down the fried fare, barely giving them any notice as he ate.

"But you're going to share it, right?"

Edie made an apologetic face. "I'm kind of on a diet."

Kappy looked from the mounds of fried foods to the lone pretzel Edie held. "And a pretzel is part of this new eating plan?"

"It's better than that." She waved a hand at all the golden-brown coating.

"Uh-huh." Kappy shook her head. "You have to share."

"Kappy has a boyfriend." Jimmy picked that moment to join the conversation.

"She does?" Edie asked.

"*Jah,*" Jimmy said.

"No," Kappy countered.

"Did you see them together?" Edie wanted to know.

Jimmy nodded. "I sure did. He couldn't

take his eyes off her."

"That is not true," Kappy returned.

"Is so."

Kappy couldn't continue without outright calling Jimmy a liar, and she wasn't up for that. She hadn't even been looking at Silas that close, more interested in the pickles than anything else. *And this, Kappy King, is why you will remain unmarried for the rest of your days.*

She pushed that voice away and turned her attention to her food. By now the fried treats were cooling off a bit too much, and the grease was starting to make her feel a little sick to her stomach. It was that and nothing else. She was sure of it.

"What about you and Jack?"

Edie tossed the last piece of her pretzel onto the paper wrapper, then blew her bangs out of her face. "There is no me and Jack."

And that seemed entirely impossible. Not so long ago, Kappy was certain that Jack and Edie would make the perfect pair, but now that the dust had cleared on Ruth's murder, other crimes had pulled his attention away. Where they had been seeing Jack Jones every day, now they only saw him occasionally.

"But there could be."

"Gross." Jimmy tossed down the piece of chicken he had been eating and made a disgusted face at his sister.

"I hope you're talking about the food," Edie returned.

"Jack Jones?" Jimmy asked. "For real?"

"What's the matter with Jack?"

Jimmy shook his head sadly, as if there were some things a person could explain, and yet others couldn't be understood with mere words.

"Tell me, brother," Edie said. "Why do you grin at the thought of Kappy with Silas Hershberger and make a face and call me and Jack Jones gross?"

Kappy shook her head. "I don't know if you want the answer to that."

Jimmy shrugged. "He's Amish."

"So if Jack were Amish —"

"May I be excused? I need to feed the ducks."

Edie's gaze dropped to her brother's empty plate. "Yeah, sure."

Jimmy nodded, put his dishes in the sink, and headed out back once again.

"I told you that you didn't want to know the answer to that."

"Oh, hush." Edie sat back in her seat and nibbled on her fingernail.

"There are more fried . . . things, if you

122

want them."

"Is it such a bad thing?" she asked. "To want to be *Englisch*?"

Kappy shrugged and started gathering up the remainder of their food. As a young Amish girl, she had been taught to eat everything on her plate, but tonight she made an exception. There were only so many fried cheese pieces a person could have before it took its toll. "Is it so bad for him to want you to remain Amish?"

"I can't remain Amish."

"You know what I mean."

Edie went back to chewing her thumbnail. "Yeah. I suppose you're right."

Kappy stacked the dishes in the sink and made her way back to the table. They could wait until they worked through whatever was bothering Edie. "What would be the worst thing that could happen if you stay here and rejoin the church?"

"I dunno."

Kappy could almost see her brain working, searching for all the reasons why she shouldn't come back, a reason for her to leave again. But after what seemed like a full five minutes, Edie shook her head. "Nothing, I don't guess. I mean, I'll be stuck doing the dishes by hand, reading by lamplight, and toting my clothes to the

Laundromat each week."

"There are worse things."

"I guess," Edie mumbled.

They sat in silence for a moment, then Edie swung her attention back to Kappy. "You and Silas Hershberger?" The grin on her face was a bit mischievous and way too knowing.

"Oh, Jimmy's just telling tales."

"Or he wants to get you away from Hiram." Edie pulled a face.

"What's wrong with Hiram?" Years had ingrained in her the habit of defending him. He was a businessman and fancy Amish, a black-topper. His family thought they ran the valley, and so on and so on.

"How much time do you have?"

"Seriously," Kappy said. "Hiram is a great man. And he was a good husband. He'll be a good husband again someday."

"But not to you." She was fishing, plain and simple.

"We may have cooled things off a bit."

"I knew it." Edie clapped her hands together and braced her elbows on the tabletop, leaning closer to Kappy as if they were about to share juicy secrets. "I thought the two of you had already set a date."

"Where'd you hear that?" Kappy frowned.

Edie shrugged one shoulder, then tugged

on the neckline of her blouse. "The Mennonites were doing laundry at the Coin and Suds."

"So not only are you eavesdropping, you're listening in on Mennonite conversations?"

"Is that somehow worse?"

"They never seem to get the story right when it involves Amish. Especially if it's about the white-toppers."

The white-toppers were the most conservative Amish in the valley. There wasn't a great deal of difference between the black-toppers and the yellow-toppers. In fact, most people couldn't tell them apart outside of their buggies, but the white-toppers were another matter altogether.

The men wore brown pants and coats and the women never wore bonnets. Kappy wasn't sure what these details had to do with God and following the church, but somewhere along the way, they had decided this was the best way to go.

"It's a good thing you're not a white-topper then, huh?"

Kappy knew when she was beat. Edie was hanging on and wouldn't let go until she got what she was after. "We're taking it a little slower. A lot slower."

"Then why has he been coming over so often?"

Kappy shrugged. "He's worried about Willie, I guess."

"He's okay with these changes?"

"He's let off a little since his brother went missing."

"He's not missing."

"How do you know that?"

Edie shot her a look. "Did anyone think I was missing when I left?"

"Oh. Right."

"I didn't know Willie. He was little when I left, but from what I hear, he comes and goes on a regular basis."

"Does that mean he really doesn't want to leave but thinks he does?"

"It means it's hard out there. When I left . . ." Her words trailed away to nothing. "Anyway, it takes a lot of commitment and stubbornness to make it out there. Whether Willie has that or not, I guess we'll find out eventually."

Kappy nodded. "That's just the thing. He's been gone for months before and this time he's only been gone for days, and Hiram is so . . . worried. I've never seen him like this."

"Maybe he knows Willie means it this time."

"I guess. But it's not like he left a note or anything."

Edie sighed. "I think this thing with Sally June has everyone stirred up. I mean, it's bad enough by itself, but coming so soon after *Mamm* . . ."

The thought shot through Kappy like a fire arrow. "You don't think . . ."

"That Willie killed Sally June? I have to admit the thought did cross my mind. But Mr. Text said he saw a woman driving."

"Mr. Text?"

"That's what I've decided to call him."

"What if . . . Mr. Text is trying to throw us off the trail?"

"Really? Kappy, think about what you're saying. That would mean he got my number and a phone and started texting me, knowing we were going to look into this." She shook her head. "That's too far-fetched even for me."

"Whew." Kappy let out a long sigh. "I didn't want Willie to have any part of this."

"I didn't say he was innocent, just that Mr. Text isn't lying to us."

"How do you know that? And how did he know that we would start wondering about the truth?"

"Gut feeling and I don't know. Maybe he knows us?"

"Do you think he's *Englisch* or Amish?"

Edie seemed to think about it a moment. "Amish."

"With a cell phone?"

"Maybe he's running around?"

"Maybe," Kappy muttered.

They sat in silence for a moment, each one mulling over the possibilities.

"Why would an Amish teen get a cell phone and text you about a possible murder?"

"Why does anybody do anything?"

Kappy wasn't sure what that meant, but with the way Edie's mouth turned down at the corners, she wasn't about to ask. "Amish or ex-Amish?"

"No idea."

"Do you think it could be Willie?"

"We could ask him, but that doesn't mean he'll tell us the truth."

The thought of Willie out there, driving around in a blue car, texting them because he was scared, was almost more than she could stand. He was just so young. And she surely didn't want to bring up the possibility of his guilt in front of Hiram; he was worried enough already. "We don't even know it's a man . . . or boy."

"True dat."

"Don't say that."

Kappy laughed, but the sound seemed too loud in the small kitchen.

"I guess this means we can't pass this off as mere coincidence."

"I guess not," Kappy agreed.

"And I suppose you want to help Hiram find out if Willie is okay? Or involved?"

"He is my friend."

"Yeah, I know."

"Friends should help each other."

"I know that, too."

Kappy smiled at her. "Does this mean that you are going to help me?"

"I suppose." Edie rolled her eyes.

"Does this mean we're friends?"

Edie grinned. "You know it."

"Does this mean you're staying?"

She nodded. "For a time."

That was all Kappy needed. A couple of weeks to convince Edie to stay in Blue Sky permanently. Either with the church or as an *Englischer.* Kappy knew this was Edie's home. Even if Edie didn't.

CHAPTER 8

"I got another one." Edie pushed past Kappy and into the house just after breakfast on Monday morning. "Look at this."

Edie thrust the phone toward Kappy, giving her no choice but to accept it or let it drop.

"There's nothing on here." Kappy held the phone where Edie could see.

"Honestly," Edie grumbled. She took the phone, tapped the screen a few times, then handed it back to Kappy. "I really need to teach you how to use this phone."

"Cell phones are strange."

"Right. Now look at it before it goes to sleep again."

Goes to sleep? Kappy shook her head, then did as Edie commanded.

Beware! Things are not as they seem. I had to leave this time. I didn't want to. But I know you will help me.

She read it a second time. Then again, but

it still didn't make a great deal of sense to her.

"Do you know what this means?"

Kappy handed the phone back to Edie. "Actually, no."

"It means we're being watched. Sally June's death wasn't an accident. And the texter really is Willie."

Kappy snatched the phone back, pressed her thumb to the screen, and re-reread the message. "How did you get all that from here?"

"Elementary, my dear Watson."

"I get to be Sherlock Holmes?"

Edie took a step back in surprise. "You know Sherlock Holmes?" She gave Kappy a sly look. "Well, well, well, aren't you full of surprises."

Kappy shrugged.

"No. Seriously," Edie said. "I'm sure old Bishop Sam doesn't have Sir Arthur Conan Doyle on his approved reading list."

"Maybe. Maybe not," Kappy hedged.

"Maybe not." Edie laughed.

"*Jah,* okay. I might not have *asked* him if I could read it. But I've never heard him say that I couldn't."

Edie clapped her on the shoulder. "You're a sneaky one, Kappy King."

"Does that mean I get to be Sherlock?"

"We'll see."

"Are you going to tell me what the text means?"

"Elemen— I mean, it's simple, really. He tells us to beware, which means we have to be in some sort of danger."

"Or someone could be following us."

"Doubtful. He tells us that things aren't what they seem, which means the accident wasn't really an accident. He also says 'this time,' which means he's left before. And that means he's Willie."

Maybe Edie would get to be Sherlock. Unless . . . "Are you sure about that?"

"Positive."

Kappy mulled it over. "If you're right, then we should ask around. Someone had to have seen something."

"They did," Edie said. "Willie Lapp saw something and now he's in hiding."

Kappy shook her head. "You've seen the cemetery. It's right across the street from the site of the accident. Do you really think that someone could purposefully run a buggy off the road and not be seen? It's the busiest road in the valley. And you and I both know that someone *had* to be in the cemetery."

"There's always someone in the cemetery," Edie agreed.

"Now all we have to do is find them and see what they saw."

"Don't you mean if they saw something?"

Kappy grinned. "I'm trying to remain positive."

"Positive it is," Edie said with a nod. "Okay, Miss Positive, what are we going to do? Go door-to-door and ask if someone saw anything?"

"As far as I can see, that's our only choice."

"Great." Edie's tone sounded anything but excited.

"Where's Jimmy?" Kappy asked, reaching for her bonnet.

"Home."

"Should we get him first?"

Edie nodded. "Probably. Plus, it'll do him good to get out of the house."

"Isn't that why you made him take a part-time job?"

"Partly." Edie followed her down the porch steps and into the yard. "We'll take my car up to get him, sound good?"

Kappy moved past her in the opposite direction. "We can't take your car to go door-to-door asking if people saw anything that day."

Edie stopped even as Kappy continued to the barn to retrieve her mare. "Why not?

We've been driving it all over the place."

"Not for something like this."

"I beg to differ." Edie held up one finger as if to make her point, but Kappy ducked into the barn. They had to take the buggy. Kappy wasn't sure how much of Edie's driving she could take. "We went to a bunch of houses after *Mamm* . . . died and we were in the car then."

Kappy came out of the barn, leading June Bug by her halter. "And look at how far it got us. They would barely talk to us." She offered the reins to Edie, who refused to take them.

"They would barely talk to us because you are shunned."

"Exactly the reason why I shouldn't be riding around in a buggy. Besides, you aren't exactly the most popular girl in the valley."

The words shouldn't have stung but they did. "The fresh air will do you some good." She shook the reins at Edie. "Either take the reins or get the buggy out of the carriage house."

Not having a further argument, Edie sighed and took the leather straps.

Kappy made her way into the carriage house and backed the buggy out into the yard. Edie frowned but handed her the reins so she could hitch up the horse.

"I should just go get Jimmy in my car. You could follow me up. That way I can leave my car at my house."

"Nuh-uh," Kappy said. "I don't trust you to start running all over the valley without me."

Edie's eyes narrowed and for a moment she looked almost . . . hurt. "Whatever."

Kappy hopped inside and pulled the reins through the front window. She did her best to hide her victorious grin. "Come on." She hooked one arm toward Edie. "We've got a mystery to solve."

"I still don't understand why we're going back to the cemetery again," Edie grumbled under her breath.

But from his place in the back seat, Jimmy still heard. "To see *Mamm*'s grave. Right, Kappy?"

"That's right." She secured the reins and hopped down. "Why don't you go on over there? Your sister and I are right behind you."

"Okay." Jimmy jumped down and started for the place where they had laid Ruth Peachey to rest. He turned around and continued to walk backward. "Just don't take long, okay?"

Edie waved. "Okay."

Satisfied, Jimmy faced front and concentrated on counting the rows of graves.

"We're here to get the lay of the land." Kappy crossed her arms and turned completely to the left. "See Minnie Peight's house over there?" She pointed to a house on the incline of Stone Mountain and partially hidden by trees.

"Yeah."

"She's too far away to have seen much, plus those trees are blocking her view. But that house there —" She pointed to the house that sat halfway between Minnie's house and the road. "They have a much better view."

"An *Englischer* lives there. I told you we should have brought the car."

"Hush that." Kappy turned a bit more, scanning the roadside. "Lorna may have seen something." She pointed toward the house on the other side of the cemetery.

"See! There's a truck in that driveway, too."

"Mennonite."

Edie let out a low growl.

Kappy ignored her and started walking toward the back of the cemetery, farthest from the road.

"Where are you going?" Edie stumbled

after her, her flip-flops smacking against her heels as she tried to keep up with Kappy's purposeful strides.

Kappy marched toward the mountain until she came to the last grave. She turned around, then scanned the scene once again. "Anyone in the cemetery could have seen it."

"Yeah," Edie agreed. "If they were here, at that exact moment in time."

"Anyone could have been here," Kappy murmured, scanning from side to side again. "As long as they have a loved one buried here. Come on." She started back toward the road and the buggy.

Jimmy had gotten his fill of visiting his mother and was wandering through the graves reading names and dates.

"Where are we going?" Edie asked, following behind her.

"We've got to find out if anyone was here at the time of the crash." From behind her the rustle-smack of Edie's footsteps stopped.

"Do you know how many people live in Kish Valley? Any of them could have been here."

Kappy tossed a quick smile over her shoulder and motioned for Jimmy to meet them at the buggy. "That's just the thing.

We don't have to talk to everyone, just the Amish and Mennonites."

"Is this, like, a real investigation? Really real? Like Jack Jones would investigate?" Jimmy's grin had nowhere else to go. If it got any wider it would stretch itself clear off his face.

"Sort of," Kappy said, pulling her eyes back to the road.

"You shouldn't have told him," Edie grumbled from beside her.

"If you don't want to leave him home alone, then he has to come with us. And if he's with us, he's going to have questions. Might as well get it all out now so we can get down to business."

Edie rolled her eyes and pulled on her ponytail to tighten it.

"Can I have my very own notebook?" Jimmy scooted forward so his face was between their respective shoulders.

"We'll see," Kappy said absently.

"Jimmy, *I* don't even have a notebook."

"I think we should all have notebooks."

"Is that why we're headed to Sundries and Sweets?" Edie leaned in closer to Kappy, forcing Jimmy to sit back in his seat. "Or did you want to see Hiram again?" she asked quietly, so only Kappy could hear.

"That's over." Kappy sniffed, but managed to keep her voice down. It wasn't like she didn't care for Hiram; she just couldn't stand the thought of him never loving her as much as he loved Laverna, his first wife and Kappy's best friend. She supposed that was what she got for falling in love with someone who was already in love.

But Laverna is gone.

She pushed the thought away. It was true Laverna was gone, and Kappy and Hiram deserved a chance at happiness, but it wasn't Laverna standing in their way. Not really.

"We're going to talk to Hiram about Willie," Kappy said as she turned the buggy into the parking lot next to the small country store.

"Why are we doing this again?" Edie asked.

"Because there's no sense in us going around the whole valley asking questions if Willie has already returned home." Kappy slid open the door and hopped to the ground.

"Do you really think that's going to happen?" Edie asked.

Kappy shook her head. "But we have to make sure." And they did.

Jimmy followed his sister out of the carriage and rubbed his hands together in obvious glee. "This is going to be fun."

Edie blew her bangs out of her eyes. "Yeah. Tons."

The inside of the store was the same as always: dim, lit only by the natural light that made its way through the high windows, and smelling faintly of dust. Kappy knew that Hiram's youngest sister, Emma, had recently begun working at the shop. It had to be a full-time chore, for every time Kappy went in Emma had a rag out wiping down the shelves. Today was no exception.

"Hi, Kappy." Emma smiled as she approached. It was good to see her come out of her shell, so to speak. She had always been a quiet girl, but until recently, Kappy had never realized the panicked look that went with that shyness. Only now that it was gone had Kappy even noticed that it had been there at all.

"Hi, Emma." Kappy came to a stop, only then realizing that just Jimmy had followed her inside. Edie must have thought she was better off outside. Jimmy stopped at the toys to pick up one of those paddleball games and started to play. Since there were no other customers in the store, Kappy had Emma all to herself. Should she ask if Hiram was available? "I just came to ask about Willie."

The young girl's blue eyes clouded over and for a moment Kappy thought she might burst into tears. Instead she shook her head, her prayer *kapp* strings swaying with the motion. "Everyone's so worried. He just disappeared one morning." She gave a quick shrug. "No one has seen him since. It's so odd."

"What's so odd?"

Behind her Kappy could hear Jimmy switching from the paddleball to some other toy, she wasn't sure what, but it sounded wooden.

Emma looked left and then right as if she were afraid that someone might be listening in. "All the times before," she said, "at least all the ones I can remember, he left in the middle of the night. I mean, there's one main road here. It's a little hard to sneak out unnoticed."

Kappy wasn't about to ask her how she knew that. Some questions were better left unanswered. "You're saying he left during the day?"

"He was heading over to the farmers' market for *Mamm,* and he never came back."

"And everyone assumed that he jumped the fence?"

"Of course he did." Her eyes widened.

"You don't think something happened to him, do you? *Mamm*'s so upset, and Hiram just keeps stirring her up." Emma clamped one hand over her mouth as if to stem the flow of words. "I didn't mean to say that."

"It's all right." Kappy awkwardly patted her arm in the most supportive manner she could muster. Thankfully, it seemed to comfort. "He's waiting for the candy delivery?"

The sweets part of Sundries and Sweets was an array of handcrafted candies made by a Mennonite woman on the other side of the mountain. Joan, she believed her name was. "The candy delivery always comes on Monday."

"That's right." Emma nodded. "Do you want me to go get him for you?"

"No, *danki*. I don't want to disturb him. Or you."

"It's no trouble, really. Hiram will be angry if he knows you came in and he didn't get to see you." She started toward the back door of the store, but Kappy clutched her arm to stop her progress.

"Really," she said, her tone stern but amicable. "I don't need to see him today. Maybe next time."

Emma looked crushed, as if Kappy had just told her that Willie was never coming home. "*Jah.* Okay." She bit her bottom lip and gave another quick nod.

"*Danki.*" Kappy started for the door. "Come on, Jimmy. Time to go."

"Hey, Kappy. Wait a minute."

She stopped.

"I want these bubbles." He held up a small plastic bottle of bubble soap. "But I don't have my money with me. I have it at home. Can you loan it to me, please?" He bounced on his toes in obvious excitement.

"I'll get them for you."

"You will?" He almost squealed in his joy.

"But it's not a loan. It's a gift."

"Are you serious?"

Kappy nodded, hating that he got so animated over a dollar gift. He needed more joy in his life. That much was obvious.

She pulled the money from the secret pocket she sewed into her aprons and handed it to Jimmy. Then she gave Emma a quick wave and ducked out the door.

"Where's Jimmy?" Edie called when she spotted Kappy.

"He'll be here in a minute."

Sure enough, Jimmy rushed out the door, small paper sack clutched in his hands.

"What the —"

"Just go with it," Kappy requested, then Jimmy climbed into the back of the buggy.

143

"Thank you! Thank you, Kappy!"

Edie tossed a suspicious look at Kappy as she hoisted herself into the carriage. "What did you do?"

Kappy shrugged and picked up the reins, turning the buggy around and setting the horse to an easy pace. "I bought him some bubbles."

"Bubbles?" Edie frowned, then tossed a look back toward her brother's ecstatic expression. "That's all? Are you sure? Because he's too excited for bubbles."

It was true. Jimmy was beyond excited. But Kappy chalked it up to unexpected gifts and him getting to go somewhere besides work and church. Most likely it was a hefty combination of both.

"That's all."

Satisfied, or maybe she was just dropping the matter, Edie turned, staring out the front as Kappy took them back toward home. "So how did it go? What did Hiram say?"

"Hiram wasn't there."

"No?"

"But I talked to Emma."

"His younger sister."

Kappy nodded. "That's right."

"What did she say?"

Kappy glanced back at Jimmy, but he

wasn't paying attention. He was staring out the back, watching the road as it ribboned behind them. "They're all worried," Kappy said. "It seems that Willie typically leaves in the middle of the night. But this time he was running an errand for his *mamm* and never came back."

"What about his buggy?" Edie asked.

"I didn't think to ask."

"You didn't think that was important?"

"Sure, it is. I just didn't think about it at the time."

Edie's frown deepened, then she faced the front once again. "Did you realize how close the accident was to the cemetery?"

"I seem to remember parking there and walking across. Twice."

"No, I mean really thought about it."

"It's not an omen," Kappy said. "Hiram's store is in the same direction. She was simply taking a load of pickles for him to sell."

"And you know this for a fact?"

"Of course."

"What makes you so sure?"

"The Daniel Eshes always take pickles to the Sundries every Tuesday."

"You mean to tell me that they make a delivery every week at the same time?"

"Well, *jah,* as far as I know. The Daniel

Eshes are organized businesspeople. They definitely have a schedule to follow." And since she and Hiram had almost been a couple, she knew that Tuesday was when the Sundries and Sweets store received their pickles.

They neared the scene of the accident, and Kappy slowed the carriage. She couldn't help herself. There was something eerie about what they had figured out. Now they knew where Sally June was headed when she lost her life.

They were barely moving when they went past the cemetery, but it wasn't the people on the west side of the road who concerned her.

"The Eshes live down that way," Kappy said, hoping to bring something else into the conversation.

"Wait." Edie clasped her fingers around Kappy's forearm. The motion held such force the horse shook her head and snorted at them. "If they get their pickles at the same time every week, then that proves it. This was no accident. Someone meant to harm Sally June."

CHAPTER 9

Shock bolted through Kappy. "But . . . but . . . why would an *Englischer* want to harm a sweet Amish girl?" The thought was ludicrous — today's word — and completely unbelievable. "Unless . . ."

"Unless what?" Edie's excitement was near palpable.

"Unless he was hired." Kappy grinned with satisfaction.

But Edie shook her head. "We are in Blue Sky, Pennsylvania, not on some cop show on TV. And what do you know about cop shows anyway?"

Kappy sniffed. "I know enough." She hadn't exactly *seen* a cop show. She had read more than her fair share of mysteries, and just to be clear, Edie made a terrible Dr. Watson. Watson was levelheaded and always cool, and Edie jumped to conclusions so often Kappy worried that she might hurt herself.

"Kap-py, why are you driving so slow?" Jimmy's whiny protest broke through their discussion.

"Sorry, Jim." She tossed the apology over her right shoulder, then set the horse at a faster pace.

"We'll finish this later," Edie murmured from beside her.

The thoughts and questions chased one another around her head as she drove them home.

First stop was Kappy's house. They piled down from the buggy, Kappy nearly unable to breathe with all the excitement coursing through her. Then she said a little prayer. She shouldn't be thrilled about the harm of another.

"Come up to the house when you're finished putting the horse away. We'll be able to talk more then," Edie said so only Kappy could hear.

Kappy nodded. "I'll have to check on Elmer first." She needed to make sure that he'd stayed put while they were gone and hadn't found a way out of the yard and down to the neighbor's.

"Come on, Jimmy," Edie called. "Let's go to the house."

But Jimmy shook his head. While they had been talking, he'd plopped himself down on

148

the porch steps and opened the little plastic jar of bubbles. The iridescent orbs floated around his grinning face. "Aren't they beautiful?"

"I never really thought about it before," Edie grumbled. "We need to go," she said louder and directly to him.

"No, we don't. It's not feeding time, I changed out the water in the duck pool this morning, and Judith isn't supposed to have her babies until next week."

"Judith," Edie scoffed under her breath. "Who names a gerbil Judith?"

Kappy released a small chuckle. "Jimmy, apparently. I think it's cute."

"I guess."

"What's wrong?" Kappy could tell something was bothering her and had been for a couple of days.

"Nothing."

"It's a sin to lie, Edith Peachey."

"It's a sin to tell all your secrets, too."

"It is not." Kappy led the mare into the barn and directed her into a stall. She grabbed a brush and began to work.

"It should be," Edie said as she followed behind her.

Kappy didn't press. Edie would tell her when the time came. If it ever did. "He's happy right where he is," she pointed out.

"Let me finish with June Bug and I'll find us something for lunch. We can talk, and he can blow bubbles until the hunger pains drive him inside."

Edie gave a quick nod and a small sigh. "Sounds like a plan."

Edie pitched in, getting June Bug a scoop of oats and refilling her water trough. Then together, Kappy and Edie started toward the house.

"You're good with him." Edie's comment sounded off-hand, just an observation, and Kappy left it at that.

"Jimmy? I like him." And she did. Others might not see his intelligence and spirit, but Kappy did. And she knew how he felt. Her entire life she had been on the fringes, never quite one of the community but as close as she could be without it. They were outliers, she and Jimmy, cut from the same cloth, two of a kind.

"Some days . . ." Edie started as they made their way into the kitchen.

Thankfully, Elmer was in the backyard and considering that Kappy hadn't been met at the door with a complaint from one of her neighbors, she had to consider it a good sign. "Some days what?"

Edie shook her head and slid into a chair at the table. "I don't know what to do with him." She leaned back, allowing Kappy to see the tears in her eyes. "I love him so much, but I don't know what to do with him."

Kappy sat down next to her and took her friend's hands into her own. "All he needs is love."

Edie let out a humorless laugh and pulled from Kappy's grasp to wipe her tears away with the backs of her hands. "He needs more than love. He needs his *mamm.*"

"We all need our *mamms,* but some of us aren't as fortunate as others."

"He's just grown up so much and yet he's not. He's big, and I know his body has matured. I don't know how to address that. What if he asks me if he can go out with a girl?"

Kappy glanced toward the window even though she couldn't see Jimmy from where she sat. "He's outside playing with bubble soap."

Edie sniffed. "You're right. He's still my little brother, right?"

"Right." Kappy tilted her head to one side and studied her friend. "Is this why you made him get a part-time job?"

"He needs to get out of the house." She paused. "Don't you think?"

"He got out of the house today."

"Not to go on an investigation."

"Was he or was he not out of the house?"

"Yeah," Edie grumbled.

"Is this why you're still thinking of leaving Blue Sky?"

"No, no," Edie said a little too quickly. "I don't know if I still belong here."

Kappy flashed her a quick smile. "Of course you do, as much as any of the rest of us."

Kappy stood and went to the fridge to get them a drink, giving Edie time to grab a paper napkin from her purse along with a mirror to repair the black stuff she wore on her eyes. Kappy returned with a glass of water and one of the cookies she had made the day before for each of them.

"Better?" she asked.

Edie sniffed again but nodded. "I'm fine. It's just hard, you know. I've never had another person to worry about and he's . . . well, you know how he is. And then not too long ago he was arrested." She was tearing up again.

Kappy took her hands and wrapped them around the water glass. "Here. Drink."

Edie did as she was told, then dabbed at her eyes again. "I've been thinking," she said.

"Does your brain ever stop?" Kappy

laughed.

"It's the lack of a television. Makes a person nutso."

"I'll say." Kappy took a drink of her water.

"What if the person was Amish, but driving a car?"

"Whose car?" Kappy asked. "The blue car?"

"Yes. The one that killed Sally June."

Kappy mulled the idea over for a minute. It was as far-fetched as they came, but still the best idea they'd had to date. "Okay. I'll bite," Kappy said. "Why would someone Amish be driving around in a car?"

"To throw us off the case."

Kappy shook her head. "They didn't know we were going to be on the case." She wasn't one hundred percent certain there *was* a case. *Englisch* drivers were constantly getting frustrated and impatient when behind Amish buggies. It stood to reason that the car went around, spooked the horse, and the rest was history.

Edie tapped her finger against her chin. "So why did they do it? Why did they run over Sally June, then drive away?"

"What if the person driving the car was *Englisch* and didn't want to stop because they were in a hurry?"

"What if they have something against Sally

June?" Edie countered.

"She was one of the kindest people I know."

"Maybe she got in their way?"

"Maybe she was simply driving," Kappy returned.

"And this was all an accident?" Edie asked. "Then why did the person leave?"

"Because they were scared. Or mean-hearted."

"Or maybe they were just trying to get rid of their competition."

"The pickles?" Kappy guessed. "Are we back to that again?"

Edie shrugged as if to say, "Of course." "It's possible that someone wants to topple the Eshes' monopoly on the church pickle market."

"There's only one person —"

Edie nodded.

The pickle lady. Bettie Hershberger.

"What do we do?" Kappy asked Edie an hour and a half later.

They had dropped Jimmy back at the Peachey household with instructions to not leave the house or open the door for anyone. They would return as soon as possible.

"We could have brought him with us, you know," Kappy said.

154

Edie shook her head. "I don't want him thinking that Blue Sky isn't safe."

"But yet, you'll take him to live in the city."

Edie's expression turned contrite. "I never said that."

She didn't have to, but Kappy kept the observation to herself. "Do you really think he's going to stay in the house the entire time we're gone?"

"What am I supposed to do? It's not like he has a phone where he can call if he needs me."

"He has his alert necklace."

Edie mumbled something incoherent and looked out at the passing landscape.

"What was that?"

"I don't know why we had to bring the buggy again," Edie said. This time Kappy was able to clearly hear her words, but she had a strong suspicion that it was not a repeat.

"When in Rome and all that," Kappy said.

"When have you ever been in Rome?" Edie asked.

"It's an expression."

"I know that. What I don't understand is why you know I'm worried about my brother being at home by himself and yet you want to take our slowest means of transportation."

"If we're going to visit with the Hershbergers about the pickles and maybe take a look around their place, don't you think we should at least show up in the proper conveyance?"

"Conveyance?"

"It's a word."

"I know it's a word. Just how did it get added to your vocabulary?"

Kappy felt heat rise into her cheeks. "I read, you know."

"That's right," Edie said. "Sherlock Holmes."

Kappy sniffed. "What's wrong with Sherlock Holmes?"

"Well, it explains a lot."

"What is that supposed to mean?"

"Nothing. Nothing at all."

Kappy turned the buggy down the lane toward the Hershbergers' house. It was somewhere between the cemetery and Mose Peachey's bait shop.

A rusty-colored dog and a couple of his friends barked out a greeting as Kappy climbed down from the buggy. Edie followed suit, and a few moments later the back door opened. Silas stepped into view.

The dogs stopped their barking and approached them with wagging tails the moment Silas appeared. He scratched one behind the ear as he made his way toward Kappy and Edie.

"Kappy." He greeted her with a smile. He gave Edie a cursory nod, then turned his attention back to Kappy. "What brings you out today?"

She couldn't very well say pickles. She mentally scrambled around, trying to remember the exact reason they had come up with for this impromptu visit. Edie elbowed her in the ribs to jumpstart her memory. "I heard that your . . . *mamm* was making birdhouses. We thought we could come take a look at them."

Silas's forehead wrinkled in confusion. "She's been making them for a couple of years now."

Kappy willed herself not to color at his words and gave a small shrug. "This is the first time I've been able to get by here."

Whereas Minnie Peight made standard birdhouses with clean lines and new paint, Silas's mother, Madeline, made decorative ones, odd-shaped birdhouses fashioned out of recycled wood scraps and rescued tin. And yes, she had been making them for a couple of years. Kappy had just never thought about coming to look at one until now. No, it wasn't the primary reason for her visit, but it was the best excuse she could come up with. She couldn't very well say, *I came to see if your aunt is running a covert pickle sting operation,* now could she?

"This way," Silas said, stepping around them. "They're in the barn."

Kappy had to admit the birdhouses were about the cutest thing she had ever seen. Well, if she were into that sort of thing.

She walked around the couple of tables Madeline had set up. She started in one direction, Edie in the other. Kappy trailed her fingers lightly over the birdhouse roofs as she passed. They came in a variety of colors, and all of them looked as if one good wind would take the paint right off them. Kappy wasn't sure if Madeline purposefully used peeling paint or if she had been lucky to be somewhere when they were tearing down an old house. Seeing as how the birdhouses were painted in a variety of colors, she had a feeling the old-looking paint was new. Strange. She had never seen anything like it. Well, nothing like it that was new. She saw peeling paint on her house every day.

"Does this one come in blue?" Edie asked. She held up a birdhouse of medium size, bigger than a shoe box, smaller than a bread box.

Silas stared at her for a moment.

Edie frowned. "Sorry." She turned to Kappy. "Will you ask him if he has this one in blue?"

"Why can't you ask me yourself?"

"I just did."

He blew out a quick breath. "Sorry. You took me by surprise is all."

"How's that?" Edie asked.

"You're Edith Peachey."

"I am." She tilted her head to one side. "Silas Hershberger! I remember you. How are you?"

He nodded. "Good. Good."

"You two know each other? What am I saying? Everyone around here knows each other." But Kappy hadn't expected it. She had mentioned Silas to Edie before. Perhaps her friend just hadn't made the connection.

Silas flashed her a quick smile. "Let me check upstairs for that house. *Mamm* keeps extra stock in the hayloft." He moved farther into the barn, leaving Edie staring after him.

"Edith Peachey. I never would have thought . . ." he muttered as he left them.

"He likes you," Edie said with a grin.

Kappy whirled toward her. "What?"

"You heard me."

"I know what I think I heard, but he

doesn't like me. Seems more like he likes you." Kappy tried to keep the grumble from her voice. She didn't succeed. So she flashed Edie a quick smile to soften her words. What was wrong with her today?

"Oh, we go way back."

"Jah?"

Edie nodded. "We were in the same youth group before I left. But we were only friends, if that's what you're thinking."

"I'm not thinking anything."

"Yeah, you are, but don't worry. He's only interested in you, and you should use it to our advantage. That's our ticket in."

"Pee-shaw."

"Shhh." Edie turned away just as Silas came back carrying the requested item.

"Here ya go."

Edie took it from him. "How much?"

He quoted the price as Edie fished into her wallet to count out the cash. She held it out toward him. He didn't hesitate before accepting the money from her.

"Well, that's refreshing," Edie commented.

"What?" Silas looked from one of them to the other as if trying to get the thread of a conversation he had entered in the middle.

Kappy shook her head. "Don't pay her any mind. She's lamenting her *Bann* status."

"You're one of the few people in Blue Sky

160

who will actually talk to me directly."

Silas smiled and Kappy realized how that small action made her stomach feel light. Or maybe she was coming down with something.

"And thanks for getting me a blue one. Blue's my favorite color. I always wanted a blue car."

"You should get one, then." Silas smiled in that friendly way he had. But otherwise he didn't show one shred of emotion over the thought of a blue car.

"I heard your aunt moved up from Lancaster," Edie continued.

Kappy gave a start at Edie's words. *Way to step in there.* She certainly hadn't been paying attention to their mission.

"*Jah,* it's been interesting since she moved back."

"Really?" Edie asked. "I would think your *dat* would be glad to have her so near."

"That's true." He leaned in close, as if someone were listening in and he didn't want them to hear. "It's the rest of us who are suffering." His dimples took the sting from his words, and Kappy's stomach did that funny little flip again. Seriously. What was wrong with her?

"I'm sure it'll settle down soon enough," Edie added.

"I hope so. The entire house smells like vinegar."

"Vinegar?"

Kappy had to hand it to Edie. Her performance was enough to win the most prestigious *Englisch* acting award.

"It's the pickles," he admitted. "She hates the white pickles and is determined to change everyone's mind about them."

Edie laughed prettily and twisted a strand of her hair around one finger. For some reason the action made Kappy want to stand in front of her until she stopped. What was she doing anyway?

"Change everyone's mind, huh? How does she propose to do that?"

"Just between me and the two of you, she's too intense about all this pickle stuff. I keep reminding myself that she was uprooted and needs a little time to settle in but . . ." He shook his head. "Anyway. What were you asking?"

"How is she planning to change everyone from white pickles to the green variety?" Kappy asked.

"I'm not exactly sure." He scratched his chin thoughtfully, and Kappy tried to visualize what he would look like with a beard. As a widower, Hiram already had one, but Silas wouldn't grow his until after he married.

What a thrill it would be to know that he'd grown a beard all because of her.

"She has been going around talking about supply and demand, flooding the market, and things like that. She's trying to talk the stores into selling her pickles."

"You can lead a horse to water," Edie quipped.

"Exactly." Silas snapped his fingers. "But I guess it's giving her life new purpose. And that's important."

"Amen," Kappy said.

"I guess we should be going," Edie said. "I have to take Jimmy to work."

"I'm glad you stopped by today," Silas said.

Edie smiled. "Me too."

"Come back anytime."

They made their way back to the buggy. Somehow Kappy was able to keep her emotions at bay until she had climbed into the carriage and turned it around.

Silas waved to them as they pulled down the drive.

"Can you believe that?" Kappy asked.

Edie shook her head and twisted around to look out the back window. "Nope. He's way cuter than I remember."

CHAPTER 10

Kappy pretended not to fume all the way back home. And Edie chatted incessantly the entire time. So hopefully, she didn't notice Kappy's silence. Kappy couldn't say exactly what was wrong, but she knew part of it had to do with Edie's indecision on whether to stay in Blue Sky or leave. Then she wanted to come flirt with an Amish man! What did she think? He was going to jump the fence for her?

"Kappy." Edie bumped against her arm, bringing her back from her thoughts. She had a feeling this wasn't the first time Edie had spoken her name.

"*Jah?*"

"Do you want to go with me to take Jimmy to work? Maybe we can stop by a few of those houses around the site of the accident."

"*Jah,* sure. Whatever you want." She turned her attention to the front and pretended to study the road.

"Why do I feel something's not right with you?"

"Why would something be wrong?"

Edie shook her head. "Not really wrong, but off . . ."

"Everything's fine."

"Sin to lie," Edie reminded her in a singsong voice.

"I'm not lying."

"You're jealous," Edie said in awe.

"I am not."

"Then what is it?"

Kappy shook her head and pulled the buggy onto School Yard Road. "It's dumb."

"Tell me."

"I don't want to say."

"Tell me or . . . well, I don't know an 'or,' but when I think of one you won't like it."

"Ever since you got back you've had a problem getting people to talk to you, then Silas practically falls at your feet."

"You are jealous."

Kappy pulled into her driveway and stopped the mare. "No. Really. It's not that at all. It's just . . ." How did she say it? "You've been gone for years and now you're back. You keep talking about leaving, and yet Silas accepts you for who you are. How can you flirt with him like that if you're still thinking about leaving?"

"Flirt? You think I was flirting with him?"

"Jah."

Edie threw back her head and laughed. "I wasn't flirting with him."

Kappy felt like a balloon that had been deflated with a pin. "You weren't? Okay. Good."

"Didn't I say that I thought he liked you?" Edie asked.

Kappy shook her head. "He doesn't like me."

Edie bumped shoulders with her, the grin on her face stretching clear across. "You keep telling yourself that. But remember this conversation when he comes courting."

He wasn't coming courting. She had been lucky that Hiram had been interested in her and it was more than obvious when she broke it off with him that her chances of ever marrying were down to zero to nil. To even imagine Silas would want to spend time with her was more than she could handle.

"Are you going with me to take Jimmy?"

"Can we take the buggy?"

"No."

Kappy sighed. "Okay. I'll come anyway."

They dropped Jimmy off at the bait shop

166

and headed back down the road. "Do you want to stop by Silas's again?" Edie asked.

"You want to run by the police station and talk to Jack Jones?"

"Touché."

"What?"

"Never mind." She cast a quick look at Kappy. "Where to first?"

"Lorna Betz's." Kappy braced one hand against the roof of the car and they were off.

"You really think Lorna saw something?" Edie asked.

"We won't know unless we ask her."

"True dat."

Kappy rolled her eyes and held on for the duration of the trip.

Lorna's house was halfway between Minnie's house and the road. The spot where it sat was flat and had a practically unobstructed view of the scene of the accident. Whether anyone there knew anything useful remained to be seen.

Edie parked in the driveway of the midsized brick house and they got out. There was a truck in the drive, a bicycle under the carport, and the sound of singing coming from the backyard.

"Should we go back?" Edie asked.

"Of course." Together they made their way

around the cute little house.

Lorna Betz stood at the clothesline, the items she had already hung flapping in the light breeze.

"Lorna?" Kappy called.

The woman peeked her round face between the sheets, her cheeks going rosy in recognition. "Kappy King, is that you?"

Kappy nodded.

"My goodness." Lorna dropped her bag of clothespins on top of the basket of clean laundry and made her way through the hanging wash to greet Kappy.

From a distance, Lorna Betz appeared no more than forty, but when she got closer a person could tell from the wisdom in her eyes that she had more years on her than that. "What brings you out today?"

Kappy gave a half-shrug. "Did you hear what happened to Sally June Esh?"

Lorna pressed her lips together and shook her head sadly. "Such a terrible tragedy. Are they having a benefit for her family?"

Kappy nodded and pulled a flyer from the hidden pocket of her apron. She unfolded it and handed it to Lorna.

"Where did you get that?" Edie asked.

"I picked it up when we were at Sundries and Sweets."

Lorna scanned the page, then lifted her

gaze to stare at Edie. "Edith Peachey? Is that you?"

Edie smiled, but Kappy could tell that it was a bit strained. "In the flesh."

"I thought I heard somewhere that you were back. So sorry to hear about your *mamm.*"

"Thank you," Edie murmured.

"Speaking of Sally June," Kappy said, trying her best to steer the conversation back to the topic they needed to discuss. "I can't believe that happened so close to your house."

The three of them stared out over the field toward the road. Thankfully, the Betzes' corn was planted behind the house, and they had a clear view of the place where the buggy had been forced off the road.

A chill shivered down Kappy's spine. She could still see the gouges in the grassy roadside, an ominous reminder of what had taken place. But why? Why had someone hurt young Sally June Esh?

"It was close, all right. I guess it would have been really scary if I had been home." Even on a still day the sound could have been easily heard at the Betzes' place.

"You weren't home?"

"I had gone over to my sister's house to help her get ready for market day."

Every Wednesday there was a huge out-door market in neighboring Belleview. Lorna's sister, Liz, was well known for her organic vegetables.

Kappy nodded. "I wanted to get out to the market last week, but I didn't make it over there."

"It was a pretty good turnout, all things considered."

"How did Liz do?"

"Not bad. She took some small Kirbys and sold out to one customer." Lorna chuckled. "Never seen that before."

"How many?"

"Four or five bushels."

"Bushels?" Four bushels alone was nearly two hundred pounds of cucumbers.

"I know, right? Her plants really took off this year. She had more than we knew what to do with. I talked her into taking them. It was either that or let them rot on the vine. She told me they would end up as pig slop, but then the second customer of the day and *bam,* they were gone."

Kappy looked to Edie. Edie raised her brows in that *go on* manner she had. "Do you remember who bought them?" Kappy asked.

"You don't easily forget something like that." Lorna ran her hands down her rotund

170

belly. "It was that Hershberger woman. Barbie . . . ?"

"Bettie?" Kappy's mouth went dry in anticipation.

"Yes, that's it." Lorna smiled. "Bettie Hershberger bought them all."

"I'm still not sure what this proves," Edie said as they climbed back into her car and headed toward the next house.

"I'm not sure it proves anything, either, but if she bought two hundred pounds or better of pickling cukes, then she means business."

"Isn't that what Silas already told us? That she was hoping to change everyone's mind, and she wanted to get her pickles in the stores and such."

"*Jah,* but this proves it."

Edie nodded. "If you say so. I was ready to take Silas at his word."

"I was, too, but this is good, too, *jah*? If she has started to can them already . . . well, it can't be long before her plans are revealed."

Edie cast her a quick glance then stopped, looking one way and then the other. "Which way?"

The houses up the side of the mountain were a long shot. The farther away they got, the clearer the sight, but the harder it would be to see any details due to the distance.

"Back toward the road, I suppose."

They drove in silence for a moment, each one contemplating the clues they had and the difficulty in finding eyewitnesses.

"We need to find that blue car," Edie said. "There was nothing to see at Silas's."

Kappy shook her head. "You didn't expect them to have it parked in the barn, did you?"

"No. And Silas didn't even flinch when I started talking about blue cars. But now we know that his house truly must smell like vinegar if she's been canning hundreds of pints of pickles."

And she would have to be with the reported number of cucumbers she had bought.

"I'll admit the whole thing sounds suspicious, but pickles? That's hardly worth hurting another person over."

"You haven't been out there," Edie said. "You would be surprised what people will do for less than pickles."

"I may not have been 'out there,' and I can't say that Bettie Hershberger has, either, but pickles?"

"I just mean in general." Edie shrugged. "I still say Silas likes you."

"Silas likes everybody," Kappy countered.

Edie didn't answer, just noted the lack of cars at the houses closer to the road. "I guess everyone's at work."

"What do we do now?"

Edie stopped the car at the main road.

"Go home and try again another day."

It wasn't what she wanted to do, the disappointed note in her voice testament to that. But what choice did they have? And chances were that if the people weren't home now, they weren't home on the day of the accident.

Kappy stifled a sigh as Edie turned the car toward the house.

"There's one thing I know about Silas," Edie said, picking up their earlier conversation. "He's a sight better than stuffy old Hiram."

Kappy sniffed. "There's nothing wrong with Hiram being . . . conservative. I like the way he balances things."

Edie shot her a frown. "What exactly does that mean?"

"You know as well as I do that I didn't have the most conventional upbringing."

"Yeah. So?"

"Hiram sort of gives me . . . I don't know . . . people looked at me differently when I was going around with him."

"Are you saying that he gave you some

sort of respectability?"

"Sort of, and I am very grateful that he took an interest in me."

Edie shook her head. "You aren't yourself when you're around him."

"I would like to think that I am better."

"Try again." Edie pulled the car into Kappy's drive, but neither one made a move to get out.

"Edie Peachey, there is nothing wrong with trying to improve oneself."

"No, but there's plenty wrong with allowing someone to change you when there's nothing wrong with you to begin with."

Kappy didn't answer.

"Why would you want someone to tone you down?"

She shrugged.

"And I know for a fact he doesn't like dogs."

Kappy turned in her seat to face Edie. "That is not true. Of course he likes dogs. He owns one."

"You can own a dog and not like them," Edie said. "But Silas . . . that man loves dogs."

Kappy remembered all the canines wandering around at the Hershberger place. There had been at least three, maybe four. But Hiram . . . did she know for a fact that he liked dogs? She did not. It wasn't like that would be how she judged his character, but it went to prove how little she actually knew about him. They might have practically grown up together and known each other their entire lives, but he was still a mystery to her. She shook her head.

"Speaking of dogs . . ." She reached for the door handle. "Do you want me to ride with you to pick up Jimmy from work?"

"If you'd like."

Kappy's only answer was a quick nod. Then she got out of the car and started for the house.

Her legs felt like rubber as she made her way up the porch steps. She really didn't want to think too much about Hiram and Silas. It was much easier to think about pickles, Bettie Hershberger, and blue cars. And even though who killed Sally June was a mystery, Kappy understood the whole thing a lot better than she understood men.

Edie honked as she pulled from the drive. Kappy waved and stepped into the house, making her way into the backyard. No shrill puppy barks greeted her and her heart sank. Where had the mischievous pooch gotten off to? As soon as one of her neighbors showed up, she would know for certain.

With a sigh she went back into the house

and sat down at the kitchen table. She had *kapps* to sew. When she had gone into her basement shop that morning she noticed a few sizes were getting low. There had also been a couple of special orders in the box. They were both from regular customers, and she had their patterns on hand. All she had to do was find the peace of mind to sit down and sew.

She pushed up from her feet and made her way to her sewing room. But the stacks of fabrics didn't give her that sense of well-being that they usually did. She found the white organdy she had bought at the dry goods store and laid it out on the small table she kept in the room. She really needed to look into getting some of that waterproof material. That was all the rage in Lancaster. At least that was what the girls were telling her. Kappy wasn't so sure, but a girl had to make a living. And if her customers wanted waterproof prayer *kapps,* then waterproof prayer *kapps* they would get.

She cleared her mind and set to work, but when she cut the same pattern on the wrong side of the fabric, she knew she needed to take a break before she ruined another one.

With a sigh, she made her way back into the kitchen. She could get a drink of water, maybe sit for a while and empty her head of some of the thoughts flying around inside. She could make a grocery list. She could get that out and, maybe then she would be able to concentrate better.

She got a glass of water, a notebook, and a pen, then once again sat at the table.

She needed milk, but she would get that from the Joseph Rabers. She had a co-op sort of thing going with him. She had bought the cow, he housed it and milked it, and in turn she made his wife, Mary's, *kapps* and didn't charge her a dime. It was good to have the benefits of fresh milk without the hassle of keeping cows. It might not hurt to see if gossipy Mary had heard anything good lately. Anything that could help her and Edie figure out who would want to hurt a sweet girl like Sally June Esh.

Kappy stopped that thought and turned her focus back to food. She could use a loaf of bread. She hadn't baked bread in years. Maybe she needed to buy some bread flour instead and make a loaf of her aunt's special potato bread.

And you know who loved potato bread? Hiram. Hiram loved potato bread. Didn't he? She thought he did.

She pushed the thought away and added bread flour and yeast to her list. She really wished she had a sourdough starter, but every time she received one she had a hard time keeping it from getting moldy on the top. Maybe she should run by the Sundries store and see if Hiram had any fresh baked sourdough. Then she could ask him if he liked potato bread.

She tossed her pen down and sighed. Too many thoughts were making her crazy. Maybe she didn't know much about Hiram. She knew he was a good man and that was a lot. She knew she wouldn't marry him until he could love her as much as he loved Laverna. Kappy didn't think that would ever happen. She wasn't trying to be negative, merely pragmatic. That was tomorrow's word of the day. She had peeked. *Pragmatic,* that was exactly what she was being.

And being pragmatic didn't mean she believed all of Edie's claims that Silas liked her. He seemed to like her well enough, but he was a good man, and she had never given him cause not to like her. But if he did . . .

She flipped the top page of her tablet over to expose a fresh sheet of paper, then she picked up her pen.

Never in her life would she imagine herself to be "boy crazy," but that was exactly what was going on. She had only had one suitor in her life and that was Hiram Lapp. Now she possibly had two, and the mere thought was sending her into a tizzy.

She drew a line across the top of the page. On the left side she wrote *Hiram,* on the right, *Silas.* She hesitated a moment longer, then began her list.

CHAPTER 11

Kappy had filled half a sheet of paper when she heard someone at the front of her house. Most everyone knew that she only conducted business at the back door and even that was reluctant. Her *kapps* were in the basement shop, set up with one box for paying and another for special orders. There was no need for anyone to be coming to the front of the house unless . . .

She dropped her pen and made her way to the door. It was Ephraim again, she was almost sure of it. She was really going to have to do something about the fence. She couldn't have Elmer getting out every day or even when his whim dictated.

But it wasn't Ephraim Jess hobbling up her porch steps, but his sworn enemy, Nathaniel Ebersol. In one hand he clutched a wilted and broken green stalk that once upon a time had most likely been a hollyhock. That could only mean one thing.

"Hi, Nathaniel. What brings you out today?" She didn't need him to tell her other than she could use the time he took in answering to get herself together. She hadn't been expecting this.

"Cut the pleasantries, Kathryn."

She took a step back. Customarily no one save Martha Peachey, her across-the-lane neighbor, ever called her Kathryn. And in the last few days she had been called by her given name not once but three times. Which meant, like Ephraim before him, Nathaniel was angry. Or senile. Never before in her life had she wished mental problems on another, but she was so tired of angry neighbors and a misbehaving puppy.

"I'm sorry." The words burst out of her before she even had time to form them in her mind.

Nathaniel stopped on the last step, staring at her. He had his empty hand on the railing and the other still held his mutilated plant. "What are you sorry for, girl?"

"Whatever it is Elmer has done to your garden."

"Heh?" He looked at the plant still clutched in his fist, then he tossed it to one side. "Who's Elmer?"

"He's my new beagle."

Nathaniel squinted at her. "One of Ruth's

pups? I wouldn't mind having one of them myself."

You can have mine nearly jumped from her lips, but she managed to keep the offer to herself. She really loved the little dog, just not as much when he got her into trouble with every neighbor on School Yard Road. "I can talk to Edie for you, if you'd like."

Nathaniel nodded. "I'll give it some thought." He looked down to where he had tossed the wilted green stalk. "You admit that your dog did that?"

Kappy swallowed hard and nodded. It was always best to tell the truth, wasn't it?

Nathaniel scratched a spot under the band of his hat without removing it. When he was finished his hat sat at a strange angle and showed off more of his bald head than before. Kappy hid her smile.

"I was hoping that we could blame it on that other neighbor of yours."

Kappy's eyes widened in surprise. "You're not mad at me because my dog destroyed your flowers?"

Nathaniel straightened his hat. "I might have been." He paused. "Was the other one upset about something?"

"Elmer killed some of his chickens."

"I see. Then I'm not upset at all. I love

growing plants. And I suppose these messed-up ones are just an opportunity to plant new ones."

"Thank you, Nathaniel."

He nodded and hobbled on back down the steps. "I'll be seeing you," he tossed over one shoulder. He stopped halfway between the house and his carriage. "Did you hear about Sally June Esh?"

Kappy's heartbeat kicked up a notch at the sound of that name.

"*Jah.* It's really sad, it is."

"That girl had so much ahead of her."

Kappy nodded, unsure what to say.

"I trade with her *dawdi.* I tell you, it's a shame. The whole family is broken up."

"I'm sure." What else was there to say?

"And Jonah," Nathaniel continued. "He's practically beside himself."

Kappy nodded again. Nathaniel was in a chatty mood today, and she should take advantage of it. Not that it would do her any good, but she should try.

"Nathaniel," she started when he stopped to take a quick breath. "You didn't happen to see anything that day, did you?"

He did that head-scratching-without-removing-his-hat thing again, tilting it much in the same way. "I'm pretty far from the road."

Kappy knew that. But she was still hope-
ful. "You were at home that day?"

Nathaniel nodded. *"Jah."*

Kappy's hopes deflated. "You weren't at
the cemetery or anything?" Nathaniel's wife
had died a few years back and Nathaniel
figured he was too old to start over with a
new one. Secretly, Kappy thought it was so
he could continue his war with Ephraim in
peace.

"That's your other neighbor's day to go."

"Ephraim?"

"I reckon."

"But he —" She had been about to point
out that unlike Nathaniel, Ephraim had
never married. He wouldn't be at the cemetery to visit his late wife's grave, but she
supposed he had his own kin who had
passed on.

"He's got plenty of people to visit there."
Nathaniel's mouth turned down at the
corners. He looked particularly angry about
something, though Kappy supposed it was
the mention of Ephraim. That would do it
every time.

"Thanks," Kappy said.

"For what?"

She shook her head. "I'll talk to Edie for
you if you want."

He frowned.

"About a puppy."

Nathaniel nodded. *"Jah.* That'd be good. *Danki."* Then he turned and hobbled toward his buggy.

Kappy watched him go, trying to put all that she had just learned into focus.

Jonah Esh was having problems dealing with the death of his sister. Understandable. Ephraim Jess might have actually been in the cemetery when the accident happened and could be an eyewitness to the crime. Fantastic. As long as Ephraim was upset about Elmer's shenanigans in his yard, Nathaniel would be forgiving. Even better. Now if she could just teach her dog which of her neighbors to visit.

Kappy went back into the house. She sat down in her seat and picked up her pen to resume making her list.

She wasn't one hundred percent certain, but she was pretty sure that this list was the hardest thing she had done. Ever. Both men were good men. Both loved God and planned on staying with the church. Both were handsome to a fault. Yet the thing that bothered her the most? She was taking Edie's word that Silas was even interested, Jimmy's, too, and she had already broken off any plans she'd discussed with Hiram. So what was she doing making a list of the good and bad qualities of each?

Kappy had just finished mopping the floor the following afternoon when a knock sounded at the door. Had to be some new girl or visitor to Blue Sky who wanted a new prayer *kapp*. Word got around fast that Kappy was the one to see. She just wished that her rule of going around back would spread as successfully.

"Go around back." Kappy yelled toward the closed door.

"Kappy? It's me."

"Hiram?" What was he doing here? She made her way to the door, but didn't open it. "What are you doing here?"

"I need to talk to you about something."

"Oh." She stared at the white-painted wood. On the other side she knew Hiram was staring at powder blue.

"Kappy?"

"Jah?"

"Are you going to let me in or are we going to yell through the door all afternoon?"

"Oh. Right." She pulled the door open and motioned for Hiram to enter. "Be careful. The floor might still be a little wet." She waved a hand toward the mop propped up next to the kitchen entrance.

"Are you still making everyone go around

back for their *kapps*?"

She closed the door and crossed her arms. "Is that what you came here to talk to me about?" It was an old disagreement between the two of them and, as far as Kappy was concerned, dead. As a doornail.

"No." He sucked in a breath, then let it out slowly. "Can we sit? Maybe at the table. Or in the living room?"

She gestured toward the couch and followed him into the living area.

"I know you don't believe me, but the women would really appreciate a gentler approach to salesmanship."

"I believe you've said that before." She settled down in the wooden rocker as he found a place on the couch.

"It's true."

She stopped herself from shaking her head. It would do no good to try to change Hiram's mind. Just as it would do no good for him to try to change hers. She didn't coddle her customers. She had the *kapps* ready in the basement, she got her special orders ready when requested, and she didn't hover over her customers as they were trying to shop. They had peace, and she had privacy. It had worked this way for years. She saw no reason to change the system now.

"What did you really come here about, Hiram?"

He leaned forward onto the edge of the sofa, clasping his hands between his knees. "I heard you've been quite the traveler lately."

Kappy frowned. What was he talking about? "Who told you that?"

He shrugged. "Emma told me that you stopped by yesterday."

"I did."

"And you went to visit Silas Hershberger in Edie Peachey's car."

"I did not." At least that one she could answer honestly and still contradict him. They had gone in her buggy.

"You didn't visit with Silas yesterday?"

"I didn't say that. I said I didn't visit him in Edie's car."

"Just Lorna Betz?"

"Get to the point, Hiram." She was beginning to lose interest in this conversation.

"It doesn't look good, Kappy. You shouldn't be running all over with ex-Amish and in a car."

So a buggy was okay? She shook those words away. "I think you're missing something here, Hiram. We are no longer a couple."

"And if I was the deacon? Or Bishop Sam?"

She rocked back in her seat and calmly studied him. He was very upset, though she couldn't figure why. Maybe because Hiram Lapp had gotten most everything he'd wanted in his life. Now he wanted her, but he couldn't have her. It was driving him out of his mind.

"But you aren't the deacon or Bishop Sam, and I haven't done anything wrong."

"If you haven't done anything, then why won't you tell me what you were doing?"

Because it's none of your business jumped to her lips, but she managed to bite it back. She didn't have anything to say to Hiram. Everything she might say would just sound defensive, and she wasn't about to defend herself to him. If her theories were correct and someone had been trying to kill Sally June Esh, then she just might be saving someone else by uncovering the killer.

Plus, it wasn't as if she and Hiram were an actual couple; they were just *almost* a couple. His attention to her had kept anyone else who might be interested at bay, but she couldn't say that she minded all that much. She wasn't sure she was cut out for marriage.

But solving a crime, that seemed to suit

her well enough. Though if she said that, she was certain that Hiram would have a fit. And tell her that there was no crime to solve. So she simply smiled and kept her thoughts to herself.

It seemed to take forever to get Hiram satisfied and out the door. She couldn't say he was happy with her answers, but it was obvious that he knew when to give up. Once he was gone, she glanced back at the table at the list she had been making. She didn't have the heart to go back to it. Her encounter with Hiram had left a bad taste in her mouth.

He didn't seem to be quite himself these days. Like the rest of the Lapp family, he was worried about Willie.

But she didn't think he would find any comfort in knowing that Willie had been texting Edie. Besides, they weren't absolutely certain that the texts were from Willie. More like strongly suspected. She couldn't say anything to Hiram until she had more concrete information.

A knock sounded at the front door. She shook her head. She'd had more visitors in the last few days than in a long time. And where was her dog, who should be sounding the alert? Most likely off terrorizing her neighbor's hostas.

"I know you're in there. I can hear you breathing."

"Go away, Edie."

"I thought you might want to go with me to pick up Jimmy."

She really needed to be figuring out how to repair her fence to keep her dog on the right side of the wire. "Can you take me by the hardware store?"

"Of course. Why do you want to go?"

"Fence."

"Right. Are you coming?"

"Let me get my money."

As much as she hated to admit it, traveling in a car was so much more efficient than a horse and buggy, but Kappy couldn't imagine traveling at these speeds everywhere she went. She wasn't sure her heart could take it.

"Penny for them."

"Huh?" Kappy dragged her gaze away from the passing landscape and settled it on her friend.

"Your thoughts. A penny for your thoughts."

Kappy made a face.

"It was supposed to make you smile."

"Nathaniel Ebersol came by the house this

afternoon."

Edie blew out a snort. "That's enough to make anyone frown."

"He told me that Ephraim Jess might have been in the cemetery at the time of the accident."

"What?" Edie nearly braked in her excitement. "How would he know that?"

"It seems they have some sort of schedule worked out. You know the two of them can barely be in church together."

"Still going strong, huh?"

"I think it gets worse every year."

"And still no one knows what they are into it about?"

Kappy shrugged. "Someone has to know, but as old as they are, most of their friends are gone now, taking that secret with them."

"And old Nate thinks that Ephraim may know something?"

"It's possible. If he was at the cemetery at the same time as the accident."

"You realize that he may be telling you this in order to harass Ephraim?"

"I know."

"Then again, he may have seen the entire thing."

They rode in silence, each one lost in swirling thoughts. Jimmy was excited to be picked up and even more excited when Edie told him that they were going to the hardware store.

"Are we going to build something?"

"I've got to fix the fence where Elmer keeps getting out."

"Can I help?" His excitement was so strong that Kappy couldn't help but smile.

"Of course."

"Bonus," Jimmy exclaimed.

"Where did you hear that?" Edie asked.

Jimmy grinned, obviously pleased with himself for remembering to use that new special word. "Some *Englisch* kids came in today to buy bait. And honey. I heard them say it." His smile stilled, then fell. "It's not bad, is it?"

Edie shook her head. "No, it's just sort of . . . worldly."

Hardly the word Kappy would have used. *Vague* or *vapid* would have been better, but Edie didn't have a word-a-day calendar like she did.

"*Jah.* Okay then." Jimmy sat back in his seat and let the wind rushing in from the rolled-down window blow his hair off his face.

"He's cute," Kappy said so only Edie could hear.

Edie's fingers tightened on the steering wheel. "Do I let him say that? Or do I tell him not to? What would the bishop do?"

"You're worrying about this way too much."

"Easy for you to say. He's not your brother. You aren't trying to raise him in a culture that you left behind a long time ago."

"That's small potatoes," Kappy pointed out. "Let the small stuff alone. It'll take care of itself. The big stuff: church, baptism, following the *Ordnung,* those are the things to worry about."

"If you say so." Edie pulled her car into the parking lot at the hardware store, and they all piled out. "What are you looking for?" she asked Kappy.

"I don't know, really. Something to keep the puppy in the yard."

"Can I help you?"

Kappy whirled around at the familiar voice. Silas Hershberger was standing behind her wearing a green vest with a store name tag and a sweet smile. "Silas? What are you doing here?"

"Working. Part-time, you know."

"No, I didn't." But it was nice to see a friendly face.

Edie nudged her in the ribs.

Kappy took a quick step away.

"What are you looking for today?"

"Kappy's puppy keeps getting out," Jimmy

helpfully supplied.

"You have a puppy?"

"A little beagle. He's about six months old now, I guess."

"I love puppies."

Edie nudged her again as if to say, *I told you he liked dogs.*

"This little guy likes to dig and then he crawls under the fence . . ."

"And terrorizes the valley," Silas finished for her.

Kappy laughed. "Something like that."

"I'm going to help." Jimmy grinned at Silas, who promptly smiled back.

"Kappy is lucky to have such a fine helper. Every master needs an apprentice."

Jimmy tugged on Kappy's elbow. "Do you hear that? Are you a master?"

"Hardly."

"She is," Silas said emphatically. "And that makes you the apprentice."

"You're funny, Silas." Jimmy laughed.

"Right this way," he continued. "I have just the thing."

They followed behind him to the area where the fencing was housed.

"How long have you been working here?" Edie asked. Then slapped a hand over her mouth. "Sorry," she whispered. It was obvious that she didn't want to get Silas in trouble for talking to her. She was under a *Bann,* after all.

"No worries," Silas whispered in return, his smile playful. "I guess I started right after Bettie came to live with us. Here we are." The conversation about Bettie stopped as Silas pointed out the features of the fencing he was showing them. But Kappy could only think of one thing. His household had increased, and he had to take a part-time job to make ends meet. No wonder Bettie was so determined to convert everyone over to green pickles. She needed the money so her nephew could quit his part-time job.

CHAPTER 12

"I know what you're thinking," Edie said as they drove home. They were almost to the turnoff for School Yard Road when they finally had a chance to talk. Jimmy had chatted nonstop about Silas, the fence, helping Kappy, and Silas. Yes, he talked enough to mention the man twice.

"You do?" Kappy asked.

At last, Jimmy sat back in his seat and was now staring out the window, that sappy yet irresistible smile that was all Jimmy plastered across his face.

"Let's drop Jimmy off at the house, and we'll go over there."

"I don't want to go," Jimmy piped in. "I need to feed the ducks. And the gerbils, and the rabbits. And the goats."

Kappy whirled to face Edie. "You have goats?"

Jimmy laughed hysterically from his place in the back seat.

"He's just wishful thinking," Edie said with an affectionate eye roll.

Jimmy laughed harder, slapping one hand against his knee. "I almost had you there."

"He thinks that if I agree to let him feed the goats, then I'm saying that he can have some."

"Jimmy," Kappy admonished, turning in her seat to look at him directly.

He shrugged. "Can't blame a guy for trying."

Kappy stifled a laugh, not wanting to encourage him.

"Yes," Edie said. "Yes, I can."

Jimmy was more than ready to get out and stretch his legs, but the sight of a familiar car kept Edie and Kappy in their seats a bit longer.

"What's he doing here?" Kappy asked.

"And I know this how?"

Kappy shook her head. The last person she had expected to see today parked in front of Edie's house was none other than Jack Jones, detective. "You don't think he knows about the texts, do you?"

"How would he?"

True, the only people who knew about the texts were the three of them and the texter. Jimmy could have let their secret slip, but when had he been around Jack Jones?

"What does he want?" Kappy asked.

Edie sighed. "Only one way to find out." She turned off the engine and got out of the car. Kappy followed behind her.

"Well, well, well," Edie drawled, sashaying toward Jack's car. It was the only word Kappy knew to describe the way Edie walked, like clothes on the line blowing in the wind. "Jack Jones. What brings you out today?"

Jack opened his own door and stood. Until that moment Kappy had forgotten how tall the man was. Or how intimidating. He had dark, dark hair and no matter the time of day appeared to have a five o'clock shadow across his firm jaw. His dark eyes were hidden behind mirrored sunglasses, which he didn't bother to remove as they came near. Instead he propped his backside against the front part of his car and waited for them to come closer. "Just checking out how the other half lives."

"Other half?" Edie raised one brow in question.

"Hi, Jack." Jimmy waved vigorously at the detective until Jack returned the gesture. Then Jimmy skipped into the barn to start his chores.

"The Amish."

"I see." Edie didn't bother to point out to

him that she was actually ex-Amish and for that Kappy was grateful. She didn't want to get into a discussion of semantics.

"There's been a lot of concern since the Esh girl died."

Kappy nodded. "We've all been worried."

"Because the *Englisch* drivers don't take it slow enough around curves?" Jack asked.

"Among other things."

"That's the strange thing about that accident," Jack continued. "There is no curve there. And no skid marks."

Kappy and Edie looked at each other, then back at Jack. She hoped her expression was less revealing than Edie's. Her friend looked as if she were about to crack and tell Jack everything they had found out.

"Really?" Edie said, the one word sounding more like it belonged to a Southern belle than an ex-Amish Pennsylvania girl.

"What does that mean?" Kappy asked. Her voice was unfamiliar to her ears, and she wondered if she sounded as strange to Jack.

Maybe not, since he pushed up from this lounging position and pointed to the tracks of fencing they had bought at the hardware store. "What's that?"

Edie waved away his question. "Nothing."

"It's supposed to keep my dog in the yard."

Jack raised one coal-black brow. "Elmer's been getting out?"

She sighed. "He's something of a pill."

"And this is supposed to keep him in?" He pointed to the flat pieces of fencing that looked more like they belonged to a barbecue grill than around the yard.

"Silas said they would. Plus, they have some sort of guarantee."

Jack gave a quick nod. "What exactly do you do with them?"

"They get buried in the affected area to extend the fence below the ground level."

"Smart." Jack nodded. "You need any help?"

"I'm sure we can manage," Edie started but Kappy was already saying, "Of course. Another set of hands would be very helpful."

"Come on, then. I'll follow you back to Kappy's." Jack nodded and smiled, then returned to his car.

"Let me tell Jimmy," Edie called toward his departing back. He lifted one hand in a pseudo-wave, but didn't bother to turn around.

Of course, Jimmy wanted to go, too, and they promised to help him feed the ducks once the fence was complete. Kappy was grateful to have both Jimmy and Jack's help and didn't want to waste the opportunity of two strong men willing and able.

"What was that all about?" Edie asked as the three of them returned to her car.

"What?" Kappy asked, though she knew what Edie was referring to.

"Jack."

"I thought we could use his help," Kappy said with a sniff.

"Liar."

Kappy sputtered. "Why . . . why would you say that?"

"You always sound like you have a cold coming on when you tell a lie."

"I do not," Kappy gasped. Did she?

"The truth this time," Edie commanded as she eased her car down the lane.

Kappy gave her a small grin. "I need his help. I can't dig all those holes to bury these fence pieces, or whatever these things are."

"And that's the only reason?"

"Of course. Why?" She sniffed again. *Hen's teeth!* She did it again.

"Jack is not Amish," Jimmy proclaimed.

"If you really needed help, why didn't you ask Silas to come over?"

"I like Silas," Jimmy said.

Kappy raised her nose a bit into the air

and managed not to make a sound. "He has a lot to do if he had to get a part-time job. I wouldn't want to take him away from any of his family time."

"And you relished the opportunity to corner me and Jack together."

"You certainly can't date if you never talk."

Edie didn't answer as she pulled the car into Kappy's drive and cut the engine.

"I wondered if the two of you got lost," Jack quipped.

"Hi, Jack," Jimmy said, then immediately started laughing at his own joke.

"Good one," Jack said good-naturedly. Kappy couldn't believe that was the first time he had heard that one.

Their time for conversation had come to an end.

"I really appreciate this," Kappy said.

"No problem." Jack led the way into the backyard and directly over to Elmer's favorite place to dig, marked with a small pile of dirt. The pooch himself was nowhere to be seen. Probably off terrorizing chickens and geraniums. "You have a shovel?"

"In the shed."

"I'll help," Jimmy said proudly.

"I'll show you where it is." Edie nudged her toward the outside storage shed where

Kappy kept her yard-grooming tools.

Edie all but shoved her inside.

"How do you know where I keep my shovel?" Kappy asked, starting to resent being nudged and poked.

"Not important. We need to get him to talk about the case."

"Who says he's even investigating it?" Kappy asked.

"Even if he's not, he'll have heard things around the station."

"True dat." Kappy smiled a little with her payback.

As if on cue, Edie frowned. "Ask him something when we get back out there."

"Me?" Kappy squeaked.

"Yes, you. You're better at this sort of thing than I am."

"I wouldn't say that," Kappy protested.

"I would."

"Stop trying to flatter me. It's not going to work."

Edie shot her a sly smile. "Of course not."

But before Kappy knew what was happening, she and Edie were back outside the shed, holding out a shovel toward Jack and a small pickaxe to Jimmy. He smiled with glee.

"What's the talk around town these days?" Jack asked after showing Jimmy where to start. Jack himself began to dig. The whole move was meant to look casual and effortless, but Kappy had a feeling there was much more to it than that.

"Oh . . ." Edie shrugged and blew out pursed lips. "You know the Amish. Mary Beth has a new recipe for creamed celery. And Chris Schrock is talking about buying a new gelding for a buggy horse."

"Yeah?" Jack seemed interested, but Kappy had a feeling he was playing along with Edie. "Exciting times. Though I haven't had creamed celery since my grandmother died."

"Sorry to hear that," Kappy murmured.

"I was ten."

Edie shot her a stern look and inclined her head toward Jack. Luckily, he didn't notice.

"What about you? What's going on at the Sheriff's Office?"

"Crime and punishment." Jack grunted as he pressed the shovel into the hard ground.

"Any word on who ran over Sally June Esh?"

Jack wiped the back of one arm across his forehead. "I was going to ask you the same thing."

"Why would we know anything about that?" Edie asked with a nervous laugh.

Jack stopped digging and braced his arm on the handle of the shovel. "See, here's the thing. I've been going around talking to members of the community and I can't get a straight answer from any Amish."

Edie pressed her lips together in mock sorrow. "That's too bad."

"I was hoping maybe you had heard something."

"Why would we have heard anything?" Kappy did her very best to keep her expression innocent, but she wasn't sure she'd succeeded. Thankfully, Jack seemed not to notice.

"The two of you appear to have a thumb on what happens around here."

Kappy scoffed. "I don't know where you would get an idea like that."

"From the fact that the two of you practically solved Ruth Peachey's murder." He lowered his voice so as to not to draw Jimmy's attention. Her respect for Jack Jones jumped another notch.

Edie gave half a shrug. "She was my mother."

Jack nodded. "I know. I just thought . . ."

"Surely you have some clues and such."

Jack went back to digging. "Of course." He grunted between the words. "We know that the car involved was black or dark colored."

"You don't have a make or a model?" Edie asked.

"Just that it's a four-door, medium-sized sedan." He lost Kappy somewhere between four and sedan.

"That's all?" Edie asked. "Nothing else?"

"Would I be here talking to you if I had more?"

"True dat." Kappy and Edie spoke at the same time, then frowned at each other.

"I suppose not," Kappy said.

Jack lined up the fencing and instructed Jimmy on what to do next, how to place the pieces into the trench they'd dug, then pack the dirt in on top. He shifted his attention back to Kappy and Edie. "If you hear anything, be sure to let me know."

Kappy and Edie waved as Jack drove away. Jimmy had already been given the important task of finding Elmer and bringing him home. He was most likely halfway to Nathaniel's by then.

"Do you think we should have told him about the texts?" Kappy asked.

"Bite your tongue," Edie exclaimed. "The last thing I want is for them to take my phone."

"But —"

Edie shook her head. "I just got Jimmy that 'ladybug' phone. It can only call my number. What good will that be if my phone is in the evidence room at the Sheriff's Office?"

"*Jah.* Okay. Do you think I should have told him that the car was blue?"

"You don't have any proof of that. Just speculation."

"I saw it in the picture myself, and if they're looking for the wrong car, they'll never find the killer."

"Jack is a professional. I'm sure he'll figure it out. He got this far, right?"

Kappy nodded.

They stood for a moment, each lost in her own thoughts. They had found out so much, but it seemed every shred of evidence or clue, no matter how small, seemed to throw their entire investigation off track. Yet there was one person they still needed to talk to.

"What do we do now?" Edie asked.

"I think it's time to pay Ephraim a visit."

"You come to bring me more chickens?" Ephraim called from his front porch. He had come outside when he heard Edie's car. Kappy still wasn't convinced that visiting with the good Amish people of Blue Sky while driving around in an *Englisch* car was such a smart idea. But it would shave some time off their trip. It was getting late and they needed to get back as soon as possible to help Jimmy with the chores.

Kappy stopped halfway between the car and the house. "Do you need me to bring more chickens?"

"Your devil pup was out here this morning. But I'm not missing any more hens."

"Good." Kappy continued toward the house, Edie right behind her. They stopped just short of climbing the porch steps. "I repaired the fence this evening, so hopefully he won't be a bother to you again."

Ephraim propped one forearm on the porch post and eyed them. "So why are you here?"

She supposed that telling him she was visiting in the spirit of good-neighbor-ness would be pushing it a bit. "I heard you might have been in the cemetery last Tuesday morning."

"I might have been." He took a swipe at the sweat beading on his forehead and tucked the rag into the back of his trousers. "Who wants to know?"

Edie nudged Kappy a few inches forward.

"I-I do." Kappy managed.

"Why would you care when I'm in the cemetery?"

"Ephraim, a young girl was cut down in her prime. Before she even got to live half of her life."

"We never know how long God will put us here."

Kappy nodded. "True. But I feel that Sally June was destined for more than dying on the side of the road with no one around."

"There were plenty of folks around."

Her heart skipped a beat. "There were?"

"Always is that time of day."

"When she di— was run off the road?"

Ephraim looked from Kappy to Edie, then waved one hand as if to dismiss them. "Quit your hovering and come sit down."

Kappy took a hesitant step forward, casting a quick glance back to Edie.

"You too, I reckon. I figure it won't go against the *Bann* if you sit on my porch for a bit. Nothing in the *Ordnung* about not sharing shade or allowing a wayward soul to get sunstroke."

"Danki." Kappy sat on the edge of the porch, turning so she could see Ephraim. He had taken a seat on the small wooden bench there next to the front door.

Edie inched forward and sat on the far side of Kappy, a good distance from Ephraim. She only nodded at him, conveying her thanks without saying a word.

"You saw Sally June that morning?" Kappy asked. "The morning she was killed?"

"Well, I thought I saw Jonah, but it turns out it was Sally June."

"You thought you saw Jonah . . . her brother?" Kappy asked.

"He usually drives by and waves. Every Tuesday just like clockwork."

"Because you go to the cemetery every Tuesday morning?" Kappy wanted to ask who he was visiting there, but as curious as she was, it had no bearing on the matter at hand.

"*Jah,* and Jonah delivers the pickles every Tuesday."

"Did you . . . did you see the accident?"

He shook his head, his mouth turning down at the corners. "No. I heard it, though. The most horrible sound."

"Did you happen to see the car?"

Ephraim tilted his head to one side and studied her with wizened eyes. "Why are you so car crazy? You thinking about jumping the fence?"

"No. No. Or course not. But the police have determined that an *Englisch* car hit Sally June's buggy. I was wondering if perhaps you saw the car."

"I did. I did. But I already told the police that."

Kappy sat back in surprise. "You did?"

"They came by here a couple of days ago."

Behind Kappy, Edie cleared her throat.

"They did?"

"What did you tell them?" Edie asked.

"What I saw."

Getting information from him was like pulling teeth.

"And that was?" Kappy prodded.

"That a black car crashed into Sally June's buggy and drove away like the devil was on his bumper."

Kappy and Edie thanked Ephraim and said they had to get back to the house to help Jimmy. Well, Kappy told him that. Edie was reluctant to speak any more than necessary. He might have allowed her to rest for a bit on his porch, but that didn't lift her *Bann* by any stretch.

"What do you make of that?" Edie asked as she eased back up the lane toward home.

"It explains why the police are looking for a black car, when there was a blue streak of paint on the back end of the carriage."

"Maybe it was a really dark blue and only looked black to Ephraim."

"Maybe." But there was something about

it that just wasn't right.

"Jack is smart. He'll figure it out," Edie said.

Any other time Kappy would have teased her about her support of the handsome detective, but not today. They both had too much on their minds.

"*Jah,* I suppose. But he's taking the word of an eyewitness."

"An eighty-year-old eyewitness with a bad back, bad knees, and terrible vision."

That part was true, but the fact that Ephraim was there at the time of the accident would carry far more weight than their speculations.

"There's something about this that's just not right." Kappy propped her elbow in the space where the window was rolled down. She tapped a finger against her chin and did her best to pretend she was Sherlock Holmes. He wouldn't miss any clues. He saw them all with an uncanny eye. It was almost as if he had God on his side.

But they actually did. She would pray about it. That would help. She would ask God for His guidance. Surely then, she and Edie would have the edge over this killer.

"We don't have a motive, you know."

Kappy stirred out of her thoughts and turned her attention to her best friend.

"What was that?"

"We don't have a motive. Someone wanted to kill Sally June. But why? Who were her enemies? Who would want her dead? Who would benefit?"

"We've been over this. The best motive goes to Bettie Hershberger."

Edie shook her head. "I'm not sure pickles are a motive."

"You've been away from the Amish too long. Those pickle deliveries are important to the families. That's their income, their livelihood. Farming land is getting scarce, so people are having to do more and more to make ends meet."

"Do they really make that much from the sales?"

Kappy shrugged. "I don't have a number, but it's enough that Jonah delivers pickles to the supermarket once a week . . ." The wheels of her thoughts started turning once again. "On Tuesday . . . Edie! Do you know what this means?"

Edie pulled into her drive and shook her head. She quickly put the car in park. "What does it mean?"

"The killer wasn't after Sally June! She was an innocent bystander. They were after Jonah!"

CHAPTER 13

"There's one person who knows the color of that car for sure," Kappy said later than evening.

While they had been at Ephraim's, Jimmy had found Elmer and placed him in his newly refenced backyard. Then the three of them somehow managed to feed all the animals and themselves before dark. Jimmy had gone up to take a bath and get ready for bed.

Kappy needed to be getting home, so she could check on Elmer. But she had too many thoughts in her head to walk away now. They were onto something — big — and she wanted nothing more than to see it through.

"Who is that?" Edie asked. "Who knows the true color?"

"The texter."

"Mr. Text? Didn't we decide it was Willie?"

"It could be Willie. But it might not be.

But whoever he is, he was there. He would know what color the car was."

"He never said he was there."

Kappy thought about it a second. "Hand me your phone. I want to re-read those messages."

Edie handed Kappy her cell phone. "I'm telling you he never says he was an eyewitness, just that he knows what happened."

"But that's almost the same," Kappy protested. They were so close. She couldn't let such a small detail stand in their way.

"Close only counts in horseshoes and hand grenades."

Kappy stopped. "Grenades? Who said anything about grenades?"

"Never mind." Edie flicked one hand as if to dismiss her words. "It means that close isn't going to cut it if we want to find out who really killed Sally June Esh."

Kappy held up Edie's phone. "Let's ask him."

"What?" Edie drew back in surprise.

"Let's outright ask him what he saw."

"Do you want to ask him who he is while we're at it?"

Kappy shrugged. "I guess. But at this point, who he is isn't as important as what he saw."

"Not to him, I bet."

"Are you going to do it?" Kappy asked. She would do it herself, but she hadn't figured out how to work the crazy device. Well, not that she had tried. But she might have to put some effort into it. That little phone was proving itself to be all kinds of useful.

"I don't know, Kappy."

"You've tried to text him *and* you've tried to call him. What's making you hesitate now?"

"What if he gets suspicious? I don't want him to stop texting."

"That didn't slow you down before."

"That was then. What if the text gets him caught by the very people he's been hiding from?"

Something that would never happen to Sherlock Holmes. Mainly because they didn't have cell phones back then. But when the detective got a clue, he followed through with it. "You don't really think that's a problem. So why are you reluctant?"

Edie shook her head. "I don't know. The whole thing gives me a bad feeling."

"I don't understand," Kappy said. "You and I ran all over the valley trying to find out who killed your mother. And *this* is making you nervous?"

"I can't explain it," she cried. "But what if

we're wrong? What if we text the person and they lie to us, tell us an innocent someone is guilty?"

Kappy sat back in her seat, her excitement dampened by Edie's sound reasoning. "But we could ask him if the car was blue or black. He might have been closer."

"That's true, but . . ."

"But what?"

Edie shrugged. "I don't know."

Kappy sighed. Aside from stealing Edie's phone and trying to work it herself, Kappy had no choice but to honor Edie's wishes. "Promise me one thing," Kappy asked. "Promise me you'll think about it."

"I promise," Edie grumbled. She didn't sound happy about it.

First thing the next morning, Kappy started for Edie and Jimmy's. She had promised to help them feed the animals and she would honor that promise. Just as she hoped that Edie would honor her promise to think about texting Mr. Text, possibly Willie Lapp.

After breakfast, Kappy made sure that Elmer was snug in the backyard with no new holes under the fence. She fed him, gave him fresh water, and tied a ball on a string and hung it from her clothesline. That would keep him busy for a while. In fact, he was chasing it back and forth as she started up the lane toward the Peacheys'.

"You're up and about early this morning," Edie said when Kappy walked into the barn.

She was usually up by this time, but not *about,* as Edie had put it. "I told you I would come help," Kappy explained. "I promised."

Edie shot her a strained smile. "I appreciate that."

"What's wrong?" She had expected Edie to be a little resistant today, but she didn't expect her to be this upset.

Edie shook her head. "I didn't sleep well last night. I keep thinking about Willie and if he'll be in danger if we start asking him questions."

Willie or whoever it was felt they were in danger or they wouldn't be in hiding. But Kappy didn't tell Edie that. She already had way too many worries on her mind. "Willie is smart. If this even is Willie. Whoever it is knows enough to stay out of sight until the killer is caught. We have to trust God to protect them until then."

Her words were meant to calm and reassure, but they only seemed to upset Edie further. "I trusted God to keep my mother safe while I was off in the big city. And you know how that turned out."

"That's why it's important we try to find this car."

"What?" Edie's remorse fled and shock took its place. "Find the car? We have no idea what kind of car we're looking for."

"Sure we do. It's medium-sized with dark-blue paint and four doors."

"Be serious, Kappy. Do you have any idea how many cars in the valley fit that description?"

"Three or four?" She shrugged.

"Thirty or forty. At least."

Kappy's hopes deflated a bit. "That's not so many. And we don't have any other clues."

"I'm not sure I'd even call this a clue. It's more of a drop in a bucket."

"Listen. I've given this a lot of thought. All we have to do is drive around and look for cars that fit that description. Then we check out those people and see if they have any motive."

"At least you're taking my advice on that one."

Kappy sniffed and raised her chin a bit higher in the air. She would not back down. Willie's life might depend on it. "What do you say?"

Edie shook her head. "I don't have time to mess with this. Mose called and wants

Jimmy to come in to work today."

"And you — we're — going to take him to the bait shop. All we have to do is watch for cars on the way there. I'm telling you, there can't be that many dark-blue sedans in Kish Valley."

That was the first thing she got wrong.

From the moment they pulled into Mose's Bait Shop and saw a dark-blue sedan parked in the packed gravel drive, it seemed everything was stacked against them.

That car ended up belonging to an out-of-state couple who were heading home and had to take some of Mose's nearly famous honey back with them.

But Kappy wasn't giving up that easily and, as far as she was concerned, everyone except the three of them — her, Edie, and Jimmy — were suspects. She even walked around the blue car to make sure there were no dents or scratches that might indicate a collision with another vehicle. Or a yellow buggy.

"Here we go." Edie started the car and tossed a notebook and a pen to Kappy. "I'll drive, of course, but you need to watch for these cars. Write down where we see them and a license plate if you can. Okay?"

"Got it, boss."

Edie rolled her eyes, reversed the car, and started back down the highway. "We need to get some gas soon."

"Can you make it to the end of the valley?"

"I believe so."

Kappy nodded. "Then let's give this one pass, get gas, and turn around. Then we can come back from the other way and see if there's a car we might have missed."

"You know we're going to miss a couple. Maybe even a lot."

"But we have to try," Kappy said. She felt the note of panic creep into her voice. "This is my hometown, and I will not have anyone terrorizing it and killing innocent teens."

"I thought you said they were after Jonah."

"Maybe. Unless they knew that Sally June would be making the delivery."

Edie shook her head as if to get her rattled thoughts back into order. "Who would know something like that?"

"The family, maybe a few friends."

"Is Jonah Esh dating anyone?" Edie asked.

"Don't you think he's a little young for you?"

Edie sniffed her disapproval. "That is not what I mean and you know it. At the funeral, didn't you say you heard someone talking about Jonah dating a girl his family didn't

222

approve of? Maybe she gave the information to a third party."

"Third party?" What did she mean by that?

"Someone other than one of them."

"Wait a minute . . . what if Willie has a girlfriend?"

Edie shook her head. "What are you talking about? I thought we agreed that we don't even know for certain if Mr. Text is Willie."

"If he is, we should definitely check it out."

Edie nodded. "If you say so."

Kappy smiled. "I definitely say so."

By the time they picked up Jimmy from work, they had five names on their list. Mrs. Robert Swanson, the new pastor's wife; Mr. Delvin Roberts, who ran the grocery store; Mabel Mast the Mennonite; Judy Ames, the pizza delivery person; and Trevor Carson, who worked at the medical clinic at the end of town.

Not bad for driving around all afternoon, Kappy thought. But they would need to do better. Even more than sitting at Edie's table and trying to regroup.

Kappy tapped the end of her pen against the paper and shook her head. "This is not a very criminally-minded list."

"Don't let that fool you. 'Who knows what darkness lies in the hearts of men?' "

Kappy raised her gaze to Edie's, not sure whether to open the door and run for her life or laugh at her friend's dramatic flair. "What?"

Edie flicked a hand in her direction and shook her head. "Nothing. It's from a movie. I think. Anyway, the point is you don't know what a person has in their heart."

"I guess not." Kappy looked at the list again. If any of these people were guilty she would eat her shoes. A preacher's wife, the mild-mannered grocery store manager, the laid-back pizza delivery person, the caring nurse, and the Mennonite. Kappy couldn't fathom how any of them even knew a young, twenty-something Amish man who worked hard for his family and kept to himself.

"We need to compare notes with Jack," Kappy mused.

"Isn't he looking for a black car?"

"He said dark-colored or black. Maybe there are a few people on this list who would be the same. And he would have access to all sorts of city and state records, wouldn't he?"

Edie nodded. "I suppose."

"Invite him to dinner."

"What?" She pushed at Kappy, causing her chair to rock a bit.

"For a pacifist you certainly are violent."

"Who said I was a pacifist?"

For all Kappy knew, Edie had given up her peaceful ways the day she took off her prayer *kapp.* "True dat."

"Ugh!" Edie growled.

"Are you going to ask him out or not?"

"I can't ask him out."

"Sure you can. You just call him up, tell him that you've been thinking about him, and that you want him to come out and have supper with you. And Jimmy."

"And you."

"Me? Why do I have to be there?"

"The same reason I have to be there."

"Whoa . . . I don't like Jack nearly as much as you do."

"And I do not like Jack at all."

But the sparkle in her eyes when she said his name was enough to turn those words from a statement to a lie.

"Pretend there's some other reason. Like . . . like helping me with the fence."

"Shouldn't you be the one to invite him, then?"

"Fine. Be that way. I'll invite him myself, but we're coming here to eat."

"But . . . but . . ." Edie sputtered.

"No buts. It'll be dark by the time we eat, and I like your new solar lights. And I have a feeling that Jack will, too."

"Humph."

"You're welcome." Kappy flashed her a quick smile. "By the way, has the bishop said anything about the solar panels?" Kappy didn't know a soul in Blue Sky who had solar panels. Not a soul in the entire valley had them, but as bold as brass, Edie had them installed. She didn't have unlimited power like she would have in an *Englisch* house, but she had a little more light at night. And she had heard through Jimmy that Edie had been watching YouTube videos after the sun went down.

"The bishop has no say in the matter," Edie said.

Though Kappy couldn't agree. The bishop had a say in all matters he chose. "Sure," she said, and Edie rolled her eyes.

"I am no longer a member of the Amish church," she said emphatically.

"But Jimmy is."

Edie stopped. "And this is why staying here is so difficult."

"Maybe you should go talk to Bishop Sam and tell him how you feel."

"I couldn't talk to him when I was eighteen. I surely can't talk to him now."

"But I would think —"

"Hup." Edie held up one hand to stop Kappy's words. She had been about to say that Edie had grown up a lot since she was eighteen. Perhaps it might even be easier for her to talk to the bishop now. But Edie was hearing none of it.

"I guess I'll invite Jack. Let me have the phone." Kappy held out her hand.

But Edie shook her head. "How do I know you won't be texting Mr. Text and asking his name?"

"Other than the fact that I can barely make a call on that crazy thing? I guess you won't."

"Then no."

"No?"

"No. You can't have the phone."

"How am I supposed to call Jack and invite him to supper?"

"I guess you won't." Edie shot her a self-satisfied look. She had effectively killed two birds with one stone.

"I could go to the shanty."

Edie shrugged, but a little of her smugness melted away. "Suit yourself."

"I will." She turned toward the barn. "Jimmy!"

He stepped into the sunshine as if he had

been waiting for her summons.

"I've got to make a call at the shanty. Want to go with me?"

"*Jah.* Sure!" He skipped toward her, his excitement palpable. "Who are we calling?"

"Jack Jones," Kappy said with her own victory grin at Edie.

"I like Jack."

"Me too. And your sister has graciously agreed to cook supper for us all."

"Hooray." Jimmy pumped his fist in the air.

Kappy laughed but Edie appeared a bit shocked. "I thought you didn't like him."

Jimmy frowned. "I never said that. I said he wasn't Amish."

"Wanna walk down with us?" Kappy asked to change the subject.

Edie shook her head. "Fine. You can use my phone."

Kappy laughed. "Not on your life."

Jimmy grinned. "Good. I want to go for a walk."

"Whatever," Edie said with a defiant lift of her chin. "I'll stay here and change out the water in the swimming pool."

Jimmy's expression fell. "That's my job. You want me to stay and do it? I will."

"Go on ahead. I'll do it," Edie replied.

The phone shanty sat on School Yard

Road, but was a stone's throw from the highway. Sure, it would have been easier to call from Edie's phone, but this was about principle. Edie couldn't dictate all of Kappy's phone calls and she wanted Edie to know that. No matter how immature the thought seemed.

The small green building was barely bigger than an outhouse, though instead of a toilet, it contained a phone for the Amish families who lived in the area to use.

Families, Kappy thought with a mental shake of her head. There was her, Nathaniel, Ephraim, Martha Peachey, Edie and Jimmy, and that was it.

"Can I call?" Jimmy bounced on his toes with excitement.

"Sure." Kappy opened the door and motioned him inside.

He seemed gloriously happy that Jack might come to dinner. Jack was just that sort of guy, likeable and fun to be around . . . mostly. But Kappy wasn't blind. She could see the spark of interest between Edie and the detective. And if she could get them to act on that . . . well, Edie might just stick around a bit longer. Like forever.

The interior of the phone shanty barely had enough room for one person. Kappy pulled Jack's business card out of her pocket and was going to dial the number for Jimmy. He protested, saying he wanted to do it all himself. Being independent was so very important to him, and Kappy nodded.

"Just tell him that we want him to come to supper Friday night at yours and Edie's house, okay?"

Jimmy nodded. "Got it."

Kappy allowed the door to close, then turned toward the road. With any luck, this long shot of inviting Jack Jones to supper would pan out. Either in another clue or even a love interest for Edie.

Her friend would be angry when she discovered Kappy had set them up, but it would be worth it. Or Jack would be angry when he found out they had used him for information. If he found out. But either way, it would be worth it. Whoever killed Sally June Esh couldn't get away with it.

The sound of a car approaching drew her attention to the highway. She had never really taken stock of how close the phone shanty sat to the main road, but it was barely a hop, skip, and a jump away, as Aunt Hettie would say.

A dark-blue car whizzed by. It was a miracle that Kappy noticed the driver at all, but there she was: a woman with long dark hair, just like Mr. Text had described!

Kappy took off toward the highway, chasing after the car as if she could actually catch it.

A car horn sounded, and she skidded to a stop in the gravel fringe that welcomed School Yard Road to the highway.

"Hen's teeth!"

Their suspect had just slipped through her fingers.

CHAPTER 14

Kappy could barely contain herself as she ran back to Edie's house. Jimmy grumbled that she was going too fast, but her excitement kept getting the better of her, and she would have to stop and wait for him to catch up.

"Edie," she called, opening the front door. "You are not going to believe what just happened."

Her friend came out of the kitchen wearing a flowery apron and a frown. "You joined the circus and promise never to darken my door again."

"Funny," Kappy quipped in return.

"Don't darken it. If we do anything we should paint it blue. Like Kappy's. I like blue." Jimmy grinned.

Both Edie and Kappy decided to ignore that comment.

"Now answer for real."

"Jack's coming to eat with us." Jimmy

hopped from one foot to the other in a sort of jiggy victory dance.

"Oh, yay." Edie rolled her eyes and started back to the kitchen.

"I saw the car. I saw our girl."

Edie stopped in her tracks. "What?"

"You heard me."

Edie whirled around, supper forgotten as she pulled Kappy toward the table. She nudged her down into one of the chairs and took the one opposite her. "Tell me everything."

Kappy started at the beginning, but the story didn't take more than two minutes to retell.

"Did you get a license number?"

Kappy shook her head. "Was I supposed to?"

"It would have helped." Edie sat back in her seat and blew her bangs off her forehead. "Without it we're no further along than we were before you saw the car."

"I messed up."

"You didn't know."

"It took me by surprise. One minute I was thinking about how close to the road the phone shanty is, and the next a murder suspect was driving by." She shivered. Had she really been that close to a killer? "What if this was just an accident?" she asked, raising her gaze to Edie's.

"I thought we had gone over this."

"*Jah,* we did, but I can't help thinking . . ."

"Well, don't. You want to believe that everything is good and right in the world, and some things are just wrong."

"I suppose."

Edie pushed to her feet and made her way back into the kitchen. Kappy could hear her but not see her as she continued. "That's the thing about Blue Sky. I mean, even the name sets up unrealistic expectations of a place that will live up to its name. And it simply . . . can't."

Kappy rose and followed Edie into the kitchen. "Smells good." She lifted one of the lids and inhaled the delicious-smelling aroma.

"So much for you cooking."

She shrugged. "Someone had to invite our supper guest."

"I'm still not sure this is a good idea."

"It's the perfect idea. Especially now that we're this close. I could practically touch her as she drove by. You can't hide in a town the size of Blue Sky."

"Amen," Edie muttered.

Kappy took a step back and propped her hands on her hips. "That's the problem, isn't it? You can't hide here."

"Whatever." She rolled her eyes.

"Make any sort of face you want, but I know the truth."

"You're just making stuff up." Edie shook her head, then laid her spoon to one side. "Okay. Fine. You're right. There's no hiding here. Everybody knows what everyone else is doing. Or not doing, as the case may be. The *Englisch* are bad enough. The Amish are even worse."

"We just care about our fellow man."

"Uh-huh. You just keep telling yourself that. Without TV and Internet, I guess you need some sort of entertainment."

Something akin to anger — or was it disappointment? — shot through Kappy. But it was gone as quickly as it came, leaving behind a new sense of awareness. "That may be true. But ask anyone here for help, and they would give you their last penny and you know it."

"That doesn't mean I want to stay here."

"*Jah.* But it's a pretty good reason not to leave."

Friday dawned as the perfect soon-to-be-fall day. The wind held a small chill, but the sun's rays were warm enough to chase it away.

Kappy got up early as promised and walked over to the Peacheys' to help with the chores. She didn't mind. She actually liked helping, but there was no way she was telling Edie that. Her newfound friend was having a hard enough time making up her mind about staying or leaving. Kappy didn't want to add any more to the mix.

But Edie was nowhere around as Jimmy and Kappy fed the puppies, cleaned the gerbil hutch, and refilled the plastic swimming pool for the ducks.

"Where's your sister?" Kappy asked as they finished up. It wasn't like Edie to leave Jimmy alone for this long. Not that he was truly alone. He was with her, but Edie seemed to hover over Jimmy. His time in jail seemed to change his sister's attitude toward him. Then again it wasn't every day that a person's brother was accused and jailed for killing their mother. Or maybe it was their mother's untimely death that had caused the changes in Edie.

Jimmy shrugged. "She said something about her hair."

That was completely not specific. She could be washing it, cutting it, combing it. Who knew?

"Did you have breakfast?" Kappy asked.

Jimmy nodded. "She gave me a bowl of

cereal before you got here."

"Cereal's not enough." They had been working hard, Jimmy especially. He needed more to eat than a bowl of cereal.

"Come on." Kappy hooked one arm toward the house. "I'll help you find something." She knew there were a lot of challenges with Jimmy and food. Like he wouldn't eat red foods. That included anything from red gummy bears to spaghetti sauce. She knew it had to be a chore for Edie, but that was no excuse to barely feed him.

Kappy pushed into the back door of the house with Jimmy close behind. It was past time she and Edie had a talk. If she thought the Amish were nosy before now, she would understand just how nosy Kappy King could be.

Right after she got Jimmy some ham and eggs.

She found a frying pan under the stovetop cabinet, then turned back to him. "Do you eat ham?"

His brow wrinkled in confusion. "*Jah.* Why?"

"It's red. Well, sort of."

"When you fry it it's brown," Jimmy explained.

"Fine." Kappy set the pan on the stovetop.

"You don't have to cook for me," he said.

"You need to eat."

"But I already had something."

She shook her head. "A bowl of cereal is not enough for all the work you do."

"I eat cereal every morning."

Kappy stopped. "Every morning?"

He nodded.

"What did your *mamm* feed you?"

A small cloud of pain moved across his features. "Cereal."

"Really?" She hadn't pictured Ruth as the kind to take modern shortcuts, but she hadn't known her neighbor *that* well.

"Well?" Edie's voice drew her attention. "What do you think?"

Kappy's eyes widened, and Jimmy stood with his mouth hanging open. Both were speechless.

Edie strolled into the room like one of those *Englisch* models on a long fashion runway. She mock tossed her hair over one shoulder and struck a pose.

"It's . . . it's . . ." Kappy couldn't find the words.

"Pink!" Jimmy squealed.

Indeed it was. Bright pink. All around the crown of her head, fading to pale pink on the ends. Underneath it was still blond.

"I know Jimmy likes it." Edie dimpled at

her brother.

"I love pink," Jimmy added with a grin.

"I love pink, too," Kappy finally managed. But it certainly wasn't a color for hair. "Why?" It was the only thing she could ask.

Edie gave a loose-shoulder shrug. "I felt I needed a change."

Kappy glanced at the clock, then placed the skillet back in the cabinet. She worried about Jimmy, but it wasn't like she could force him to eat. "At eight thirty in the morning?"

"It's always a good time for a change." She moved farther into the room and sat down at the table as if everything were as normal as yesterday. Come to think of it, they hadn't had many normal days as of late. But that was beside the point.

"Does this have anything to do with Jack Jones coming for supper tonight?"

Edie's face twisted into something that made her look like a squinting duck. "Pul-lease."

"Please what?" Kappy asked.

"Please don't ask me dumb questions."

"If it's so dumb, then why haven't you answered it yet?"

"Because it's so dumb that's exactly why I'm not answering."

"That means *jah,*" Jimmy chimed in.

Edie turned her attention to her brother. "Have you brushed your teeth?" She didn't even wait for him to respond. "Go on upstairs and take care of that."

"But I already —"

"Then do it again."

Jimmy looked from one of them to the other. "Why do I always have to leave when things are just getting good?" He started for the door.

"And comb your hair," Edie called behind him.

"What has gotten into you?" Kappy could barely wait until Jimmy was out of earshot before asking.

"Nothing."

"At the risk of calling you a liar, that is not the truth."

Edie sniffed and raised her chin, like a duck letting water roll from its back. "Believe what you want."

"I believe what I see." Kappy waved a hand in her general direction. "Your clothes . . ." She trailed off with a shake of her head. "Your hair is pink, and you're treating Jimmy like a child. What has gotten into you?"

"You bought him bubbles."

"Everybody loves bubbles. Why are you acting like he doesn't have a brain?"

Edie sighed, her body deflating as the starch went out of her demeanor. "I worry about him, okay?"

"You worry about him?"

"Yeah. I worry. It's been so long since we've been around each other. And you seem more comfortable around him than I am. That can't be right. I'm his sister."

"He knows that."

"But what if —" She stopped. "Never mind. Did you want something to eat?" She nodded toward the pan Kappy still held.

"You're not getting off that easy." Kappy shook her head. "Finish what you were going to say."

For a moment, Kappy thought she might not answer. When Edie finally spoke, her voice was barely above a whisper. "What if I can't protect him?"

A wave of understanding washed over Kappy. "I used to think that about my family. Why couldn't I save them? Why was I the only one who lived? We don't have answers to those questions, but we still have to move on, move forward."

"I suppose." Edie dropped her gaze into her lap and picked at an imaginary spot on her stretchy orange pants. Mixed with today's green-and-gold shirt and two-toned pink hair, she looked like someone who had been in one of those races where they throw paint on a person. Kappy never saw the draw in running, then having paint tossed at her when she was hot and sweaty, but she never saw the draw in the running itself. So who was she to judge?

"Now," Kappy began again with a smile, "what are we going to feed Jack tonight?"

To Jack's credit, he didn't blink an eye when he saw Edie's hair. Kappy was a little concerned that he would turn around and not even come into the house, but he simply nodded and handed her what appeared to be a store-bought lemon cake repackaged to look as if it had been made at home. It was hard to tell for certain, but with all the fancy swirls of icing and the fact that the cake was almost too pretty to eat, Kappy figured he had stopped and picked it up somewhere.

"Smells good in here." Jack sniffed appreciatively.

"I hope you like chicken Alfredo." Edie clasped her hands in front of her and locked her elbows, looking like a young girl at her first singing. If she didn't loosen up a bit, they would never get any information from the detective.

"I do."

Pleasantries aside, Kappy directed everyone including Jimmy into the dining area. Jimmy had already set the table, and everyone found their seats.

"This was a nice surprise," Jack commented after Jimmy said grace, and they started to fill their plates.

Edie shrugged. Thankfully, she had found herself again and was once more acting like Edie. "Oh, you know, when you are a part of a community, you have to be a part of the community, don't you think?"

What was she talking about?

Jack frowned. "I suppose. Yes." He looked anything but convinced.

"We just had this terrible tragedy, and it made me realize how short life can be. We should reach out to the others around us."

Kappy closed her eyes and willed Edie to stop talking. She wasn't one hundred percent certain, but she suspected that she preferred the starstruck, giggly Edie to this one.

"Blue Sky is a great place to live," Jack commented. Kappy couldn't tell if he was sincere or merely being kind.

This conversation was not going in the direction she needed for it to go if they were going to find out what Jack knew about the accident.

"I love it here." Jimmy grinned.

"How are your puppies?" Jack asked and the conversation turned to dogs until everyone had finished their salads. Edie enlisted Jimmy's help to bring in the next course while Kappy said a little prayer that the creamy Alfredo sauce would work its magic on Jack's bachelor stomach. Kappy had never been one to court much, but she had heard it said that if a girl wanted to make a man fall in love that she should cook for him. This was the same thing. Sort of. They didn't want him to fall in love, just be full and content enough to spill some of the case evidence their way.

"How's your spaghetti?" Kappy asked after everyone had been served.

Jack looked down at his plate in confusion. "It's not spaghetti. It's fettuccine."

Jimmy shook his head. "I don't like spaghetti."

"I remember," Jack said with a sad smile.

When Jimmy had been arrested for his mother's murder, he had been served spaghetti in jail and had gone into a fit. Jack had been very concerned about him.

"You know who really liked spaghetti?" Edie asked with a too-bright smile. "Sally June Esh."

"I didn't know that," Kappy blurted

before she could stop herself. What had happened to their plan? Edie was supposed to subtly lead him into a conversation about the girl. This lead-in was anything but subtle.

"Me either," Jack said, looking as wary as a sparrow in a room full of cats.

"How do you know that, Edie?" Jimmy asked.

Edie's cheeks turned almost the same color as her hair. "Her . . . mother told me. At the funeral."

"Interesting topic of conversation for a time like that." Jack wiped the corners of his mouth.

Edie shrugged. "You know how grief can be. Makes people all wacky."

So does love. Or extreme like. And that was exactly what Edie had for Jack Jones. She could deny it all she wanted, but Kappy could see it now as plain as day.

"Any luck locating the driver of the car?" Kappy asked.

Edie gasped and Jack's eyes narrowed. Kappy figured the direct approach was best now. They had thrown subtlety out the window a while back.

"No." He looked from one of them to the other. "Are you two trying to figure out who did this?"

"Of course not."

"Why would we do something like that?"

Luckily, Jimmy was too engrossed in his supper to pay them much mind.

Jack sat back in his seat and pushed his plate forward as if finished with the meal. He had barely eaten half, and Kappy wondered if he might leave without even eating a piece of the scrumptious-looking cake he'd brought. "It seems that the two of you keep turning up. Sort of like when Ruth was killed. And then this invitation to supper . . ."

"We're just concerned about our community. That's all," Edie said with a sniff.

"Right. Because I could use a little help."

"What?" Edie and Kappy spoke at the same time.

"I know there are some witnesses out there who have information, but no one in the Amish community or the Mennonite community will talk to me about it. I was hoping that maybe the two of you could help me."

CHAPTER 15

"I'm just saying," Kappy said the following morning, "maybe we should have told him about the texts."

Edie rolled her eyes in Kappy's direction, then turned back to the road ahead. "You know why I can't tell him about the texts —"

"*Jah, jah,* and you don't think he'll give us real information about the case."

"Why would he? He knows we'll just be underfoot."

Kappy stared out the window, then closed her eyes as everything grew fuzzy. "Or maybe you should trust him."

Edie scoffed. "Whatever." She paused so long that Kappy opened her eyes to make sure she was okay. "This is much better. We run down our own clues."

"Or we could take up a hobby. You know, like painting or gardening."

"Art is prideful. You aren't allowed to paint."

"You would be."

"And we already have gardens. That's where the vegetables are, remember?"

"I'm just sayin'."

Edie turned her car into the church parking lot and pulled into the line of vehicles waiting off to one side. "Time to quit sayin' and start listening."

"Do you really think we're going to find out anything at the church car wash?"

"We have to be open about these things."

"And what exactly are we open to?"

Edie sighed. "Anything. But mostly we need to find Delilah Swanson's car and see if it has any damage on it."

"Can I help wash cars?" Jimmy chirped from the back seat.

"Of course," Kappy said while Edie said, "No."

Jimmy sat back with a pout. "I should have just gone to work."

"I told you," his sister said, her patience beginning to slip a notch or two. "You can't just show up at work because you're bored."

"Can so. Mose told me I could come anytime I wanted."

"Mose was just being polite."

Kappy took hold of one of Edie's arms.

"Let him wash cars. It might be good for him." Anything would be better than just following the two of them around town while they checked for clues. "Besides, the preacher's wife is in charge of the fundraiser, *jah*? So we ask her if Jimmy can help and that gives us an opening to talk to her."

Edie cut her eyes to the side, then put her car in park. "You know, this would be much easier if you would decide whose side you're on." She got out of the car. Kappy and Jimmy followed suit.

"I wasn't aware there were sides."

Edie looked from the long line of cars to the preacher's wife, who seemed to be directing everything from where they drove in to who did the windows. "There are always sides."

Mrs. Robert Swanson, Delilah to her friends, wasn't exactly what Kappy had pictured for a preacher's wife. Preacher Sam's wife, Mary Ann, was . . . well, different. Delilah looked like she'd stepped from the glossy pages of an *Englisch* magazine. Her hair was a sprayed helmet of unnaturally black curls that somehow seemed to suit her. Thick blue eye makeup, satiny pink lipstick, and a little black dot at the corner of her mouth.

"She's a perfect combination of Liz Taylor and Marilyn Monroe."

"Who?" Kappy asked.

"Never mind."

"Her pants are a little . . ."

"Short?" Edie supplied.

To Kappy they looked a lot like the bottom of a snow-white bathing suit. Her button-down cherry-red shirt was tied in the front and her shoes had thick cork soles. None of it looked like appropriate wear to wash a car. Not that Kappy had washed many cars. But no one else there was dressed as . . . fancy. Most had on patterned shorts and stretched-out T-shirts.

"Hi!" Edie quickened her steps and waved toward the polished woman.

Delilah stopped midpoint and directed her attention to them. She drew back a bit, then quickly recovered. "Well, hello there."

Kappy wasn't sure where she had picked up her accent, but she was fairly certain it wasn't from anywhere in Pennsylvania. Maybe somewhere south . . .

"This is my brother, Jimmy." Edie gestured to where Jimmy was coming up behind her.

Delilah Swanson's impossibly blue eyes flicked to Jimmy in his Amish hat, pants, shirt, and one diagonal suspender and back to Edie's eclectic ensemble of lime-green stretchy pants and an animal print shirt that continually fell off one shoulder. "O-kay." The poor woman looked positively afraid.

"He wants to know if he can help you with the cars for a bit."

Delilah sputtered. "The monies we're making are for the church." Her gaze darted nervously around as if she were about to be pranked, and she was preparing herself for the worst.

"We know that. He knows that, but he likes to help people."

"I see." The preacher's wife looked as if she was about to take off running. "I'm sorry. I didn't catch your name."

"Edie Peachey." Edie stuck out one hand. "This is my brother, Jimmy."

"Well, Miss Peachey, I suppose it wouldn't hurt for your brother to help a bit. As long as he understands that he's probably going to get wet."

"I know." Jimmy flashed her his trademark infectious grin. "I always get wet when I water the ducks."

"Yes, well. Go over there and talk to that girl in the purple shirt. That's my daughter, Didi. She will tell you what to do, okay?"

"Okay." Jimmy skipped off, leaving Kappy and Edie to face the questioning look of

Delilah Swanson.

"What brings you out today?" the preacher's wife asked. "I assume you didn't come here just so your brother could help with the cars."

Edie shook her head. "My car is in line to be washed. Just helping out in the community."

Delilah sucked in a deep breath, then blew it out without saying anything. Which was strange. Kappy fully expected the questions to fly.

"We appreciate that very much."

Edie smiled. Kappy smiled. Delilah smiled as if waiting for them to leave. "Is there something else?" she asked.

"Which one is yours?" Edie nodded toward the line of cars.

"Didi. In the purple shirt. She's our only child."

"Not children. Which one is your car?"

The perfectly practiced look on Delilah's face slipped an inch or so before she pulled it firmly back into place. "Oh, my car isn't here. Goodness, no."

"No?" Edie asked while Kappy watched with interest. So her car wasn't in the lot. The one thing they had come to look at.

"I had a . . . uh, little accident the other day and, well, I didn't want the pastor to know." She flashed them a beaming smile, one that was too big for the occasion.

"An accident?" Kappy asked.

Delilah waved one hand about like a dizzy bumblebee. "Oh, nothing big. Just a little fender bender, but it did require a little bodywork. But that's just between us girls, right?"

Edie returned her smile. "Right." But her tone was anything but conspiring.

"What do you make of that?" Kappy asked once they had moved away.

"A fender bender? A young woman loses her life, and Beauty Pageant over there calls it a fender bender?"

"We still don't know that it was her." And they wouldn't without seeing the car. But there was something strangely . . . flippant about the woman. Like everyone around had been placed there simply for her amusement.

"I'd bet good money that it is."

Kappy looked at all the cars waiting to be washed. "This is a lot of cars, *jah*?"

Edie glanced around. "I suppose."

"Maybe one we missed?"

Edie jerked to attention, her anger gone in a flash of new hope. "Maybe." She pointed toward the washing section. "You look over there, and I'll look over here. We'll meet back up when my car is done, 'kay?"

Kappy nodded. "Sure."

Edie headed off, and Kappy slowly wandered around the area where so many *Englisch* teens — plus one Amish young adult — washed the cars, then stood back as the driver maneuvered to the next station to be rinsed. There were so many helpers and so many suds that it was a little difficult to see what colors the cars really were until they moved under the hoses. Kappy moved a little farther down.

The girls waving the hoses didn't appear to be the most trustworthy of the bunch, and Kappy backed up a bit to stay out of the spray of water.

"I heard her parents grounded her for a month!"

The young girl's companion gasped, and Kappy hid her smile. Such drama at an early age. She wondered if it was just the *Englisch* kids or all of them. All of them, she decided. Teenagers were the same the world over. Only how they got into trouble was different.

"Are you kidding me?"

Kappy chanced a quick look at the girls. They were sitting on a concrete log-looking thing in the parking lot. Kappy knew they were used to keep people from driving straight through, but she had no idea what they were called. That surely wasn't a word on her word-a-day calendar.

One girl had long blond hair and the other short dark hair, which meant neither could be their girl. Not that she thought they were looking for a teenage girl. These girls were more interested in who was grounded for what than the pickle problems among the Amish.

"I wonder if she'll go out with him again. If she has the chance, I mean."

"Of course she will. Have you seen that guy?"

"His hair is weird."

"Who cares about his hair? It's his eyes. All dreamy blue."

"I guess so. I just can't get past that haircut."

Kappy looked back just as the blonde nudged the tiny brunette. "You went out with Dustin Moore and his hair was much worse than the chili-bowl cut."

"A man bun is very popular these days."

"Yeah, on a man."

"Why you . . ." the girl started, but the words had no sooner left her mouth than both of them dissolved into giggles. "He's okay. I guess. For an Amish boy."

Kappy stopped in her tracks. They were

talking about an Amish boy? Dating an *Englisch* girl? She was sure the Amish parents were even more upset than the *Englisch* ones. Chances were, those two were never going out again.

She set her feet into motion once more. It really wasn't any of her concern. She was looking for cars that had possibly been in an accident, not picking up on teenage gossip.

"Kappy! Kappy! Did you see me?" Jimmy came bounding up, his grin as wide as she had ever seen it. "Those kids over there —" He turned halfway around as he pointed. "They let me help them. And they weren't mean to me or anything. That's good, *jah*?"

The thought of someone being mean to sweet Jimmy made her heart hurt. She swallowed back the feeling and returned his smile. "Did you do a good job for the customers?"

He puffed out his chest. "*Jah.* Of course I did. I even washed Edie's car. Come see." He motioned her to follow him as he half ran, half skipped to where Edie's car sat gleaming in the sun. "Look at it!" he cried. "Look at how shiny it is."

"It is shiny," Kappy agreed.

Edie nodded but frowned. "It should be, for what I paid."

Kappy glanced over to where a couple of girls stood by the road with poster signs declaring this to be a car wash for donations. "Doesn't that mean you only pay what you can?"

"My brother came here and insisted on washing the cars. That I had to pay anything was too much." She shook her head and got into her car. "Are you coming?"

Kappy went around to the passenger side, allowing Jimmy to climb in before she did so as well. "Do you really want to go home now?"

"We can't sit out here all day waiting on the cars. Plus, that preacher's wife is giving me the creeps."

"What's wrong with her?" Kappy could admit that she didn't appear to be a holy woman, but that was between her and God. Kappy had no say in the matter.

"She keeps looking at me like she can see right through me."

"Of course she can't," Kappy said.

"Maybe she likes you," Jimmy added.

"It means that she looks like she knows all my secrets."

Kappy frowned. "Why didn't you just say that?"

Edie shrugged. "No idea. Let's get out of here before —"

"There you are!"

Edie slapped one hand over her mouth to hold back her scream.

Kappy gasped, and Jimmy laughed. She could only assume that he had seen Delilah Swanson coming.

Edie sucked in a deep breath. "Here I am. But uh . . . we were just leaving."

"Oh, heavens no!" Delilah exclaimed. In fact, everything the woman said seemed to be louder than necessary. It was like when Kappy was in school and they were practicing for the Christmas pageant. The teacher kept telling them to project their voices. That was how Delilah talked, like she was projecting to a room of admirers.

"No?" Edie asked.

"I mean you can't go before I have a chance to talk to you."

The corners of Kappy's mouth twitched, but she managed to keep them from rising . . . much.

"What — what would you like to talk about?"

Delilah didn't notice, but Kappy could tell that it cost Edie a lot to ask that question.

"I came to invite you to church on Sunday. You and all your friends." She gave them a guarded look. Kappy couldn't figure out exactly what it meant. "Everyone is welcome in our church."

"That's nice. Thank you." Edie reached for the keys to start the car.

"Please say you'll come."

Edie gave her a pained smile. "Sorry. I can't make any promises."

Delilah drew back a bit, obviously unaccustomed to not getting her way. "I thought . . . well, with your friends and all . . . See, I figured you must be ex-Amish and good for you, but I know that you can't go to church with your . . . people. So please feel free to join us. Our congregation is big enough for everyone."

Edie put the car in gear and let it roll a tad.

Delilah took a quick step back to keep it from running over her feet.

"Thank you, though," Edie said.

Delilah beamed them all another smile. This one, Kappy noticed, didn't reach her blue, blue eyes. "Come anytime."

Without another word, Edie hit the gas. The car lurched forward. She had to slam on the brakes to keep from rear-ending the car in front of them, but Delilah Swanson took the hint and stalked away on her ridiculous shoes.

"What was that all about?"

Edie drummed her fingers against the steering wheel. "If I couldn't stay in my own church, what makes her think that I would want to join hers?"

Kappy shrugged. "I don't know. Isn't that what they do, try to get people to come to church?"

"I suppose. But if I wanted to go to church, wouldn't I already be there?"

"Are you saying you don't want to go to church?"

"Hardly." But there was something she couldn't identify in Edie's tone. Regret? Remorse? Longing?

"Don't you miss God?" Kappy asked.

Edie laughed. "How can I miss God? He's all around. All the time."

"Amen," Jimmy said from the back seat.

She was right, of course, but there was something about the conversation that didn't sit well with Kappy, though like Edie's tone, she wasn't sure what it was. She barely had time to contemplate it before Edie exclaimed, "There she goes!"

"Who?" Kappy and Jimmy both sat up straighter in their seats. "The woman in the blue car?" Kappy asked.

"Bettie Hershberger."

It couldn't be anybody else. Bettie Hershberger was the only one in Big Valley with a gray-topped buggy. Kappy knew it was only a matter of time — if it hadn't happened already — before the deacon had a little talk with Bettie about conforming and community. She might be allowed to get away with bringing green pickles to church, but a Lancaster buggy was taking it too far.

"Should we follow her?" Edie asked.

"Yes," Jimmy hollered from the back seat.

"Sit back," Edie instructed.

"She's going to the grocery store," Kappy said.

"How do you know that?"

Kappy shrugged. "Just a hunch, I guess."

"Follow her," Jimmy chanted, but at least he had moved back in his seat.

"Should I?" Edie asked.

"Absolutely."

Edie pulled out behind Bettie's distinctive buggy. "You wouldn't think so, but that buggy sticks out like a sore thumb."

"It does."

It also made it easier to follow.

"You think she's going to ask Mr. Roberts about carrying her pickles in the store?"

"Maybe," Kappy said. "But how is she going to make all of these pickles if she gets everyone to carry her product?"

"I don't know much about business or supply and demand," Edie said. "But if she can't keep up, that will ruin her business before she even gets started."

"Supply and demand? What does that mean?"

"It's like your *kapps.* You're the only maker in Blue Sky, so you have the only supply to meet the demand."

"What does this have to do with Bettie Hershberger?"

"Not a lot," Edie agreed. "Except . . . now that the Eshes aren't making nearly as many pickles, then Bettie's business should be taking off."

It was the same reason she was at the top of their suspect list. Right above Delilah Swanson.

"I found out what happened to that preacher lady's car," Jimmy said.

Edie stomped on the brake, then realizing she was still in the middle of the road, started forward again. Thankfully, most everyone in Blue Sky was at the church car wash so there weren't many other vehicles on the road.

"What do you mean you know what happened to her car?" Edie looked in the rearview mirror.

"You wanted to know, right?" Jimmy asked.

"Of course," Edie and Kappy said at the

same time.

"I asked someone."

Edie shot a proud smile at Kappy, obviously tickled that Jimmy was helping in the investigation.

"So what happened?" Kappy asked.

"She hit a buggy."

CHAPTER 16

"Coming." Kappy wiped her hands on a dishtowel and hustled toward the front door. She sidestepped Elmer, who had abandoned his breakfast in order to rush to the door. He had to get his visitor-barking quota in. Or at least he thought he did. When he was barking at unknown visitors he wasn't biting at her ankles. Kappy considered that a plus.

It was Sunday, but this was an "off" Sunday for her district. That meant no church as the members either visited with their loved ones or had church in another district. For Kappy it meant a quiet day at home. Except . . .

The knock sounded again.

"I said I was coming." She wrenched open the door without even looking.

Edie marched in as Elmer retreated back to his food bowl, his job done. "You didn't ask who it was," Edie accused. "You didn't even look through the peephole."

Kappy shut the door and eyed her unlikely friend. "How do you know that? You were on the other side of it."

"I was peeking."

"Who else would knock on my door this early on a Sunday morning?"

"My point exactly. You don't know," Edie said. "I could be a killer or something."

"Do killers usually knock on the door before they murder people?"

"Laugh all you want." Edie propped her hands on hips swathed in cherry-red jeans. "But there's a killer on the loose in Blue Sky, and we need to find her."

She couldn't argue with that fact. Except . . . "It's Sunday. I'm fairly certain tracking down killers on Sunday is against the *Ordnung.*" Written or unwritten, she knew the bishop wouldn't approve.

"What Bishop Sam doesn't know won't hurt him."

Kappy had to think about that one for a moment. "I don't know . . ."

"We can go for a drive. There's nothing wrong with going for a drive on Sunday."

"In my buggy?"

Edie sighed. "I suppose that's the only way I'll get you to go around with me."

"That's right." Kappy gave a quick nod.

"Fine," Edie grumbled.

"Do you want some coffee first?"

"That sounds great. And we can go over all the notes we've made so far. Did you get a chance to read over them last night?"

Kappy poured them both a cup of coffee and placed them on the table. "I looked over it right before bed." And she had, but Edie's handwriting was so bad she could barely make out letters much less words.

"Let's see." Edie picked up the notepad lying on the table and started to read. "Wait a minute. These aren't my notes. These are *your* notes." She looked at Kappy with a huge grin on her face.

Those were her notes about Hiram and Silas! Kappy lunged for the notebook, but Edie held it out of her grasp.

"What do we have here?" Edie stood, using her superior height to keep the notes from Kappy's reach. "Hiram: kind, generous, upstanding in the community." Edie made a face.

Kappy quit trying to grab the notebook and instead crossed her arms as if Edie reading what she had written for her eyes alone was no problem at all.

"Silas: kind, generous, upstanding in the community." Edie dropped her arms, allowing Kappy to swoop in and take the notebook from her. She immediately slammed it shut. Like that mattered now.

"Why are their good qualities the same?"

Kappy ran one hand over her prayer *kapp,* her fingers automatically checking the hairpins to make sure everything was still in place. "They have similar good qualities."

Edie shook her head. "It's not the good qualities that you should be worried about. It's figuring out if you can live with the bad ones."

Kappy waved away Edie's words. "I don't know why I did that. It's not like I'm getting married or anything." Hadn't she reconciled herself to being single her entire life? It wasn't so bad. She was used to being alone most of the time. Though here lately . . .

"Thank heavens." Edie flopped back into her chair and started spooning sugar into her coffee. "I mean, Silas isn't bad, I suppose. And he drives a yellow-top. That's a plus."

"I guess I just got caught up in Jimmy saying that Silas liked me and all." It was silly. More than silly. Ridiculous.

"It's only human, I suppose."

"*Jah.* I suppose." Kappy eased back into her seat and took a sip of her coffee.

"The notes on the case?" Edie asked.

"We don't have a case."

"Fine. No case. But we do have notes. Where are they?"

"In my room." Kappy quickly made her way to her bedroom, then back to the kitchen. "I couldn't decipher them." She tossed the notebook onto the table.

Edie grinned. "That's because they're in code."

"Seriously?"

"It's very authentic, don't you think?"

"I have no idea."

Edie took up the notebook, her eyes scanning the page. Then again.

"Is something wrong?" Kappy asked.

"Yeah. I can't remember how to translate it."

"That's great, Edie."

"Sorry. I guess we'll have to write them all again."

Kappy sat back down, feeling as if the morning were going to go on forever. "*Jah.* I suppose."

"Let's see. Here's what we know," Edie said a half hour later. "Sally June was run off the road and killed. The car that hit her buggy was blue and was driven by an *Englisch* woman with long dark hair."

"We don't know that she was truly *En-*

glisch," Kappy pointed out. "She could be Amish and learned how to drive during *rumspringa.*"

"True." Edie made a few more notations on their new, not-coded list. "It's a four-door sedan."

"If you say so." Kappy took another sip of her coffee. "This would have been so much easier if the preacher's wife had been talking about an Amish buggy instead of a shopping cart."

Edie nodded. "Who knew they called them buggies wherever it is she's from."

"Tennessee or Georgia, I heard someone say."

"That doesn't take her off my list of suspects. She could have been covering up a slip."

"True. But I don't know." Sure, Delilah Swanson was about as different as any preacher's wife she had ever seen, but that didn't make her guilty.

"Neither do I and that's why she's still on my list."

"What about the others?"

"That's what we're going to do today. Drive around and see if we can see anything funny going on with the rest of them. One thing is certain. One of them killed Sally June Esh, and we need to figure out which who."

Jimmy stayed behind to read to with Martha Peachey. Kappy even heard him promise to come back later in the week and help her clean out her chicken coop. It was a nasty chore, but he seemed to be looking forward to it. He loved animals that much. Even chickens.

"I think we should swing by Mabel Mast's house first, then we'll try to find Judy Ames," Edie said as Kappy pulled her buggy onto School Yard Road and headed toward the highway.

"If she's working tonight, we could just order pizza," Kappy quipped.

"Great idea."

"I was joking," Kappy said.

"Never joke about pizza," Edie returned.

It seemed to take an hour to get just a few miles down the road. It had to be because Edie told her how much quicker it would have been if they had only driven her car.

"That's her house there." Edie pointed to a modest-size house with a red front door. The siding was a gray-blue and the trim white. All in all, it was a cute dwelling, well kept, with flowers blooming in planters and the beds that lined the front.

"That must be the car." Kappy cocked her

head in a side nod.

"Okay, what's the plan?"

"Plan? I don't have a plan. If we needed one maybe we should have come up with it before we headed over here."

"Okay, here's what we do. You go knock on the door, and I'll stay here and look at Mabel's car."

"Why can't I stay and look at the car?"

"Because you've got to knock on the door."

Kappy opened her mouth to protest, then stopped.

Just then the front door opened and a small, round woman stepped onto the porch. She cupped one hand over her eyes to shade them as she scrutinized her visitors.

"Too late. She's seen us."

"Great," Kappy muttered.

"Go see if she has any produce to sell."

"It's Sunday. She can't sell on Sunday."

"She's not Amish."

"I am, and I can't buy on Sunday. You should go. She'll talk to you since Mennonites don't shun."

Edie rolled her eyes and let out a small growl. "Fine. But give that car a once-over."

"How —" Kappy was going to ask how she was going to justify examining Mabel's car, but Edie was already on her way to the door. It wasn't like she could crawl out the back of the buggy to avoid being seen. Well, she supposed she *could,* but she wasn't going to.

She could water her horse, though. That was a neighborly service that wouldn't raise any eyebrows, and the water trough was just to the other side of the car. The perfect excuse to walk around it.

Kappy hopped down from the buggy and waved toward the house. "Water my horse?"

Mabel waved in return, and Kappy set about backing up the horse and buggy to position the mare to get a drink. She wasn't following the conversation at the porch, but she prayed that Edie kept talking. She needed all the time she could get.

She looked back toward the house. So far, so good. Edie was talking to Mabel, though Kappy couldn't hear the actual conversation. Things appeared to be going smoothly. Mabel hadn't stomped her foot and pointed her finger toward the road in a "get off my land" sort of fashion. Instead, she turned and led Edie toward the side porch where tables of produce were displayed.

The minute their backs were turned, Kappy hunched down and hurried around the side of the car. It was a nice car, she supposed. Clean, as if Mabel had just had it washed. Maybe the day before at the church car wash? Was she hiding something? Kappy hadn't seen her at the car wash, but they couldn't hang around the entire day. That would have been terribly suspicious.

Kappy popped up a bit to check on Edie and Mabel. They were still under the porch covering. Kappy crouched back out of sight and started looking at the car. She went around it twice. There were a few weird spots on the fenders that looked a little like they had been pushed in by a giant hand, but since both sides were like that she figured it was supposed to be that way. There were chips out of the paint close to the door handle and a small dent that looked like it had been hit with a golf ball from the side. But no marks that looked as if the car had hit a buggy — Amish or grocery.

"Okay," Edie called. "Thanks so much. These are going to be great tonight."

Kappy duck-walked around the car and managed to climb back into the buggy before Edie.

"Come again." Mabel waved, her brow smooth. She wasn't suspicious. Whew. That was a relief.

Kappy waved in return, then gasped when

she caught sight of Edie. "What do you have?"

"Red peppers, strawberries, and tomatoes."

"Isn't that sort of . . ."

"Red?" Edie supplied.

"I was going to say random, but red works."

"I'm hoping I can get Jimmy to try some of it. I read about it in a book. It's called 'food expansion.' "

"And he's okay with this?"

"I didn't say that, but I'm tired of making two meals or eating what he eats. It can't be good for him."

Kappy shrugged. "He's made it this far."

"True, but I would feel better if he ate more fruits and veggies."

Spoken like the overprotective sister that she was. And what an overwhelming task: trying to get him to eat foods of other colors. Tan was his hue of choice and red was definitely out. The only thing green Kappy had ever seen him eat was a sliced apple. And it could be argued that it would have been as beige as the rest of his diet if someone had cut off the skin.

No wonder Edie felt so frustrated with the changes in her life. As long as Kappy had known Jimmy, she'd never seen him branch out while eating.

"Where to?" She stopped the buggy at the end of the lane that led to Mabel the Mennonite's house.

"We could swing by the pizza place and see if Judy Ames is working."

Kappy nodded. "Maybe she'll be there and we can get a look at her car."

"That's the plan." Edie grinned. "And speaking of cars . . ."

"Nothing," Kappy said. "Well, nothing big. There were a few scratches, but nothing that looked like it had been in a bad accident."

"The bad part is, it's been long enough since the accident that a good body-and-paint man could have fixed it and had it back to her."

Kappy thought about it a minute. "I suppose. Are we wasting our time running down these cars?"

"Not everyone would be as neat and orderly as Mabel."

"True. *Jah.*"

"So maybe they still haven't taken their car in to be repaired."

"We should be so fortunate." The words had no sooner left her mouth than a blue car whizzed past them from behind. The honking horn trailed behind the vehicle as it sped out of sight.

"Was that . . . ?" Edie asked.

"I believe so," Kappy replied.

"And was that a dark-haired girl driving?"

"Looked like it to me." Though the car had been moving kind of fast.

"Then follow her!"

Kappy flicked the reins over the mare's back and urged her into a trot. She only gave a fleeting thought to what they would do once they caught up to the car.

"Faster." Edie slapped her hands against her thighs. "We've got to go faster."

The blue car was getting smaller and smaller, then it disappeared over the next hill.

"Faster," Edie said.

"I'm going as fast as I can." Any faster and they would flip over at the first bump in the road.

"But —" Edie sputtered. She raised up from her seat, peering off into the distance for the dark-haired girl driving a blue car. It was almost out of sight. And then it was gone. Edie flopped back onto the bench seat. "I told you we should have brought the car."

True, if they had driven Edie's car they might have been able to catch up with the blue car, but the thought of driving pell-mell down the road sent shivers down Kappy's spine. She shuddered.

"Did you get a good look at the car? Was it damaged?"

Edie sighed with frustration. "No. She went by too fast."

Kappy slowed her horse and silently promised the faithful mare an extra scoop of oats tonight as thanks for all her effort today. "Now what?"

Her friend gave a one-shoulder shrug. "I guess the pizza parlor. Let's see if Judy Ames has anything to offer."

But Judy wasn't at work. Or rather her car wasn't. Most likely she was out delivering pizzas.

"You don't suppose it was an accident? You know, like the whole thirty-minutes-or-it's-free policy so many pizza delivery places have."

Kappy frowned. "I'm not sure what that means."

"You really have to get out more." Edie shifted in her seat as if gearing up for her story. They were still parked outside of Frank's Original Italian Pizza. "If the pizza driver doesn't make it to your house within thirty minutes of you ordering, then you get it free."

She knew her eyes were as wide as saucers,

but she couldn't contain her surprise. "Are you kidding? And Frank's OIP has such a policy?"

"It's right there on the sign."

Kappy looked back at the building. The only sign she saw was the open sign in the window flanked by two flyers. One announced that Bettie Hershberger had pickles for sale and the other told of a battle of the garage bands the following week. Neither one was of much interest to Kappy. And neither one said one word about free pizza.

"Not that sign. That one." Edie pointed to the marquee sign with change-out letters. Sure enough. THIRTY MINUTES OR IT'S FREE.

"Let me get this straight. You're saying that Judy was going to be late so she ran Sally June off the road in order to keep from giving away a free pizza?" Kappy shook her head.

That was the worst one yet. There was a lot of evil in the world, this she knew. But someone so evil that a pizza was more important than another's life? She couldn't fathom.

"I can't believe that," Kappy concluded.

"Yeah, well, it sounded better inside my head."

"Besides, it was barely lunchtime when we went to pick up Jimmy, which means Sally June was killed even before that. Who orders a pizza at ten in the morning?"

"Good point." Edie blew her rose-colored bangs out of her eyes, something Kappy had noticed she did when she was frustrated.

"Now what?" Kappy asked.

Edie shook her head. "Home, I guess, unless you want to see if we can find her on her delivery."

Kappy shook her head. "That doesn't sound like a good way to spend our time."

"I've got it." Edie snapped her fingers. "We'll go home and order a pizza. With any luck, she'll come to us."

"Good plan. I think." Kappy pulled the buggy onto the road and started for home. They were almost to the cemetery when Edie's phone chimed. She pulled it out of her shirt and tapped on the screen.

Kappy would never understand the *Englisch* love of cell phones. They seemed to be more interruptive and distracting than anything else.

"Oh, my stars. Pull over."

"What is it?"

"Pull over."

Kappy turned her buggy into the packed gravel lot of the cemetery, stopped the mare, then turned to face Edie. "Tell me."

Edie sucked in a deep breath and pushed her bangs off her forehead, another sign that she was agitated. As if her trembling fingers weren't enough.

"Mr. Text just texted me again. Listen to this. *It's not the car. Look for the repair.*"

CHAPTER 17

By Thursday, Edie, Kappy, and Jimmy were all sick of pizza. Well, Jimmy was okay with it as long as they ordered thin crust with chicken, onions, and Alfredo sauce. It wasn't bad the first time, but after four nights of eating the same non-pizza pizza, Kappy was ready to throw in the towel and declare Judy Ames completely innocent of any crime. Four nights of pizza and not once had she been their delivery driver.

"I think we should go in and talk to her boss," Edie said as they drove Jimmy to work on Thursday. "What if she's on vacation? Or out sick?"

"On vacation . . ." Kappy mused. "That would be almost an admission of guilt."

"Admission?" Edie asked.

"Yesterday's word," Kappy replied.

"If she's on vacation, she might not ever return," Edie said.

"Maybe not if she knows we're looking

for her."

"And if she's guilty."

"That's a lot of ifs," Jimmy commented from the back seat.

And he was right. That was a lot of ifs, a lot of questions that when answered might change everything.

"Has Bettie Hershberger been in to ask Mose about selling her pickles in his shop?"

Jimmy made a face. "Why would Mose want to sell her pickles?"

Edie shrugged, her hands loose on the wheel. "I don't know. Helping out another member of the community?"

Jimmy vigorously shook his head. "That's yuck. Pickles and bait."

"Mose sells honey," Edie pointed out.

Jimmy stopped. "That's different."

"How so?" Edie glanced at him in the rearview mirror.

"Just is," Jimmy grumbled.

"I thought we had crossed Bettie off our list."

"No one's off our list. In fact, I'm wondering if there's not a few people we should add to it."

"Like who?"

"I don't know," Edie said. "But we're missing something here."

"Maybe if we could figure out what Mr.

Text means by find the repairs."

"Yeah, how do we find the repairs without finding the car?" Edie turned her car into the lot at Peachey Bait Shop.

"The honey is Mose's," Kappy said.

Edie stopped the car. "What?"

"The honey belongs to Mose. He has the bees and everything."

Jimmy looked from one of them to the other, then got out of the car. "Pick me up at three, *jah*, Edie?"

"Yeah." Edie's reply was absent at best.

Jimmy turned to Kappy.

"I'll make sure she's here."

"Thanks, Kappy." Jimmy smiled and skipped into the bait shop.

"But there's no place that Bettie has to sell her pickles," Kappy said.

"They have that stand there at the house."

"But she needs reach if she's going to convert the whole valley."

"True." Edie nodded.

"So we're back to pickles being the motive."

"When you put it that way . . ."

That was the biggest problem of all. They couldn't find a motive. Sally June had no enemies, she was a fine member of the community, a perfect candidate to join the church next fall.

Without a clear motive, they were running around almost chasing themselves as they tried to figure out not only who but why. And was the killer after Jonah or Sally June?

They both jumped as a car horn sounded next to them.

Kappy sucked in a calming breath as Edie slapped a hand over her heart. "Jack Jones, that was totally uncalled for."

He smiled. Even through two car windows Kappy could tell that the ever-present shadow still darkened his cheeks.

"How's your investigation going, Detective?"

He glanced away, then looked back with a shrug. "As well as can be expected."

Kappy had a feeling that meant not well at all.

"Any new clues?" Edie asked.

"You're not . . . investigating on your own, are you?"

Kappy stared at her hands, unable to look at Jack and tell an outright lie.

Edie had no such problem. She blew out a breath, her lips vibrating with the motion. "Of course not. What would we be investigating?"

"I hear things, you know. This town is small. The whole valley is small."

"Don't I know it," Edie muttered.

"I thought you wanted our help," Kappy said.

"Listen," Jack said on an exhale. "I can't stop you from poking around. Even if I tried, you would probably do it anyway. So at least do me this favor: If you find anything, let me know. The longer this case goes unsolved, the harder it will be to solve it."

"What do you think about that?" Kappy asked after Jack had pulled away.

"I think he has no leads."

"Maybe we should tell him about the texts," Kappy mused.

"Why are you so gung-ho about giving him my phone?"

"I don't know." Kappy shrugged. "I guess I sort of feel sorry for him."

"Well, stop. He's trained to do this and if he can't find out what we have, that's his problem."

"I suppose so."

"I know so. Besides —"

"I don't want them to take my phone." Edie and Kappy said the words simultaneously.

"Yeah, I might have mentioned that a time or two."

"Just a couple," Kappy said with a laugh.

"I've got an idea." Edie bit her lip, her

eyes sparkling with something akin to excitement.

"Jah?"

"We've got three primary suspects, right?"

"Jah." Mabel, Delilah, and Judy. The women.

"Mabel is pretty much cleared, right?"

"If she didn't have her car repaired before we went to see her."

Edie half turned in her seat. "That's the thing. Any of them could have already had their car fixed before now. So we check out the body shops. See if anyone has brought in a car fitting that description to be repaired."

"Maybe that's what Mr. Text meant by the repairs."

Edie nodded. "That's exactly what I'm thinking."

Blue Sky boasted two main body shops. Edie and Kappy's plan was simple: Visit both of them.

Body by Black was the closest of the two, and they went there first.

Edie pulled to a stop in their asphalt parking area and frowned at the sign overhead. "It sounds more like a personal trainer than someone who works on cars."

Kappy didn't have any idea what she was

taking about, so she just nodded to be polite.

They got out of the car and went straightaway into the dirty white building that squatted between impossibly high stacks of crumpled cars.

"Looks more like a salvage yard than a body shop."

Again, Kappy nodded for the sake of politeness.

Before they got to the door of the shop, a man wearing a frown and an oil-stained pair of coveralls came out. He had an unlit cigar in one corner of his mouth, and he squinted as if he was used to it smoking.

"Help you?" he asked. He switched the cigar from one side to the other without using his hands and looked at each of them in turn.

"Yes, we were wondering if you've had any cars of a particular model and color come in for repairs recently."

His squint narrowed until Kappy could barely see his eyes. "You got a court order or a warrant?"

Edie took a step back. "N-no. We're just asking out of curiosity and such."

"I'm not answering any questions without a warrant." He folded his arms across his barrel of a chest, the movement pulling on the sleeves of his coveralls and exposing forearms liberally decorated with fading tattoos.

"We're not here to search the place." Edie glanced toward Kappy. She could only shrug, then nod as if to say, "Go on."

"What's your purpose?"

"Uh . . . we . . . It's just that . . ."

Kappy took a step forward. Her feet must have been propelled by God because she didn't know what she was going to say until she opened her mouth and heard the words for the first time. "No purpose. A friend of ours feels one of her kids may have wrecked their car. Nothing big, just a couple of dents and a few scratches."

His defensive pose softened a bit. "What does this have to do with me?"

"See, our friend thinks her daughter might have brought in the car and had it repaired without telling anyone in the family."

He switched his cigar back to the original corner. "Yeah?"

"Young girl, long dark hair, dark-blue car. Little sedan."

"They probably didn't go through the insurance," Edie added.

The man laughed. "Not many of my customers do, so that's not a help."

"Would have been last week," Kappy said.

He shook his head. "Can't remember anything like that. But if you want to leave me your card . . ."

"We don't have a card," Kappy said, a bit confused.

"The other cops had a card. They gave it to me first thing."

"And did you let them in to look at your shop?" Edie jerked one thumb over her shoulder toward the long metal-sided building that sat behind the smaller one as well as the stacks of crumpled cars.

"Yep."

"Can we go in?" Edie asked.

"You got a badge?"

"No, we don't."

The man shook his head and turned on one heel. "Then have a good day," he said as he walked back into the office.

Kappy and Edie watched him go.

"That was useless," Kappy said.

"Not entirely. We know that the police have been here, and they didn't find anything."

"That doesn't mean a lot," Kappy said. "I don't like to talk bad about people, but . . ." She let her words trail off to nothing. She didn't need to finish for Edie to understand her meaning.

"I know. He's probably running a chop

shop and knows what to hide and when to hide it."

Chop shop. Kappy didn't know how she came about the information but she knew what that was. "You don't think that maybe the killer brought the car here to hide it?"

"Just hide it?"

Edie shook her head. "I was just speculating. Come on. Let's go check with Pete's shop. Maybe he'll have better information."

With one last look at the dusty, run-down shop, the pair got back into Edie's car and headed across the valley to Pete's Paint and Body.

In terms of inviting and clean, Pete's was the complete opposite of Body by Black. Pete's seemed to be a one-man show and everything was out in the open.

"That looks like an airplane hangar," Edie whispered to her as they got out of the car.

Airplane hangar. Kappy had heard that term before, though she couldn't recall ever seeing one herself. She would have to take Edie's word for it. The building was tall, at least two stories, with a large pull-up door in the front that left the contents of the building in plain view.

Three cars were inside in various stages of restoration. One didn't even have tires on it while another looked to her to be ready to drive away any moment.

"Can I help you?" A fifty-something-year-old man came out of the building to greet them. He wore coveralls like his across-town counterpart, but his were clean with only a couple of paint splatters to mar the fabric.

"Hi, my name is Edie Peachey, and this is my friend, Kappy King."

"Pete Baldwin. Nice to meet you." He shook hands with the both of them, patiently waiting for them to state the nature of their business.

Edie gave him the same story as Kappy had at Body by Black, including the part about no insurance and a girl with long dark hair.

Pete listened intently without a single disparaging look crossing his features. When she was finished, he nodded thoughtfully and stroked his chin.

"I can't say that I've seen a car fitting that description. I mean, I've seen one. I even own one, but I haven't had anyone bring one in for repairs."

"You own one?" Edie pinned Kappy with one of her stares. The look might have been meaningful if Kappy knew what it meant.

"Yeah."

"And it hasn't had any problems?"

"Of course not."

"Can we see it?" Edie asked.

Pete opened his mouth to answer. He closed it again and seemed to think about her question a bit more. Finally, he shrugged. "Why not? I don't have anything to hide."

Edie smiled. "Yes. That's right."

The man led the way to the personal garage that sat behind the house. Three vehicles were parked inside: a pickup truck, a shiny white sedan, and the blue car they had asked about.

Edie walked around the car looking at this and that while obviously trying to appear like she wasn't looking at anything at all.

"Nice car," she finally said.

"It belongs to my kids."

Edie snapped to attention. "Really?"

"I have a boy and two girls. Well, only the oldest two drive."

"And they share the car?" Edie asked. "That's sweet."

Kappy wasn't sure what Edie meant by all that. The words sounded straightforward enough, and luckily, Pete didn't seem to find them odd. If he did, he didn't let on.

"Dad?"

They all turned as a young girl came into the garage. "Mom says you need to come into the house. Someone called. You have to call them back."

Kappy's heart gave a hard pound as she realized the girl had long dark hair, but she was small. And too young to drive. Kappy might not know much about *Englisch* customs and laws, but she didn't need anyone to clarify this. Pete's daughter was barely ten, if her guess was correct.

Pete patted at his pockets, then shook his head. "I guess I left my phone in the house." He looked torn for a second. "Is that all you need?"

Edie nodded. "If you could just keep us in mind if anyone brings in a car like we described to be repaired."

"Of course." But Kappy didn't think he had any intentions of thinking about them again after they walked out of his sight.

"Follow me." He stepped from the garage, then shut the door as soon as everyone was back in the warm early-fall sunshine. The young girl skipped ahead, but looked as if she had no plans of going into the house. She stopped at the swing set/jungle gym combo set up in the yard and started to play.

Pete walked toward the house, clearly expecting them to leave.

Kappy and Edie followed behind him, their pace slowing with each step.

Edie shot her another look. Kappy just

shrugged.

"Thank you for your time," Edie said.

Pete stopped. "Say, have you talked to anyone at the high school?"

Edie shook her head. "Why would we do that?"

"If I had a car that needed body work and I didn't have insurance, that would be the first place I would take it. The auto-body shop class is always looking for real cars to work on. And they wouldn't charge anything to fix it, no insurance."

Could it be that simple?

"Is that a fact?" Edie asked.

"Yeah, my boy even takes that class." The pride in his voice swelled with each word. "Learned a lot there."

"I'm sure he has," Edie murmured.

"Is that him?" Kappy answered. She nodded toward the teenage boy striding across the lawn.

"Yeah. That's my boy. Jeff." He waited until his son drew near enough that he could sling one arm around the boy's shoulders.

Actually, calling him a boy felt a little strange, even in her own thoughts. Jeff was as tall as his father, though not so big around. In a couple of years, he would fill out and be at least the same size if not bigger. Unlike his father and younger sister, Jeff had blond hair, the color of the wheat just before harvest.

"Mom says dinner is almost ready."

Pete looked back at them with an apologetic twist of his lips. "We have a concert tonight, so we've got to get an early start." He turned to his son. "Did you get all your homework done?"

"Yes, sir."

"And Jennifer?"

He shrugged. "I dunno. I'm not my sister's keeper."

Pete frowned. "That's one of the reasons why we put you two in the same classes. You have to help her."

Something Kappy couldn't readily name flashed in the boy's eyes, then it was gone. Sibling rivalry? Resentment? Kappy wasn't sure. It was there and gone too fast. But she could add, and Pete's unequal treatment of his children summed it all up.

"Please go back in and help her. We have things to do, remember?"

He stalled.

"Jeff."

"I'm going." He turned on his heel, but looked none too happy about it as he stalked back to the house.

Pete cast them another apologetic glance.

"It's hard enough to have children, and then when they are so different . . ."

"I can only imagine," Kappy murmured.

"What kind of concert?" Edie asked. It was a pitiful attempt to keep the man engaged in conversation, but it was all they had.

"Guitar. Jeff plays." He shook his head. "It's more than that. He's a master. A prodigy, they said. All I know is it sounds like angels' wings when he picks up an instrument."

A father's pride couldn't be more apparent.

"Da-ad!" A loud screech came from the house and a blond-haired girl about seventeen stormed out. "Tell Jeff to get out of my room."

"I told him to come help you."

"I don't want his help."

Kappy inched a little closer to the car. This family seemed a little off. One child got all the pride and praise, while the other two seemed almost invisible.

The girl marched across the yard, her eyes blazing with each step. "I may be grounded, but that doesn't mean I have to do what *he* says."

Pete turned back to them, red rising up from under his collar to stain his cheeks.

Kappy wasn't sure if it was from anger or embarrassment. "Twins," he said sheepishly. "If you ladies will excuse me." He nodded toward their car parked at the end of the driveway, a clear hint that their time was at an end.

Before either one of them could answer, he spun on his heel and herded his daughter back into the house.

Left with no other choice, Kappy and Edie turned to leave.

"*Psst . . .* hey." The sound came from around the far side of the shop. The dark-haired daughter was motioning to them to come closer. Kappy was certain she was out of the sight of anyone in the house.

"What is it?"

"You want to know what's going on, don't you?"

"I beg your pardon?"

"You want to know about the car and the buggy wreck, right?"

Kappy nodded despite herself. What could a preteen know about buggy wrecks and the rest?

"We do," Edie said. "We're trying to help a friend."

The girl waved away the words as if they were pesky flies. "Whatever." She rolled her

eyes. "If you really want to know what's going on, go talk to Jonah Esh."

CHAPTER 18

"It's ridiculous," Edie said as they drove to the bait shop to pick up Jimmy. They'd had the entire afternoon to scope out clues, and they'd come up with nothing.

"You think talking to Jonah is ridiculous?"

She shook her head. "I think trusting that a ten-year-old knows what's going on when even the police don't is."

"In all fairness," Kappy started, "she never said she knew what was going on, just that we should talk to Jonah Esh."

"And how does she know that?"

"Exactly. How does she know who Jonah Esh even is?" She was an *Englisch* girl, a young *Englisch* girl. It wasn't like she and Jonah hung out in similar groups.

"Maybe it's true. Maybe he is hanging out with *Englisch* kids."

"Who said that?" Edie asked.

"Mary Raber. I mean, she said she believed that Jonah Esh was dating an *Englisch* girl. And if the younger daughter gets carted around with the twins and their friends, there's no telling what she might have heard."

"Yeah, and there's no telling what she might make up to get attention. You saw how her dad treated her. She was all but invisible."

"I suppose." Okay, it was true. Beyond true. One of the most accurate statements she had heard in a long time, but it didn't really mean anything. "And she could be telling us this to get her brother into trouble."

"Siblings." Edie sighed.

"What do we do now?"

"I say we head over to pay a visit to the Eshes."

Except they had to pick up Jimmy first.

"Yay!" He cheered and clapped his hands. "They have these little tiny pigs. Chris Esh was telling me about them at church."

"Oh, yeah? Why didn't you tell me about them?" Edie asked.

Jimmy frowned. "You'd just say no."

"Of course I wouldn't. I would love to take you over to see the pigs."

"But I don't just want to see the pigs; I want to own one."

Edie was shaking her head before Jimmy even got the words out of his mouth. "Oh, no. No more animals, Jimmy. They're too much to take care of."

"Kappy and me do most of the work. And I love taking care of the animals. Please."

"No."

But Jimmy wasn't about to give up. "I'll pay for it myself."

"And how do you suppose to do that?"

"I have a job, you know."

"I do."

"And I've been saving my money."

"To buy a skateboard."

"Well, *jah,* but now I changed my mind. A pig would be so much more fun than a skateboard."

"But skateboards don't eat and demand attention."

Kappy knew Edie was going to cave even before she did. She loved her brother even if she didn't quite know what to do with him. And he could take care of the animals. Every time he got a new one he carefully named it. He logged it in his books and never forgot one. He was meticulous in business when it came to his stock, much better than his sister. And although Jimmy had a few mental challenges, he was still a savvy businessman.

"Ah, Edie," he groaned. Kappy had a feeling he would own a "little tiny pig" by the end of the week.

The Eshes lived on the same lane as Sundries and Sweets. Kappy couldn't keep the thoughts of Hiram from leaping through her head as they drove past.

What was he doing? Had he heard from Willie? Should she tell him about the texts? She pushed that last thought away. She wasn't going to tell him that. Edie suspected that it was Willie, but she had been known to be wrong.

"Look." Jimmy grabbed the back of Kappy's seat and pulled himself forward. "Did you see them?"

"See what?" Edie turned her car into the Esh driveway as she asked.

"The goats. They have baby goats." He all but squealed.

Edie rolled her eyes and shut off the engine. "Jimmy —"

His attitude immediately deflated.

"We're not getting a goat."

"*Jah,* I know."

They piled from the car, Jimmy's attitude bouncing back the second he spotted Chris Esh over by the barn.

"Hey, Chris." Jimmy waved and loped over to where the ten-year-old stood.

Kappy was certain there had never been a kinder soul than Chris Esh. He had been born with health problems, though with good doctors and a lot of prayers, he had made it through. But his illness-riddled infancy had left him smaller than his peers, pale and weak, with a bright smile that seemed to have captured the sun. It was as if God had saved all Chris's energy and poured it into his smile.

She supposed with all the differences Jimmy had faced growing up, he felt a sort of kinship with Chris. And despite the nearly ten-year age difference between the two, they seemed the best of friends.

"I'm glad Chris treats him . . ." Edie shrugged.

Kappy looked over to where the two boys stood, laughing about something she didn't hear. "I think Chris feels the same."

"Kappy King, is that you?" Nancy Esh stepped out onto the porch. Kappy could only imagine what the woman was going through, losing her daughter only to have rumors about her son blazing through the district. Looking at her, one would never know. Her dress looked perfectly pressed, her apron without stains. She was barefoot, but her feet seemed unnaturally clean as if she stopped often to wash them. Prayer *kapp*

303

carefully pinned and perfectly in place.

"Hi, Nancy," Kappy greeted. "How are you?"

Nancy glanced from Kappy to Edie, then back again. "I'm canning pickles."

She had asked *how* she was, not *what* she was doing, but Kappy couldn't call her on it.

"We came to talk to Jonah for a bit." Edie shaded her eyes as she stepped forward.

Nancy continued to smile politely at Kappy. Edie may have spoken, but it was apparent that Nancy wasn't about to answer.

"I thought I would bring Jimmy by," Kappy said. "He wanted to see your pigs, and I thought I would check on Jonah."

Nancy pressed her lips together and nodded. *"Danki."*

"Don't mind me," Edie grumbled.

Kappy nudged her in the ribs. Not hard enough to hurt, but enough to let her know the next one just might.

"Jonah's in the barn. I suppose that's where Chris got off to as well." She shook her head. "That boy loves his animals."

Edie smiled. "Jimmy, too."

Nancy stared at Kappy.

"Are you doing okay?" Kappy asked.

Nancy gave a small shrug. "As well as can

be expected." For a moment Kappy expected Nancy to tear up, perhaps even start to cry, but her expression remained calm and impassive.

She nodded. "You'll let me know if you need anything?"

"Of course." But Kappy had a feeling she would never hear from Nancy Esh. She was deep in grief and denial. Or maybe she had convinced herself that she was moving forward, but Kappy could see it in her eyes. She had stopped living. She might be going through the motions, but she was as good as dead inside. And until she shook that she wouldn't recognize that she needed any help.

"Good." Kappy turned to go to the barn, then stopped. "Has Alma been by to see you?"

"Comes by every day."

That was good. At least someone was checking on Nancy. In the upcoming months she was going to need all the caring she could get.

Like most barns, the one belonging to the Esh family was cool, dark, and smelled like hay.

"I don't know why I put up with that," Edie grumbled as she followed behind Kappy.

"Because you have no choice."

"Harrumph."

"Stop," Kappy commanded. "At least it gives you something to complain about."

"Like I want to complain." She crossed her arms. "Are we going to look at these pigs?"

She shook her head. "We're supposed to be talking to Jonah."

"Like he's going to talk to me."

"Fine. Stay here."

But apparently, Edie couldn't stand the thought of being on her own. "Ugh. I'll go look at the pigs. Surely that won't be a violation of the *Ordnung.*"

"I don't believe there's anything about pigs in the *Ordnung.*"

The pigs were adorable. Something Kappy never thought she would say about pigs. Edie thought so as well. She didn't say as much, but Kappy could tell by the look on her face.

Jimmy was equally enchanted. He sat with Chris in the hay with the little piglets, watching them tumble over one another in their play.

Jonah was a different matter altogether. He stood to one side, leaning against the slatted wall of the barn. His arms were folded across his front and a gloomy look played around his eyes.

Edie touched Kappy's arm and nodded in his direction. Kappy dipped her chin in acknowledgment and went to stand next to him.

He barely moved as she slid in beside him. "How are you, Jonah?"

He cleared his throat and stood a little straighter. "I'm fine."

"I apologize for saying so, but you don't look fine."

A sad smile toyed with the corners of his mouth. "You usually tell it like it is, Kappy King. Why are you apologizing now?"

Kappy jerked a thumb over her shoulder. "I think I've been hanging around with Blondie too long." She leaned a little closer to him. "It's making me soft."

She actually got a chuckle out of him with that one. "I would say hi, but you know."

"*Jah.* I know. And she does, too." She paused for a second. "I hate to bring it up, but did you know there are rumors floating around about you now?"

Jonah shook his head. "I know. People can't leave well enough alone."

"Are the rumors true?"

He straightened to his full height, casting a dark shadow over Kappy. She wasn't afraid of him. She had known him his entire life, but there was something a little menacing in his new posture. "What difference does it make if they are? If I want to date an *Englisch* girl, isn't that between me and God?"

"And your parents?"

His gaze hardened until it was blue ice. "My sister died. She was run off the road, and it should have been me. I make the deliveries. But not that day. And look what happened. I'm not that concerned about what other people think about my dating habits. I all but killed my sister myself."

"What do you make of it?" Edie asked once they were back at her house.

Kappy mulled over all that had happened between her and Jonah Esh. "He seemed defensive." She nodded as if she needed to reinforce her own words. "Like people have been hassling him about it, and he was tired of answering questions."

"His parents?"

"Maybe, but it sounded to me more like other people."

"His friends? Youth group?"

"Probably. You know how tight those kids get during *rumspringa*."

"And he's already joined the church," Edie added.

"Right. So if he leaves now —"

"He'll be shunned," Edie finished.

"I'm not sure he cares as much about that as he does losing his sister. That was all he wanted to talk about. How it was his fault, and he should have been the one."

"It's possible," Edie said. "We know he's usually the one who makes the deliveries."

"But at first I thought that was just, you know, he should have been the one because it was usually him," Kappy said. "But what if he feels he should be the one because he should have been the one?"

Edie frowned. "I'm not following."

"What if whoever killed Sally June wasn't after pickles?"

"What were they after then?"

"I don't know." Kappy shrugged.

"That takes out our number-one suspect."

"But should Bettie Hershberger be our number-one suspect if she isn't guilty?"

"You got me there." Edie sat back in her chair. "There's something we're missing here."

Kappy couldn't help but feel the same. It was as if the answer was right under their noses, but they couldn't see it because they were so close. Or maybe it was the opposite and they were so far out they weren't even in the same area.

"Maybe we should go over it again."

Kappy shook her head. "Going over all the facts isn't going to change anything."

"Maybe not, but at least I would feel like I was doing something."

"Maybe we should go by the school and talk to the auto teacher about the car."

"You really think whoever owns the car took it there instead of to a regular repairman?"

"Why not? Delilah Swanson didn't want her husband to know that she had hit a shopping cart in the parking lot at the grocery store. In the big scheme of things that was nothing, right? Whoever hit Sally June has to worry about car repairs, people finding out, and going to prison for murder."

"Or manslaughter."

"Last time I heard, they lock you up in the same prison for either one."

Edie nodded. "It's a little late anyway." School was already out for the day.

"We could go Monday."

"Monday it is. In the meantime, we can say a little prayer that we get another text."

Kappy agreed. "Amen."

Sunday dawned a bright and beautiful fall day. Kappy had always loved Sundays. Even though she was thought of as an outlier, there was something about church that made her view herself as if she wasn't any different from the others in her district. Sunday was special. Sunday brought everyone together and on Sunday the only thing that should have been on her mind was attending church and learning more about God's word.

Yet all she could think about was having an excuse to see Silas again. She was being ridiculous, but something in the way he smiled at her made her feel . . . safe. Accepted. *Jah,* accepted. As if she hadn't been raised on the fringes. As if she were just like everyone else. And yet the way he smiled at her made her feel singled out. As if she were the only woman in the world. Special. Weird how both feelings came on at once.

When she and Jimmy pulled up to the Esh farm and parked the buggy, there was something different in the air, almost a crackling electricity that happens just before the storm.

Jimmy shuddered.

"What is it?" Kappy asked. The weather was turning cooler, but it was by no means coat weather.

"I don't know. Things just feel different."

She could feel it, too, but she didn't want

to say as much and alarm Jimmy. "I'm sure it's nothing." Maybe an out-of-town visitor.

"There's Chris." Jimmy pointed toward his young friend.

"Go on ahead," she told him.

Jimmy smiled and loped after his buddy.

"Kappy." She whirled around at the sound of her name. A small part of her jumped at the chance that it would be Silas calling her name, but Hiram strode toward her. The look on his face was as far from peaceful as possible. He looked as if he hadn't slept all night. His clothes weren't wrinkled and his hair — what she could see of it from under his hat — was neatly combed. But something about him was pinched and sad. Maybe even a little worn-out.

"Can I talk to you?" he asked.

"Of course."

He motioned her through the other church members who were waiting for the start of today's service and directed her toward the horse pasture on the far side of the chicken coop. The locale gave them a measure of privacy without taking them too far from the rest of the congregation.

"Are you okay?" Kappy asked. Frankly, his expression was starting to worry her. Something had happened. "What are you doing here, anyway?" This wasn't his church.

"Willie called last night."

"He called?" Somehow Kappy kept her voice to a reasonable level. Only one person turned to see what the commotion was.

"He left a message." Hiram moved a bit closer so she could better hear him. She could also inhale the scent that belonged to only him, that mixture of spicy aftershave and clean detergent. He looked so handsome today in his starched white shirt and black fitted vest. Yet she hadn't thought of him in days. Not since she wrote her pros and cons list for him and Silas. Neither man won. But neither man lost, either.

"What did he say?"

"He said he wanted to come home, but he couldn't. Not yet. He said that it wasn't safe. What do you suppose that means, it's not safe?"

Probably just what he said, was on the tip of her tongue, but she managed to bite it back. Hiram didn't need her pragmatic side. He needed a supportive friend, and that was just what she would be. "Maybe he's just scared."

"*Jah.* But of what?"

Kappy didn't have an answer for that. Well, not one that would make him feel better and allow her to keep the investigation a secret. She and Edie hadn't talked about whether or not to tell Hiram about the text exchange. Mainly because they didn't know if it was truly Willie on the other side. But this sealed it. Who else could be sending the texts? No one save Willie Lapp.

Indecision warred within her. No, they hadn't talked about it. But Edie hadn't wanted the police to know. Well, knowing the content of the text wasn't a problem; it was the fact that she would lose her phone to them if she let them know that a witness to the Sally June Esh accident had been texting them. Kappy just didn't know what to do.

Hiram worried his lip, then shook his head. Maybe there was something that he wasn't telling her. "It's just . . ." he started.

"What?" Kappy asked.

Hiram sucked in a deep breath. "Before Willie disappeared, he'd been hanging around Jonah Esh. And Jonah . . . well, I've heard that Jonah was hanging around *Englischers.*" He shook his head. "It worries me. I know I'm supposed to trust God. I just don't trust the world and that's exactly where he is, Kappy."

His expression was so raw and earnest that she couldn't stop her next words. "I'm sure he'll be fine, Hiram."

He looked at her then, his expression full of pleading hope. "You really think so?"

Kappy smiled, looked right into his green eyes, and lied. "Of course I do."

CHAPTER 19

Lord, please forgive me that lie.

They were nearly at the end of the three-hour church service, and Kappy had barely heard one word. The entire time she had been silently praying for God to forgive her the lie she told Hiram.

She wasn't in the habit of lying to people, but sometimes the truth was too much to bear. And in this case with Hiram, there was no truth. Only speculation, and she would prefer to speculate that Willie would come out of this completely unharmed. If she could choose, she wouldn't have it any other way.

The congregation stood, turned around, and knelt to pray. Kappy did her best to clear her mind of her own prayers and pray for others. So many people in the community were hurting. So many things to pray for, yet something in Hiram's eyes after she told him that Willie would be just fine haunted her. And she knew if something happened to Willie, she wouldn't be able to forgive herself. Yet she couldn't tell Hiram anything else.

The congregation stood and faced front while the bishop went over a few last-minute announcements. Then they were dismissed for their after-church meal.

According to tradition, the men set up the tables from the church benches while the women brought out the food. The first tables of congregants were served and ate, then the second.

Perhaps she could get Jimmy to consent to leave early, and they could head out as soon as the meal mess was cleaned up. Most everyone there had an animal of some sort that needed afternoon care. But if she could convince Jimmy that he needed to get home and give his critters the upmost attention, then she might be able to avoid the feeling of dread that plagued her. Hiram had left as they had started to file into the house for the service, but the regret and heaviness had stayed with her the entire morning.

As it had been for the last couple church Sundays, Bettie Hershberger brought her green pickles and stacked the jars neatly on the table next to the Esh family's white church pickles. This Sunday a few more brave souls had ventured to the green side. It wasn't that there were no green pickles in all of the valley, but church pickles . . . they were supposed to be white. At least in Kappy's district they were.

After she ate, Kappy did her part of the cleanup, then went in search of Jimmy. She spied him on the other side of the pasture talking to Chris Esh. A litter of black-and-white puppies tumbled in the grass at their feet.

Oh, no! Puppies. Like he didn't get enough of those at home. It might take her an hour or better to get him away from the adorable creatures.

She had to try. She started toward the pair, then someone called her name.

She turned to find Silas Hershberger, and she stopped in her tracks. Silas smiled, maybe because she was waiting for him to catch up with her. Or maybe he seemed so happy and carefree because Hiram had seemed so worried.

"I'm glad I caught you," he said, drawing near.

"*Jah?* You wanted to talk to me about something?"

"Not really."

"Did you need me to do something special?" She and his aunt had talked about special-order *kapps* a couple of weeks ago.

But Silas shook his head. "No." He smiled.

She started to ask if he was having a problem, but he spoke before she could get the question out. "I just wanted to talk to you."

She hooked a thumb back at herself. "Me?" she mouthed, then instantly wished she hadn't.

"*Jah,* you." He continued to smile at her with those so-fantastic-they-almost-looked-fake teeth. "*Mamm* said she would like for you to come to supper sometime next week."

Kappy's grin froze on her face. She had barely been invited to Hiram's mother's for dinner. It was well known that Janet Lapp didn't exactly approve of Hiram and Kappy as a couple. Some of it, Kappy was sure, had to do with the fact that she was Byler Amish instead of Renno as they were, but somehow she knew it went a little deeper than that. Janet was always cordial to Kappy, but she could never say even once that the woman had been genuinely friendly. "You want me? To come to supper?"

He nodded. "*Jah.* Of course. You can bring Jimmy, too. If you need to."

"I would like that."

His smile deepened. "Good. I'll come by

sometime tomorrow, and we can work out the details."

"Sounds great."

He gave her a quick bow, then turned to work his way through the crowd.

Kappy stared after him, wondering if this was a date. It sure felt like one. The mere thought made her feet feel as light as the clouds. She floated over to Jimmy so they could go home.

"I told you he liked you." Jimmy grinned at her from across the table.

The first thing that Kappy had done when she got home was grab Elmer and get back up to Edie's. She had to tell Edie about Silas's supper invitation.

Edie shot him an affectionate glare. "Don't you have puppies to feed?"

He nodded. "And ducks and gerbils. But I don't have any goats or pigs to feed. I really would like to feed a pig."

Kappy hid her smile at his unveiled attempts to get more pets. Kappy figured if he had his way, he would have his own Noah's ark.

"I believe you've mentioned that," Edie said.

"Just making sure." Jimmy winked and let himself out of the house.

"Did he . . ." Kappy started.

Edie laughed. "He did. Not sure where he picked up that one, though."

"There's no way to know," Kappy agreed.

"Anything else happen?"

"I almost forgot. Hiram."

"What about him?"

"He looked terrible. He pulled me aside and started telling me that Willie called the shanty yesterday."

"He was at church? Your church?"

Kappy nodded.

"And you're just now telling me?"

True. She had lost her focus in a pair of deep blue, bottomless eyes. "I sort of got distracted."

"I would fuss, but I would like to hear the story first."

"There's not a lot to tell. Just that Willie called and was worried that someone was going to hurt him. He said something about wanting to come home but he couldn't."

"Hiram talked to Willie directly?"

Kappy shook her head. "He left a message at the phone shanty. But you know what this means?"

"It means Willie is our Mr. Text."

"Agreed. But should I tell Hiram that we've been in contact with him?"

"Absolutely not."

Kappy wanted to protest. All she could see was the sad and worried look in Hiram's eyes. He was fretting for his brother, not that she could blame him. "What about Jack?"

"Why are you so determined for me to hand my phone over to Jack Jones?"

"Something's wrong with the whole thing."

Edie nodded. "Of course there is. Someone was murdered. And you think that's right?"

"Not exactly what I meant, but *jah.* We've been collecting all this information, and we still can't figure it out. Maybe it's time to give what we have to the professionals and let them handle it."

"I don't know." Edie frowned. "If we give it to them, you know Willie will stop texting. Are you prepared for that?"

"He might continue to text. If he's scared and hiding, maybe if he knows that the police are looking into this, then he'll come home."

"Because he feels so safe?"

"*Jah.* No." Kappy shook her head. "We need to help him, and I believe now that giving the phone to Jack is the only way."

"I understand."

"So you'll do it?"

"No. But I'll think about it."

That was all Kappy could ask.

But Monday brought no clear answers. Kappy got up and ate, got dressed, and headed over to Edie's to help feed the animals.

She no sooner set foot onto the property than Edie was dragging her inside. "You'll never guess what happened."

"You bought new clothes at an all-night department store."

"Funny. Ha-ha."

"What happened?"

"I shouldn't tell you, you know. Not after that crack."

"Okay." Kappy made to leave, but Edie grabbed her arm, effectively stopping her.

"I got another text last night."

"You what?"

Before she could repeat the words, Jimmy came into the kitchen. "Good morning, Kappy. *Danki* for coming to help me this morning. Are you ready to go?"

"In a minute," Edie said. "We need to talk about a couple of things first."

Jimmy's expression fell. "But Kappy came to help me."

"And she will. In a bit. Okay?"

For a minute Kappy thought he might

protest more, but that just wasn't Jimmy's way.

"*Jah.* Okay," he said, then trudged out the door.

Kappy glanced at the phone, remorse hitting her like a strong north wind. "This needs to wait, Edie."

"But —"

"I'm just as anxious to see it as you are to show it to me, but Jimmy . . ." She trailed off with a small nod toward the door he'd just exited.

It took only a moment for her meaning to sink in. "You're right." Edie pushed up from the table and together they walked out to help Jimmy.

His smile alone was worth solid gold as far as Kappy was concerned.

"I think he's jealous," Kappy said as they stood back and waited for Jimmy to finish using the water hose. He was a good aim most days, but there were enough times when he wasn't exactly watching where the stream was pointed that Kappy and Edie knew to stay well enough back.

Edie scoffed. "Of what?"

"The time you spend with me."

"Thinking pretty highly of yourself, are you?"

"It's not that. You were gone for so long.

He didn't see you for years. Now you're back and spending a lot of time with me. I think he needs some sister-brother time, is all."

"We get plenty of time together."

"Do you?"

Edie thought about it, but didn't actually answer.

"It might help if you make a decision about whether you're staying or going. He's smart enough to figure out that if you leave he will have to go as well."

Kappy could almost see the realization click in Edie's thoughts. "I wouldn't take him away from here. This is his home. I know that."

"You would leave him here to take care of himself?"

"Not exactly. I would find someone to take him in. Like you or Martha Peachey."

"That's not what he wants, and you know it. He's scared out of his mind that you're going to leave and never come back. That's why he's working so hard and begging for new animals. Because if he can get you to commit to more animals, the less likely you'll be to move."

"I never . . ."

Kappy touched her arm in a measure of support. "I know." She gave Edie the most encouraging smile she could muster. "But it's time to make up your mind for good. For Jimmy's sake."

Once they finished the chores, Edie sent Jimmy in to wash his hands. When he was out of sight, she pulled her phone from inside her shirt, thumbed it awake, then handed it to Kappy. "What do you make of this?" she asked.

Kappy studied the screen. "This is from Mr. Text?"

"Aka Willie Lapp."

"Aka?"

"Don't worry about that. What do you think of the text?"

Kappy read it again.

No one understands.

"It's correct. I don't understand it, either." Kappy handed the phone back to Edie.

"But it sounds more frustrated than the last ones, don't you think?"

Kappy shrugged. "I suppose. But why?"

"Exactly my question."

"Now I'm really confused."

"I think Willie is getting tired of being out and not able to come home."

"But he could come home. I mean, why not?"

"Because there's a killer on the loose, and

he witnessed the murder."

She nodded. All the doubts were starting to fall away. "Unless . . ." she started, but quickly trailed off.

"Unless what?"

"He's hiding because he knows that the killer was after him first." Even as Kappy said the words she knew they held no merit, but they served to make her think more about the situation. Or was it differently?

"Why? Why would the killer be after Willie Lapp? It makes more sense if they were after Jonah. He was supposed to be driving the buggy that day."

"Why would anyone be after Jonah?" Edie asked.

But the answer came to them at the same time. "Because he was dating an *Englisch* girl," they said simultaneously.

Edie grabbed her arm and dragged her toward the porch. They sat on the steps, each mulling over this new theory.

"But I thought Mr. Text was Willie Lapp." Kappy nibbled on the end of her thumb as she mulled over the changes to their theory.

"I did, too. But why would he text me?"

"Why would Jonah?"

Edie nodded. "Good point. So it's safe to say that we have no evidence as to the identity of Mr. Text. Just theories."

And bad ones at that.

"If Jonah truly was the original target, then he could be in danger, *jah*?"

"I suppose. I mean, if the killer is still after him."

"The woman with long dark hair."

"We think," Edie added. "I mean, we've been wrong about a few other things."

"All the more reason to give what we have to Jack."

Kappy could almost hear the thoughts arguing with one another in Edie's mind. "Maybe," she finally grumbled.

But Kappy knew as well as Edie did that there was more to this situation than met the eye. Too many ifs that took their ideas in too many different directions.

Just then the sound of a car engine floated in from the lane, mixed with the baying howl-barks of the beagles. Elmer jumped to his feet and joined in, and a moment or two later, Jack Jones's familiar unmarked police car came into view.

"What does he want?" Edie muttered.

"My guess is to talk to you."

"Funny," Edie said.

"This is the perfect time, you know."

Her lips pressed together in a thin line of a frown. "I don't know, Kappy."

"If we make the wrong decision, another

young person might lose their life."

Edie didn't answer. She just pushed to her feet and made her way across the yard toward Jack.

"Be quiet, puppy," Kappy said. Elmer whined a bit, but stuck close to her, flopping back onto the grass and watching Jack with wary brown eyes.

"I heard Willie Lapp came back last night," Jack said in lieu of an actual greeting.

Edie whirled around and nailed Kappy with a look.

Kappy was on her feet in a heartbeat. "We hadn't heard."

Jack nodded. "You know how things get around in Blue Sky. Strange, though. I thought you and his brother were thick."

"We're friends," Kappy muttered, as she and Elmer made their way over to the pair.

Jack gave a stern nod. "I came to ask a favor." The wind ruffled his inky-dark hair as he stared off in the direction of the puppy pens. The dogs had barked out their initial warning and were settling down a bit. Only the newest of the puppies continued, obviously seeking the attention of this newcomer.

Edie's eyes narrowed, and she crossed her arms, shifting her weight as if to tell him without words what she thought of his request.

"What sort of favor?" Kappy asked.

"Willie Lapp disappeared just after Sally June died. It might just be a coincidence, but I have to make sure."

"No stone unturned," Edie muttered.

"Something like that."

"What does this have to do with me?" Kappy asked.

"We went there yesterday, but no one is talking. I was hoping that perhaps you could swing by and see what they are saying."

Kappy shook her head. "I — they're my friends. I can't spy on them for you."

Jack shifted his weight, obviously uncomfortable with the imbalance of power. "Listen. I know it's a lot to ask, but if I can completely clear Willie, then I can get on to finding the actual murderer. Sally June was your friend, too, right?"

Kappy nodded, though warily.

"Don't you want to bring her killer to justice?"

Kappy wanted nothing more than to help him solve this case, but spying on her friends . . . ? "I don't know . . ."

"I think you should."

Kappy whirled around to see if Edie was serious. Her expression appeared somber enough. Her eyes weren't twinkling with laughter. Her lips weren't twitching with barely controlled mirth.

"You mean that?" Kappy finally asked.

"I do. It's time to work together."

"Does that mean you're showing him your phone?"

"Phone?" Jack echoed. "What about your phone?"

"You just had to, huh?" Edie grumbled. She tossed her pink hair and leveled her gaze on Jack. "Someone's been texting me."

"O-kay."

"I think they might be involved with Sally June's death."

"When did the texts start?"

"The day after the accident."

"You're just telling me about them?"

Edie shrugged.

"You have your phone right now?"

She nodded.

"You keep the texts on there?"

"Yes." Edie's voice was filled with a begrudging growl.

Jack held out his hand. "Fork it over."

"But —" she protested.

"No buts. You may have been harboring evidence that could have solved this case over a week ago." He curled his fingers in a "give it" sort of way.

"Fine." Edie blew her bangs out of her face and fished her phone from the back pocket of her bright yellow jeans. She handed it to him but not without a piercing stare. "I need it back yesterday. It's the only one I have."

Jack took it and slipped it into his own pocket. "You know I could arrest you for impeding an investigation."

"Then arrest me." Edie gave him her best tough-girl shrug. Kappy had seen it a couple of times, and this time was no different: It didn't work.

"I still might."

They appeared to be at an impasse, neither one willing to back down. But Kappy knew one thing for certain: Jack could arrest Edie. Unless she did something to convince him not to.

She took two giant steps forward and stood between them. She turned her attention to Jack. "I'll do it."

CHAPTER 20

"What?" Both Edie and Jack spoke at the same time.

"I'll go over to the Lapps' and see if I can find out anything from Willie. But if I do, you have to promise not to arrest Edie." She wasn't sure it was something Jack could actually promise — not to take Edie to jail — but Kappy had to ask.

"You'd do that for me?" Edie said.

Kappy ignored her. Besides, she had a feeling the admiration she heard in Edie's voice was faked for Jack's benefit.

"Go visit him as a friend and if you happen to see something or hear something, then let me know, okay? That's not too much to ask."

It was a lot. But too much? She shook her head. "I won't tell you if he's guilty. Because I know he's not."

Jack raised his stubble-darkened chin. "Fair enough. When can you go?"

Kappy sighed. "This afternoon."

"The sooner the better," he said. "Then call me when you're done."

Kappy nodded. "*Jah.* Maybe I'll swing by the station."

Jack gave them a quick smile. "I'll be waiting."

"I can't believe you're doing this," Edie grumbled as she drove Kappy to Willie's house. He still lived with his parents, of course, and Hiram had built a house next door when he and Laverna married. It wasn't completely out of the question for her to drop in and see Hiram, then check on Willie.

"Would you rather go to jail?"

"He wasn't going to take me to jail."

Edie's voice sounded confident enough, but Kappy didn't believe it for a second. This case was different from Ruth Peachey's. Kappy could see it in Jack's face, in his eyes. He had said that he needed their support and she believed him.

"I still think we should help him."

"We're helping him, all right. Who knows when I'll get my phone back." She held up the small plastic "ladybug" phone that she had bought for Jimmy.

"You took his phone?"

Edie rolled her eyes. "I can only call my phone with it, but I gave this number to the service that monitors his alert necklace. That way if he pushes his button at least I'll know it."

"Good idea."

"You know what would have been a better idea?" Edie asked. "Not letting Jack Jones have my cell phone."

"He said he'd give it back."

"Yeah, right." Edie turned onto the lane leading to the Lapp farm and pulled to a stop in front of the barn.

"I guess I'll wait here," she said.

Kappy frowned. "*Jah.* Do that. Because that doesn't look strange at all."

"What am I supposed to do? Go in and tell them that I was worried about Willie and wanted to come by despite the fact that I'm under the *Bann*?"

"Let me think about it a minute. *Jah.*" Kappy got out of the car, surprised to hear Edie do the same.

"Fine. But no one's going to talk to me."

"Even better." Kappy shot her a saucy grin. "Maybe you'll talk less, too."

"Ha-ha. Very funny."

The door was pulled open almost as soon as Kappy knocked, as if whoever answered had been waiting for them to stop in.

"Hi, Emma. Can we come in?"

"Jah." Hiram's sister stepped back to allow them to enter.

"You probably don't know Edie Peachey," Kappy said. "But don't worry about it. You don't have to talk to her. She's under the *Bann.*" She whispered the last three words as if they were some dark, ancient secret.

"Oh." Emma's blue eyes widened in surprise. "I won't."

"Thanks a lot," Edie muttered under her breath.

"We wanted to come by and check on Willie."

Kappy wouldn't have thought it possible, but Emma's eyes grew even wider. "How did you know he's home? We haven't told anyone."

"Uh . . ." Kappy couldn't find the words she needed. And she needed them desperately. *What do I say? What do I say?*

"You know how Blue Sky is." Edie chuckled. "You can't blow your nose around here without a write-up in the paper."

Emma looked from Edie to Kappy. Then from Kappy back to Edie. "What do I say?" she whispered to Kappy.

"You don't have to say anything," Kappy assured her. "Can I see Willie now?" At least Edie's boldness had saved her from having to answer the question she had no answer for. No one knew that Willie Lapp was back in Blue Sky? Then how did Jack Jones know? It seemed the detective knew more about the case than he was letting on.

"*Jah.* Of course." She nodded her head and motioned for Kappy to follow her. Left with no other choice, Edie trailed behind. "Hiram's with him," Emma said as she made her way down the hall.

Somehow Kappy managed not to stumble over her own feet at the mention of his name. She hadn't counted on Hiram being there. Just her and Willie. Now there were five of them. Almost a party.

Emma stopped outside a bedroom door. She rapped lightly on the wood, then pushed it open and motioned Kappy inside.

The room was dark, the curtains drawn, and it seemed a sheet had been tossed on top of the fabric to block out even more light.

A young man sat on the end of the made bed, head bent, elbows braced on his knees.

Kappy took one look at him and relief flooded her system.

It was true: Willie Lapp had come home.

"*Shhhh . . .*" Hiram grasped her arm and pulled her farther into the room. "We don't want everyone knowing he's back."

"Why not?"

"We just don't, okay?"

Kappy shook her head. "Okay."

"What are you doing here?"

Emma ducked out of the room, leaving Edie and Kappy alone with Hiram and Willie.

"What is *she* doing here?"

"She . . . we were just worried about Willie."

Hiram's gaze narrowed. "How did you know he was home?"

"Martha Peachey told me." How many times was she going to lie before the Lord struck her down? She added the transgression to the mental prayer list she kept.

"How did she know?"

Kappy blew a raspberry much the same way Edie did when she was put on the spot. "Who knows how Martha finds out half the stuff she does?"

Hiram thought about it a moment, but to Kappy it seemed like a piece of forever. "True." He gave a small nod of consent, then took a step back. "I'm sure Willie can use the friendly face."

Kappy looked from Hiram to Willie. He seemed just the same as when she had seen him a couple of weeks ago. Maybe a little sadder, a little more worried. Had he not wanted to come home? Kappy wanted to ask him, but the words wouldn't come. In fact, she had a lot of questions she wanted to ask him, but she couldn't. Such as if he had been texting Edie. If he had seen the accident that killed Sally June Esh, and why he had come back. And why didn't they want anyone to know.

"Hey, Willie."

He lifted one hand in greeting.

"Did you know the police came by yesterday?" Hiram asked.

Kappy did her best to look surprised, but the expression felt forced. "What did they want?"

Hiram shook his head. "They think Willie had something to do with Sally June Esh's death."

"That's not what they said," Willie protested.

Kappy wanted to ask what Jack Jones and his buddies had asked Willie, but she managed to hold in the question. She needed for them to tell her, not go digging for information. She had already told Jack as much.

"They might as well have." He turned back to Kappy. "They were everywhere. And all of them seemed to be talking at once. *Mamm* took to bed with a sick headache. It was terrible."

"What did you say to them?" Kappy asked. She could feel Edie vibrating behind her and she knew that her friend was having as much trouble as she was containing her own questions.

"We told them that we didn't want anything to do with this."

"*You* told them that," Willie countered.

Hiram ignored him, but corrected himself all the same. "I told them that the district was still grieving Sally June, and we didn't need to keep talking about it. We need to heal."

"True," Kappy murmured. She was certain those words hadn't settled well with Jack.

"He was just doing his job," Edie said.

Willie looked at her, but Hiram didn't even flinch to acknowledge her words.

"He was only doing his job," Kappy said. "I'm sure he meant no offense."

"Wanna bet?" Edie murmured behind her. Thankfully, she had lowered her voice enough that no one save Kappy heard her.

"I didn't do it," Willie said. "I know everyone thinks I did because I left about the same time, but I didn't do it."

"You don't have to say anything," Hiram

said. "In fact, I would prefer that you didn't."

"Why?" Willie jumped to his feet. "If I don't say that I'm innocent, then they're going to arrest me. You heard what they said last night."

"I did, and that's the exact reason why you shouldn't say anything. That's what these men are trained to do, get you to confess. Whether you mean to or not."

Willie flopped back onto the bed and let out a frustrated growl.

"Were you the one texting me?" Edie asked.

Willie and Hiram both swiveled to face her.

"Text you?" Hiram asked. "Why would my brother text you?"

"Oh, now you want to talk to me."

Kappy nudged her in the ribs. "Did you text Edie, Willie?"

The young man frowned. "How would I text you?"

"With your cell phone." Edie rolled her eyes. She was more than convinced that Willie had been the one, but the longer they stood in the dark bedroom and talked, the more she began to wonder.

"I'm Amish. No cell phone." Willie held his arms out as if Edie were about to conduct a search.

"Rumspringa," Edie singsonged.

"I may be running around, but I don't have a cell phone."

Kappy turned to Edie. "I think he's telling the truth."

"How do we know for certain?" Edie asked.

"We don't. We just have to trust him."

"I'm sitting right here," Willie said.

"Good," Edie interjected. "At least you can't say we were talking behind your back."

"Is that why you came here?" Hiram asked.

For the first time since they had entered the bedroom, Kappy was glad for the cover of darkness. The heat she felt rising from her neck into her cheeks was hot enough to roast marshmallows. "Of course not."

"I think it's time for you to go." Hiram took a menacing step toward her.

Kappy didn't believe for a second that he would hurt her, but she retreated all the same. She had come here under false pretenses, and she deserved his scorn.

"Sorry, Hiram," Kappy said. "I'm glad you're home, Willie."

"Danki, Kappy."

She turned to make her way from the room. Hiram followed behind him.

"Are you telling me you've been getting texts that you thought were from Willie and you didn't tell me?"

"It's not like that," Kappy protested. "We didn't tell anyone."

He raised one brow, his mouth twisted into an angled frown. "That's not a comfort, Kappy. I thought we were friends. I gave you the space you said you needed. I knew that we would make it through whatever doubts you were having, but now? Now, I'm the one with the doubts. Good-bye, Kappy."

"Intense," Edie said as they climbed into the car.

Kappy shook her head. "You can't blame him."

"Sure I can." She started the car and turned it around in the side yard.

"He feels I betrayed him."

"I know what he feels. I'm just saying he was intense."

"Wouldn't you be?"

Edie gave another of her one-shoulder shrugs. "I suppose." She pulled onto the side lane and made her way to the main road. "Which way?"

Left would take them to the police station, but did they really have anything to tell Jack? No. Right would take them home.

Even farther and they would be at the grocery store.

"We could go see if Bettie Hershberger talked Mr. Roberts at the market into selling her green pickles," Kappy said.

"For real?"

"You got anything better to do?"

"I thought Silas was coming by."

He was, but did Kappy really want to get her hopes up again?

"Oh, I see," Edie said. "Playing hard to get."

"If you say so," Kappy reluctantly agreed.

"Then to the grocery store." She turned onto the main road and started toward the supermarket.

"You still don't think Bettie had anything to do with this, do you?"

Kappy sighed. "No, I guess not. Though it would have been a lot easier if she had. I just want to see how successful her pickle campaign is becoming."

"Do you think she'll get the church members to convert to green pickles?"

"No. We love the tradition too much, but I would like to see her pickles get a little more attention. They're not bad pickles at all." A little too spicy for her taste. But she had grown up eating white church pickles that were made for everyone to enjoy. *Jah,* if that might make them a little bland, then so be it.

Edie slowed her car as they neared a yellow buggy driving in front of them. She pulled into the left lane, checking the traffic before executing her pass. The buggy didn't slow. The driver kept going. Most times the buggy driver would pull to one side to allow the car more room. Kappy always did this. It felt safer to her to be off to the side and stopped when dealing with so many cars on the not-so-wide two-lane highway.

Edie passed the car and something made Kappy look back.

"Edie! That's Bettie Hershberger."

"What?"

"In the buggy. That was Bettie Hershberger."

"Free country," Edie said, barely taking her eyes from the road to glance in the rearview mirror.

"What do you suppose she's doing?"

"Driving somewhere."

"But where?" Kappy mused.

"Hard to say."

"She could be headed to the grocery store. I mean, she's almost there."

"Or she could be headed to the market stand just down from the convenience store."

"I guess we'll see."

"Maybe." Edie pulled into the parking lot and turned off the engine. "I get to do the talking."

"I don't mind talking to him." Kappy got out of the car and smoothed a hand over her dress and apron.

"Yeah, maybe not. But these are my people and they talk to me. Gotta give me that."

Kappy smiled. "It's yours."

They were just about to walk into the store when one of the flyers taped to the inside of the window caught Kappy's attention. "Edie . . . come look at this." She pointed to the window.

Edie scanned the area. "The spaghetti supper at the church?"

"No. This." Kappy tapped the glass. This flyer was different from the rest. This one was in full color instead of black lettering on brightly colored paper. BATTLE OF THE BANDS, ran across the top of the page. COME SUPPORT LOCAL BAND, BABY SISTER, AT THE UPCOMING BATTLE OF THE BANDS. All the members of the band had long hair and wore dresses, but something in how they stood had Kappy registering that they weren't females but boys in skirts and wigs.

"Why would boys do this?" she asked.

Edie gave a disinterested shrug. "It's a gimmick."

"Gimmick?"

"Not on your word-a-day calendar?"

"I know what a gimmick is. I just don't know how it applies in this situation."

"It's a way for them to be remembered."

Kappy wasn't sure how dressing as a girl would accomplish that. But she had long ago given up trying to understand the ways of the *Englisch.* Wouldn't it be better to just play really good music?

"Wait. Isn't that Jeff?"

"Jeff? Jeff who?" Edie asked.

"Baldwin. Pete's son."

"The auto-body repairman?" Edie squinted at the picture. Despite the fact that it was in color, it was still a bad image and was printed on flimsy printer paper. It was a little hard to see. "It sort of looks like him. It's hard to tell with that wig he has on."

"And remember? His father said he played the guitar." Of the five guys on the flyer, the one in the middle seemed to hide his face a bit more than the others. Coincidence? She didn't know.

"He's definitely got a guitar. Were there any other marks? You know, like a scar or a mole?" Edie asked.

"There's no way we could see it on this flyer. The picture is just so bad."

"And that hair." The words had no sooner left Edie's lips than the idea struck. Well, actually it fell on her like a stack of bricks from heaven.

"He's got on a long black wig," Kappy said.

Edie stopped. "And he has a car like the one involved in the accident."

"And he had access to repair the car without having to tell his father or claim it on his insurance."

It was falling into place, all the pieces of the puzzle. Except one. Every shred of evidence they had was pointing toward Jeff Baldwin as the murderer.

"But why?" Kappy asked.

CHAPTER 21

Kappy took a step back as a woman left the store. Until that moment, Kappy hadn't been thinking about what she and Edie had looked like, standing out front, staring at the flyers posted in the large plate-glass window.

"Why?" Edie repeated.

"His sister," Kappy said. She slapped one hand over her mouth to contain the rest of her words, but her excitement was palpable.

"That's right." Edie snapped her fingers. "His sister has been dating a boy her family doesn't approve of."

"And Jonah Esh has been dating an *Englisch* girl."

"Do you realize what this means?" Edie took another step back as a frowning woman brushed past.

"That we need to go talk to Jack Jones?"

Edie looked as if she had been slapped. She pointed to the full-color flyer. "It means we have to get to the Battle of the Bands."

"I'm still not convinced this is the best choice," Kappy said as Edie drove to the concert. It was at the edge of town in the small park next to the post office. The weather was still nice enough to have out-door events, but in another month or so, listening to music outside for hours would not be pleasant.

"Why not? If we have to stop and talk to Jack, we'll be even more late to the concert. And we can't call him since he has my phone." She shot Kappy a glaring frown.

"So that's what this is about. You're not telling him because he took your phone."

"I'm not telling him yet because he took my phone and I have no way to contact him."

"Even if you wanted to."

"We'll call him from the concert, okay? I mean, someone needs to watch this guy and make sure he doesn't get away while we wait on Jack and his posse."

She couldn't argue with that. Someone did need to keep an eye on the young man. He had killed an innocent woman. It was such a shame. Two young lives forever ruined by one bad decision.

"How — ?"

"I'll borrow a phone, okay?"

"Okay."

Edie pulled up to the park. She turned off the car and set the brake, then together they made their way through the crowd of people toward the stage.

Kappy didn't know who was playing, but after seeing the full-color picture of Baby Sister, she knew it wasn't them. These guys wore faded and ripped jeans, flannel shirts, and boots that looked like they were biker-gang castoffs.

"I wonder when they'll go on," Edie mused from beside her. Well, she more or less yelled to be heard over the loud music.

"What if they've already played?" Kappy hollered in return.

"It's a contest. They'll stick around to the end to see who wins."

Kappy nodded, wishing she had Edie's confidence, but she knew they weren't going anywhere until they saw Jeff Baldwin and Baby Sister.

Two more bands were introduced, played, and left the stage. Edie found a program, but there was no set list for the order of the bands. After a few well-timed questions between bands, they learned from the announcer that Baby Sister hadn't played their turn.

"Maybe we should go to the back area and talk to him," Kappy suggested.

Edie thought about it a moment. "What if he runs?"

"And you think he'll stay onstage once he realizes that we are after him?"

"Maybe. I mean, he's a teenage boy. He's probably still dreaming of being a rock star. He's not going to leave the stage when his dreams of fame are so close."

Kappy thought back to the pressed and proper young man they had met at Pete's auto-body-repair shop. She was still having trouble believing that young man and the boy on the flyers were the same person.

And the *whys* still plagued her. Was this truly about his sister dating an Amish boy? Or was there something more sinister at hand?

She shifted nervously. "Shouldn't we try calling Jack?"

"Do we really have something to tell him?" Edie countered.

"*Jah.* We do. He needs to come here so we can tell him about Jeff Baldwin. These bands are only playing one song. If we wait until they go up onstage before we call, they'll be done before Jack gets here." Blue Sky was small, but not that small.

"Maybe you're right . . ." Edie looked

around as if to find a phone she could bor-row. At least that was what Kappy hoped. But it was too late.

An announcer with an earring in his lip and a scruffy beard on his chin announced that Baby Sister was up next.

"Call him, Edie."

But she seemed frozen in place. "What do we do?"

"Call Jack."

Edie shook her head. "It's too late for that."

"We need the police." Kappy wasn't up for running through a cornfield and hiding from a killer again. Though the boy on the stage — it was strange calling him that since he was wearing a dress and pigtails — seemed as harmless as a newborn puppy. And the doubts started to set in. What if they were wrong? What if he didn't kill Sally June? What if he wasn't trying to keep Jonah Esh away from his sister?

The loud drumbeat seemed to tick off precious minutes. Time was wasting.

"We'll go talk to him."

"What?" Kappy asked.

"That's the best plan. We'll wait until they've finished, and we'll go backstage and talk to them . . . him."

"And then what?"

Edie bit her lip. "I don't know."

"We have to have a plan."

More loud drumbeats. More precious seconds lost.

And time was up.

Baby Sister had finished their song. The crowd cheered and clapped. Edie grabbed her hand and dragged Kappy around to the back of the outdoor stage.

Jeff and his friends were coming off the stage, all smiles and high-fives.

"Dude, we nailed it." The blond-haired drummer clacked his sticks together as if he was still playing.

"If we don't win this thing, you know it's rigged." That came from the brown-haired piano player.

As Edie and Kappy drew closer to them, it became apparent that Jeff was the only one not celebrating what the rest of the band considered to be a great success.

"What's the matter, J?" One of the band members patted Jeff on the shoulder.

He shook his head.

"Still worried about telling your old man you'd rather be a rock star than a highbrow classical composer?"

"Cut it out," Jeff said. He scratched his wig. He wore a pinafore dress, no-heel black shoes with buckle straps across the instep, and ankle socks with ruffles.

Kappy didn't know much about music, but she had a feeling that Pete the auto-body repairman with his man's man attitude would not approve of his son's choice of gimmicks.

"You are going to tell him, right? That we're heading to Hollywood after graduation."

Jeff shook his head, but not hard enough for it to be considered an answer. "There's just a lot going on right now."

"Uh-huh. This have anything to do with your sister?"

Jeff's expression grew dark. "Leave my sister out of this."

"Dude, I like your sister. And I would totally date her if she would forget about that Amish guy she's been hanging around with."

"The Amish guy is history."

The closer Kappy and Edie drew to the boys, the harder it was to figure out a reason why they were inching closer like stalkers.

"Hey. You guys were awesome!" Edie gushed, flouncing toward the group of boys as if they were her teenage idols come to life. "Can I have your autograph?"

The boys all jerked to attention, each one swinging their gaze to take in all of Edie's loud ensemble and brightly colored hair.

"Uh, sure."

"Awesome," Edie gushed. "I think I'm a little older than their average fan," she said so only Kappy could hear.

"You think?"

"Stay here," Edie said from the corner of her mouth. She moved closer to the band while Kappy held back.

"Do you have a pen?" one member asked.

As far as Kappy could tell, she didn't have any paper, either.

"As a matter of fact . . ." Edie held up a permanent black marker. "Anywhere," she invited, holding her arms out at her sides. "Pick your place, boys."

The band members gathered around her, but their conversation about Jeff's sister came to a close.

"I've never signed anyone's shirt before," the brown-haired piano player said.

"Me either," said another band member. Kappy thought he was the drummer. "At least not while they were still wearing it."

"Groovy outfit," one of the guys said.

"Great hair," another added.

Kappy rolled her eyes. That was all Edie needed: encouragement for her crazy style.

"Thanks." She gave them a sweet smile.

Edie stood patiently while they signed her

shirt. Other than autographs, Kappy had no idea what her plan was. If she had a plan. And Kappy hoped she did.

"You look familiar." Jeff stopped signing her shirt, pulling away so he could look at Edie from a different angle.

"I get that a lot." Edie scoffed. "I guess I have an average face."

"And less-than-average clothes," he muttered. He looked as if he was about to start signing her shirt again, but he stopped before he actually touched the pen to fabric. He looked around and spotted Kappy.

Something flashed in his eyes. Something that told her he remembered who they were.

"You came out to my house the other day."

"Whoa, dude. A stalker."

"Killer," one of the others said.

"I, uh . . . Oh, yeah. I remember now. I went out there to see about your father repairing my car for me," Edie told him.

Jeff's eyes narrowed. "Your car looked fine to me."

"Well, you know," Edie stuttered. "In case I ever need a body repairman. I'm new to the area."

Jeff swung his gaze to Kappy. "But you're not." His eyes widened as if he had finally put the last piece into the puzzle and was shocked by the picture he saw.

"You . . . you . . ." He dropped the pen and backed away from Edie, shaking his head as he continued his retreat. He stopped, sucked in a deep breath, then ran.

"Dude, what is up with you?"

His band mates called after him, but he didn't slow his steps.

Kappy took off after him with Edie close behind. The band seemed to have delayed her and Kappy had the jump on her friend by at least twenty feet.

"Jeff, stop!" Kappy called. "We just want to talk."

He didn't reply. He didn't even look back to see how close she was, he just ran.

Edie pounded the ground behind her, but even with her longer strides, she wasn't able to catch up.

"Call nine-one-one," Kappy called to anyone who was listening. "Call Jack Jones."

She wasn't sure if anyone was doing as she asked as she flew by.

The boy had legs like a deer, and Kappy was beginning to get winded. But she couldn't quit. He had killed Sally June for whatever reason, and she owed it to the young girl to bring him to justice.

Jeff glanced back to see how close she was to him, then he skidded to a stop.

Jack Jones was standing directly in front

of them, merely waiting for her to deliver Jeff to him.

But Jeff wasn't going down easy. He looked back at Kappy, then took off to the left, darting through the crowd. His long black wig streamed behind him like smoke from a tailpipe.

As if they knew he was coming, the crowd parted and allowed Jeff to dash along. Behind her, Jack's footfalls had joined Edie's as they all three chased the boy through the music lovers gathered in the park. Jeff seemed to be getting away.

Kappy only had one choice. She leapt toward him, barely catching the back of his dress in one hand. She wasn't a big person, but the velocity plus the fact that he was running mixed with her weight and she tumbled on top of Jeff Baldwin, bringing him to the ground.

He landed with an *"Oof."*

Kappy pushed herself up into a sitting position, though she was right on top of the teenager.

"Get off me," he yelled. But Kappy wasn't budging. Despite her smaller size, she had the upper hand. Jeff could squirm all he wanted, but she wasn't moving off him.

"What do you think you're doing?" Jack practically roared as he came upon them.

"That was the coolest thing ever!" Edie was breathless, a huge smile spreading across her face.

"Is somebody going to get him?" Kappy asked.

Jack and Edie were in motion once again. Edie helped Kappy to her feet while Jack hoisted Jeff to his. He snapped handcuffs on to the teen.

"Am I under arrest?" the boy asked.

"You bet your sweet boots you are." Jack recited a bunch of rights and instructions to him.

Everyone around them had stopped to watch, gap-mouthed, as Jack handed the teen over to a uniformed officer who had just arrived. Jeff Baldwin had tears on his cheeks. His chin trembled, and he sniffed.

"I'm sorry," he said, shaking his head. "I didn't mean to hurt her."

"You don't have to talk, son," the uniformed officer said.

"It was my father," he cried. "I did it so he would be proud of me."

After hearing Pete Baldwin sing his son's praises as if he were the Eighth Wonder of the World, how could Jeff feel that his father wasn't proud of him?

"I just wanted him to accept my music. I wanted him to be so proud of me for keeping Jennifer away from that Amish boy that he wouldn't care what kind of music we played or how we dressed."

"Son, really." Another uniformed officer had come up. "You don't need to say another word."

Jeff Baldwin was crying as they led him away.

"That was impressive." Kappy turned her attention to Jack.

"What?"

"How did you know to come here?" She had been calling out for someone to call him, but there was no way enough time had passed between her request and him showing up.

"You're not the only one around here who can solve crimes. In fact, some of us get paid to do just that."

Edie propped her hands on her hips. "That doesn't sound very grateful. We just helped you solve the biggest crime around here in . . . well, a month or two at least, and all you can do is criticize?"

"First of all . . ." Jack took a step toward her. Only Edie's own above-average height kept him from towering over her. "No one helped me do anything."

"I gave you my phone so you could read the texts."

"You should have done that weeks ago. When you first got them."

Kappy rolled her eyes as they continued to argue. Wasn't the important thing that Sally June's killer had been caught? She grabbed Edie's arm. The gesture must have taken her by surprise for she stumbled backward and allowed Kappy to pull her along, even as she continued to fuss with Jack.

Finally, she stopped and walked of her own accord. But her arguing didn't cease. "I mean, really! Who does he think he is? We have just as much right to protect our community."

Did they? Kappy had no idea.

"He can't come over here and criticize us. We did what we had to do, and if it weren't for us, he wouldn't have Jeff Baldwin in custody."

She supposed that was somewhat true. Maybe mostly true. But she had no words to calm Edie's anger. "Come on," she said. "Let's go home."

"You really should let him get a goat."

"And a pig?" Edie asked. She rolled her eyes. It had been hours since they left the Battle of the Bands contest at the park, and Edie's frustration with Jack hadn't diminished. Kappy needed to head home and feed Elmer, but she wanted to make sure Edie was in a happy place before she left. "Not a chance."

Maybe *happy* was too strong of a word. Perhaps she should shoot for *less homicidal.*

They were sitting on the porch as the sun began its drop in the sky. Jimmy had gone to feed the puppies and the rest of the critters he adored so much.

"Are you going to help him?" Edie grumped.

"He doesn't need my help, and you know it."

"Needing help or not . . ."

"You should be proud, not grumpy. We helped the police catch a killer."

"Oh, sure we did. We chased him, you tackled him, and they took all the credit."

"The important thing is Sally June's killer is off the streets." There was one thing Kappy knew for certain and that was a lot of Amish people would feel a bit safer as they traveled the roads in the upcoming weeks.

"I guess. But that look on Jack's face! Who is he to tell us that we had no right to be there?"

Kappy turned over a couple of answers in her head, but none seemed appropriate.

They were all true, but she wasn't sure that Edie needed reminding that Jack was the real deal while they were playing at solving crimes.

But before she had the chance to come up with an answer that wouldn't be like pouring gasoline on the fire of Edie's temper, the man himself pulled up.

"What's he doing here?"

"I wouldn't know," Kappy said. She was not falling into that trap again.

They remained there on the porch as Jack got out of his car and came to the edge of the yard.

"I just wanted you to know that we still have Jeffrey Baldwin in custody. He's a couple of weeks from turning eighteen, but the DA is asking to try him as an adult."

A shiver ran through Kappy. A young boy who had so much going for him. It was tragic. But it could easily be argued that Sally June Esh had as much if not more going for her, depending on your perspective.

"For murder?" Edie's eyes widened.

"Involuntary manslaughter. He claims that he didn't mean to kill her or even hurt her. Well, Jonah. You know what I mean. He thought it was Jonah until he was already engaged in the accident. By then it was too late to turn back. He wanted to scare Jonah into leaving his sister alone. But when he pulled up alongside the buggy, he was shocked to find Sally June there. The turn of events rattled him so much that he forced her off the road. Once he realized how serious it was, he panicked and ran.

"I figure the judge will go easy on him. He's just a kid seeking the approval of others." Jack shook his head. "Too sad, any way you look at it." He stared off into the distance, then turned back to the two of them. "Anyway, I thought you would want to know."

Kappy nodded.

But Edie shook her head. "Then who was sending me all those text messages?"

"Jonah Esh," Jack said. "Though by way of Willie Lapp."

"What?" Edie exclaimed.

"Willie came forward last night. Apparently, he was out the morning of the accident, meeting with the person who was to help him leave. He saw the wreck and hid out in the Eshes' barn. I guess he didn't want anyone to find him since he was a witness."

"He probably thought he would be next," Edie mused.

Jack nodded. "He was giving Jonah all the details, not knowing Jonah was turning

365

around and texting you."

Kappy thought back to each one. They had read into it what they wanted to see, when Jonah had been pleading for direction.

"I still don't know how he got my cell number," Edie said.

Jack gave a small shrug. "It's not so hard if you really want it."

"I suppose," Edie murmured.

"He was trying to help," Jack explained, "not muddy the waters."

Edie let out a low whistle. "Just wait till the bishop finds out he has a cell phone."

"Oh." Jack patted at his pockets as if he couldn't remember what was in each one. Then he produced Edie's cell phone from the one at his hip. "I guess you'll be wanting this back."

"I can have it now?"

He nodded and handed it to her. Amazing, but that little handheld device did wonders for her attitude. "We have Jonah's phone with all the original texts to your number."

"Thank you," she murmured. For once Edie was near speechless.

"I guess I'll be going." Jack gave them each a small wave and started for his car.

"Wait," Edie called.

Jack turned around. "Yeah?"

"Would you like to stay for supper?"

He hesitated.

"We're having fried chicken and gravy," she added. "And maybe strawberries, if I can get Jimmy to try them this time."

That last bit made Jack smile. "I'd like that," he said. "I'd like that very much."

EPILOGUE

"Kappy! Kappy! Kappy!"

Kappy was in her side yard tending the last of her vegetable garden when Jimmy came running up her drive.

"Back here," she called. She stood and dusted off the skirt of her apron that had taken the brunt of her kneeling position in the dirt. Elmer set to howling his little heart out, but the minute he realized that Jimmy was not alone, he tucked tail and ran for shelter behind Kappy. He stuck his head out and growled, but remained under her protection the entire time.

"Look! Look! Look!" The smile on Jimmy's face was as big as all of Pennsylvania and half of Ohio. In one hand he held two leashes. There was a baby goat at the end of each one. "Edie got me goats! And she said in a week or two that we could go talk to Nancy and Daniel Esh about a couple of pigs."

That was big news, huge, but Kappy didn't want to ask what it meant for them. Was Edie staying in Blue Sky?

"Well?"

Kappy turned as Edie sauntered up, looking quite satisfied with herself. "Does this mean . . . ?"

Edie gave one of her half-shrugs. "I guess I can stay around a while."

"This doesn't have anything to do with having supper with Jack Jones the other night, does it?"

Edie scoffed and blew a raspberry. "Of course not. I just . . . well, maybe a little. We're just friends," she clarified. "And you, too. The entire time I was out of Blue Sky I never had one friend as good as the two of you are to me and Jimmy. I would be dumb to walk away from that."

Kappy had a feeling there was a lot more to it than that, but she wasn't calling her friend out on what had influenced her decision. It didn't have to be said out loud to be true. Edie liked it in Blue Sky. She might not have felt like she fit in all those years ago, but she was *Englisch* now, and the community was changing, growing. Why, before long they might even be as big and progressive as the Amish there in Lancaster County.

Or not.

She smiled a little to herself.

"I'm glad you're staying," she said. "If only for a little while."

"Me too."

"Are you glad I got goats?" Jimmy asked.

"Very glad." She smiled at Jimmy.

"And I'm glad everything has settled down."

But with the annual pie-baking contest and the county festival coming up in a couple of weeks, Kappy knew anything could happen in Blue Sky.

ABOUT THE AUTHOR

Amy Lillard is an award-winning writer who loves reading romance novels from contemporary to Amish. These two genres met in her first book, 2012's *Saving Gideon.* Born and bred in Mississippi, she now lives with her husband and son in Oklahoma.